THE PAYBACK GAME

Sixteen Days of Terror

TEMPE BROWN

ISBN: 1535564652
ISBN 13: 9781535564656
Library of Congress Control Number: 2016913140
CreateSpace Independent Publishing Platform
North Charleston, South Carolina

The Payback Game: Sixteen Days of Terror is a work of fiction. Names, characters, businesses, organizations, places, events, and incidents are either the product of the author's imagination or are used fictitiously. Any resemblance to actual persons, living or dead, events, or locales is entirely coincidental.

OTHER BOOKS
BY TEMPE BROWN

The Seed

The Little Dirt People

DEDICATION

I dedicate this book to my son, Tommy Brown, and my dear friend, Shirley Moran. You are both in one of the toughest, most challenging and thankless businesses there is. You work long, grueling hours and go many nights without sleep to make others' adventures and enterprises go as smoothly as possible. Thank you for your hard work, for your love and for your help with this book.

ENDORSEMENTS

"Mystery/suspense lovers take heart, Brown has done it again. Assassinations inside the Beltway, a chain of mysterious riddles, and the regrets of a love gone wrong, all wrapped in a plot so real you'll think you're reading front page news. Gripping, insightful and compelling, *The Payback Game* is a novel you don't want to miss!"

Keith Clemons—5x Award Winning Author of "Stretching Heaven"
& "Mohamed's Moon"

The Payback Game takes the reader on a wild limo ride into today's headlines. Tempe Brown's characters are real, dealing with regrets, fear, and hope, as evil hides in our nation's capital. Hang on tight!

Robert W. Kimsey Author: Air Swimmer

Tempe Brown's *The Payback Game* could be the script for a modern day movie. This action-packed, fast moving story captivates her reader's interest from page to page, chapter to chapter without interruption. Because this novel contains a true life-changing message, *The Payback Game* is a must read!

Linda R. Abrams
Author: *Properties from Our Father*

ACKNOWLEDGEMENTS

A special thank you to my dear friend, Shirley Moran, for letting me work with you on site at some significant Washington functions, for helping me get the real feel and a better understanding for the very complex transportation business. You're amazing!

Many thanks to my dear friend, Rachel Schindel Gombis, whose areas of responsibility in the government are more vital today than ever. Thank you for your encouragement and inspiration. You're the best!

A big shout out to my Marine friend and former driver for the White House, Rod Hemphill. Your ideas and encouragement kept me writing. Thank you.

Many thanks to Tony Snesko for a great idea regarding the "little black book." That sparked a fire in me and sent me on a really fun journey.

A huge thank you to my veterinarian cousin, Dr. David Mitchell, for your expert advice concerning Beau. You made it real!

To my long-time friend, Carol Lyles, whose editing expertise was precise and thorough, you gave my first draft your loving touch with skill, kindness and encouragement. Thank you, dear one.

Thank you, April Summer, for your intelligent questions and keen suggestions to help get this book in good order. You have my heart, sweet daughter.

Barbara McKenzie Stewart, your candor regarding a couple of areas in the early stages of this book was extremely helpful and made it a better book. Thank you, my friend.

Thank you, Tommy Brown, Founder and Owner of *His Majesty Coach*, for your technical help and for your insight into the transportation business. You're a great businessman and a great son.

Keith Clemons, if I had half the writing skills that you do, especially in the area of description, I'd be one happy gal. Thank you for your helpful hints and encouragement.

"Eagle Eye" Nancy Taylor, your meticulous editing of this book is without equal. Thank you for your good work and for being such a big "Sabyl fan".

And last, but by no means least, when one's time is as limited as yours, Robert Kimsey, I can only shake my head in wonder that you took such care in using your "fine-tooth comb" edit of my manuscript. You made it a better book. Thank you, Friend.

DAY 1

MONDAY, JANUARY 5

A sense of uneasiness began to creep into Sabyl Martin's mind as she waited in the forecourt of Washington's posh Grande Continental Hotel. The cold air, smelling of snow, nipped at her cheeks. Once the government sedans were finished discharging their bigwigs and the principals were safely inside, an agent would signal her to advance her limousines.

The presence of the Secret Service was everywhere. Some wore tuxedos, blending in with the guests; others wore dark suits and heavy, unbuttoned overcoats. Underneath were weapons with which they were highly skilled and would use without timidity if the occasion arose. Their trained eyes scrutinized and mentally recorded everything and everyone around them. Sabyl examined the agents' expressionless faces and wondered how many more were in the shadows around the complex.

The press jostled one another to get the best angles of the titled VIPs as they stepped out of the long gleaming sedans. Cameras flashed like splintered lightning. Onlookers watched with a mixture of awe and envy. Secretary of State Douglas Fredericks and his wife, Joan, emerged, his hair gray as a squirrel, wire-rimmed glasses glinting, her red gown sparkling like tiny fireworks in flashes of the camera lights. The agents quickly escorted them through the ornate glass and metal doors where, once safely inside, the welcoming committee greeted them warmly. Another car approached. National Security

Advisor Wayne Brassfield and his petite wife, Gloria, smiled politely for the press as they were hustled inside. One by one the grand cars advanced, each discharging its notable cargo. The men were handsome in their tuxedoes, their necks stretched out like roosters about to crow. The ladies were stunning in their latest designer gowns.

To receive an invitation to Audrey Aberholdt's soiree was the supreme honor. She threw her parties this time of year to welcome back the reconvening Congress and to celebrate a fresh new season of political verve in the most powerful city in the world. The social butterfly of Washington was bent on outdoing herself.

The Secret Service Advance Team had been sent to sweep the hotel and the surrounding areas as there had been an increased level of "terrorist chatter" in the wake of the previous week's café bombing in Sweden. Security was tight for the attendees, as was duly noted by the press.

An agent nodded to Sabyl, who then quietly radioed her lead driver to pull up under the massive hotel canopy. She watched with an appraising eye as twelve of her limousines slowly advanced one at time and the clients stepped out.

Sabyl wore her warmest wool pantsuit and overcoat, but cold crept into her boots and assaulted her toes. A wayward lock of caramel-colored hair fell on her forehead from beneath a hat that fit snuggly over her ears and turned up in front. Her long eyelashes, thick as a doll's, swept upward over enormous hazel eyes. Sabyl's gloved hand raised the Push to Talk (PTT) cell phone to her mouth and spoke to her lead driver, "Go to parking area B." Everything was running like clockwork, just the way she liked it. A half-hour later, satisfied that all was well, she walked over to the drivers who were huddled together for smokes and small talk.

Burt Hastings, a retired *Greyhound* bus driver from South Carolina, smiled as she approached. He threw down his cigarette. "Hey, Sabe," he drawled. "How long is this shindig supposed to last?"

"Not sure. You know how these things can be."

Her lead driver, Ramose Abana, whom she nicknamed "Rudy," asked in a fatherly tone, "Have you eaten yet?"

"No. I'm going to get a bite now and then head back to the office and catch up on some paperwork. If anyone needs anything, call me."

Lawrence Washington, the oldest of the drivers, smiled and saluted, "Okay, boss."

"Stay warm. See you in a few hours." She turned and walked toward her SUV that was parked across the street from the hotel. Braced against the cold, she looked up and down the wide avenue preparing to cross, when a familiar voice called out to her.

"Sabyl, wait!"

She groaned, "Oh, please, God, no." For the past two years, she had tried to mentally prepare herself for this moment, knowing that she was bound to run into Scott Terhune at one of these events. Pretending she didn't hear him, she stepped out in the street just as a car came racing toward her, causing her to nearly lose her balance. Scott grabbed her arm and pulled her back to the sidewalk and held her for a moment. She felt the strength in his arms—arms that had held her on so many occasions.

"Whoa! You trying to get yourself killed?"

"No, just trying to avoid you."

Her words stung. His smile evaporated as he gently let go of her. Stepping back, he folded his arms. "So, how are you?" His gray overcoat hung well on his six-foot-two athletic frame. Physical fitness was paramount to working the Protective Division of the United States Secret Service. His soft brown eyes were sad—eyes that more than once had raised her heart rate.

She stiffened. "I'm fine, no thanks to you."

"I've, uh, wanted to talk to you," he said nervously.

"We have nothing to talk about."

"Sabyl, I want to explain—"

She cocked her head to one side and lifted a well-arched brow. "You know what? I'm really not interested."

"I know I don't deserve to ask this, but let me—"

"I told you. I'm not the least bit interested in your explanation." She turned away and began looking up and down the boulevard, wanting desperately to get away from him.

"I know I hurt you. I was a complete—"

She swung around. "Jerk?"

The air went out of him. "Yeah, that pretty much sums it up."

Her eyes flashed. "No, that hardly sums it up!"

"I deserve any names you call me for doing what I did."

"You bailed on me when I needed you most, Scott. That makes you a total—"

"I know," he grimaced.

She took a deep breath. "Look. That was a long time ago. I've gone on with my life and I don't need you to complicate it now."

"Let me have just one hour of your time, please. Maybe dinner—"

"I am so over this and I do *not* want to talk to you. And I'm definitely not having dinner with you! And furthermore—"

Frowning deeply, Scott pressed his finger to his earpiece and held up his hand to quiet her.

Sabyl glared at him. "Don't you shush me!"

The agent's training kicked in. "Get in your car!"

"What?"

A man came running out of the door of the hotel shouting, "He's been shot! The Secretary of State's been *shot!*"

"Oh, my God! Scott!"

"Get in your car!" He pulled his weapon and raced toward the hotel entrance.

She yelled after him, "Scott! My clients!"

He disappeared through the doors, the press shooting pictures and shouting questions. She ran over to her SUV, jumped inside, locked the door and spoke into her PTT. "Rudy!"

"Yes, boss."

"There's been a shooting! Tell the drivers to get in their cars and stand by!"

"Boss! Where are you?"

"I'm in my car across from the entrance. I'm okay—just stay put!"

Sirens began to fill the air as police cars arrived by the dozens, their blue strobes darting about like pyros at a rock concert. Within minutes, an ambulance from nearby Georgetown University Hospital pulled under the hotel canopy. Men in dark suits hustled the paramedics inside. Sabyl recognized the ambulance driver, Jeff Ellis, who was dating one of her reservationists. Sabyl wanted desperately to run into the hotel to see about her clients. She held the button on the side of her PTT. "Rudy."

"Boss! What's happening? What about our clients?"

"I don't know yet. Just pass the word along for everyone to start their engines and sit tight until I tell you otherwise." She lowered the sun visor to protect her eyes from the stabbing strobes. Her cell phone chirped. She answered quickly. "Sabyl Martin."

"Sabyl, it's John." It was her night dispatcher. "What in blazes is going on? I heard the police scanner. Sounds like all hell has broken loose. Cops are going by here by the dozens!"

"The Secretary of State has been shot." The words sounded strange in her mouth.

"What? Fredericks? There at the hotel?"

"Yes. That's all I know. We're going to wait it out 'til we can get to our clients." Hearing a helicopter overhead, she pushed the visor up. "Medivac is landing on the roof of the hotel."

"Man! Keep me informed, will you?"

"Yes, and if you hear anything on the police scanner or see anything on TV, call me."

Press vans began to converge on the scene like bloodhounds on a scent. The reporters on site got the news story first, which would soon be going out over the major networks. Sabyl started the engine for heat and turned on the radio. The story was breaking, but they had no more news than she already knew.

Twenty minutes later, the paramedics brought out a body bag.

The agents had moved the reporters away from the doors. Camera flashes lit up the night once again and questions flew. Sabyl's hand covered her mouth. *Oh, God! I hope that's not the Secretary.*

One of the Secret Service agents spoke into the small microphone just inside his sleeve next to his wrist and began motioning for the State Department and other government drivers to pull up their cars. Waves of dignitaries came out of the wide doors, their spouses clinging to their arms. They approached the waiting limousines as a firestorm of camera flashes blinded them. Sabyl saw Scott and another agent hustle National Security Advisor Brassfield and his wife to their waiting limo. The other agent jumped in with them. Scott slapped the top of the sedan and it sped away. He ran across M Street, now blocked off both ways. Sabyl jumped out of her car. "How is he?"

"Get back in the car!" She obeyed immediately and lowered her window. "How is he? Was that him in the ambulance?"

"No, that was the shooter. They're putting Fredericks on Medivac to Bethesda. Chest wound. He's in bad shape."

The dark blue helicopter lifted and veered north toward Bethesda Naval Hospital. News helicopters, after getting permission to enter the 17-mile radius of restricted airspace around Washington, converged on the scene and supplied aerial photos to a shocked nation.

"When can I get to my clients?"

"It may be a while. There are a lot of witnesses and they're getting names and stories."

"Was anyone else hurt?"

"No. Just Fredericks. I've got to get back inside. Stay in your car and make sure your drivers do the same."

"Of course, but how on earth did he get in with a gun?"

"Can't talk about it." He turned and sprinted across the street.

She watched him disappear behind the wide doors. The anger she felt toward him had subsided for the moment, but if she let herself think about what he had done, it would rise like a smoldering volcano all over again.

She closed her eyes and prayed silently for Douglas Fredericks and her clients. She jumped a little when her phone chirped again. It was Stubby Jones, a former New York cop and one of her drivers attending the Counter Terrorism Driving Course in Winchester, Virginia. He had just seen the story breaking on TV in his room at the Holiday Inn where the course was being held. "Sabyl! I just heard about the shooting! You're there, right? You okay?"

"I'm fine, Stubby. We're all fine here."

"You want us to come back?"

"No. You stay there. What you'll learn there is more important than ever now."

"Yeah, I guess you're right. So what's going on? Where are you now?"

"I'm in my car across from the hotel waiting until our clients are released. They've let some people leave. Probably taking them to a safe location. Who knows? Maybe there's more than one shooter in there. Guess we'll find out soon enough."

They talked a few more minutes and hung up. Sabyl looked at the green digital clock on her dash, then turned the radio back on. Nothing new.

Two hours went by. She leaned back in her leather seat. The strobes of the police cars were almost hypnotic. Without warning, her mind reached back to two summers ago. It had taken a long time to feel right about having another man in her life, but over time, she began to be comfortable with him, like slipping into a favorite pair of jeans. He was intelligent, witty and handsome with his strong athletic build, square features and a dimpled crease that ran the length of his cheek when he smiled. They shared their deepest thoughts, dreams and emotions. Their philosophies were alike, they enjoyed the same things; she was fascinated with his stories and he with hers. He didn't share her faith, but he respected her choice. They were so in love—or so she thought. After twelve years, she never thought she would love again but she did. And in one day he was gone.

That pain was second only to the loss of her husband Gary and eight-year-old son Mike, who died in a plane crash in the Rocky Mountains near Leadville, Colorado. After a three-day hunting trip in Montana, they were on their way to Albuquerque for an overnight visit with Gary's sister, Laura, and then head back to Pittsburgh the next morning where Gary had a thriving accounting practice. The news of the crash came through a knock at the door by a sympathetic policeman who had received a call from the FAA. The words had broadsided her. She crumbled to the floor, her heart shattered, and wept until she thought she would go blind.

Smiling bravely at those in attendance, her body and mind remained numb throughout the double funeral and burial. Even though it had happened sixteen years ago, the pain was still there. She remembered thinking after the funeral, *what will I do now? Do I go to work? What kind of work?*

A few weeks later, she got a call from a friend in Italy who worked for a limousine company in Milan. "Come to Italy," she prescribed. "It will heal your soul and help you to get your head on straight." A week later she boarded a plane and flew to Italy. Meaning to stay only a few weeks, she wound up staying two years. Sabyl fell in love with Italy, learned the language, made new friends and basked in the warmth of the people. It was there that she learned how to laugh and enjoy life. As a child, she had never known the joy of laughter. It wasn't allowed in their home.

Her friend got her a job at the company she worked for. It was a perfect fit for her. A plan began to form in her mind that one day, she would return to the States and she would have the best limousine company in the country. Now, fourteen years later, her impeccable reputation as a proven and savvy businesswoman earned her an impressive list of clients: CEOs, rich sports figures, pop singers, and movie producers, plus a multitude of government contracts.

Hers was not the largest, but it was the most successful limousine company in Washington, D.C. To Sabyl, success wasn't measured by the size of the company, but by how it treated its clients. She genuinely loved people and took their security and comfort very seriously.

And now they were unreachable inside the hotel—now a crime scene—going through probably one of the greatest traumas of their lives.

Her eyes were fixed on the door through which Scott had gone. He wants to explain, he says. What kind of explanation could he possibly have? She felt her stomach constrict. She knew she could never trust him again.

The doors of the five-star hotel finally opened, dismissing the frazzled attendees of what was supposed to have been an enjoyable evening. She called her drivers and told them to stand by. Scott emerged, looked in her direction and signaled that her cars could pull up.

⋏

The elaborate decorations for the Aberholdt party were a stark contrast to the grim drama that was now playing out. Forensics techs were quietly gathering evidence. Photographs were being taken of every possible angle of the room, especially the areas where the shooter had gunned down Secretary of State Douglas Fredericks. Scott was winding up his interview with the hotel manager.

For years, the Secret Service had not been accustomed to sharing its turf with other investigative agencies; but they were no longer with the Department of the Treasury. Now the agency was under the umbrella of the Department of Homeland Security. They were all there: FBI, NSA, DIA, IAI. Most likely the CIA would be involved covertly. Scott turned and saw his boss walking toward him. The gravity of the matter was evident on the face of Special Agent in Charge (SAIC) Ron Keefer, a veteran of the Protective Division.

"Hey, Ron," Scott said quietly.

He nodded to Scott and looked around at the agents gathering information from various sources. "You were here with Brassfield, right?"

"Right."

"Outside man?"

"Right."

"I need to talk to an inside man."

"Over there," Scott said, pointing to a group of agents in the center of the room.

Keefer approached an agent and asked, "What have you learned so far?"

Agent Jack Hubbard read from a small note pad. "The shooter's name is Ja'bar al-Mansur. Hotel employee. Worked here for three years. He was a student at AU. His employer said he was a good worker. Co-workers told me he was friendly enough but mostly kept to himself."

"Walk me through the scene."

The agents headed to the center of the room. "According to witnesses, he came through the kitchen door over there, carrying a tray full of hors d'oeuvres. He wove through the crowd, walked up to the Secretary, pulled a gun out from under his waiter's jacket, hidden by the tray, and shot him point blank." He pointed to a bloody stain in the carpet. "There."

Keefer bent over the area where a short red-faced man was focusing intensely along with another forensic tech. "Hey, Fred."

Without looking up he said, "Ron."

"What have you got so far?"

"A shell that belonged to the shooter and one that belonged to the agent that brought him down. The shooter used a snub-nosed 9mm-magnum revolver," he reported as he held up a plastic bag holding the gun.

"Anything else?"

"Not yet."

"Thanks."

The two agents rose and looked at each other, knowing that the Secret Service Protective Agency, their agency, had failed and everybody in the room knew it. In fact, everybody in the world knew it.

DAY 2

TUESDAY, JANUARY 6

L̲ast week's snow littered the ground in gray speckled patches like forgotten debris. Sabyl marveled at how quickly the nation's capital came out of the Christmas season, taking down all the street decorations as if it were more of an obligation than an observance, and rushed right back into "business as usual". She thought, *after last night, nothing in Washington will ever be "business as usual" again.* Beau, her beagle, sniffed the trees, eyed a squirrel, barked at it, and finally did his thing.

Thirty minutes later, her cheeks red from the cold, she came in from the invigorating morning walk, unleashed her dog, and, after pouring herself a second cup of coffee, headed for the sofa and turned on cable news. Beau lapped happily from his stainless-steel bowl and, with water dripping from his mouth, followed her, sat down, and leaned against her leg.

Blowing on the steaming liquid, she listened to the news commentators hash over the shooting again. Secretary of State Douglas Fredericks was in critical condition. The bullet had entered his left ventricle and had done major damage to the surrounding area of the heart. His wife Joan was by his side.

The shooter was identified as Ja'bar al-Mansur, a Saudi-born student at American University studying International Business. He had worked at the hotel for four years. Investigators thought he had most likely hidden the weapon, a snub-nosed 9mm magnum revolver, somewhere in the hotel, perhaps months ago. They showed the now-familiar photograph they had obtained from the shooter's green card. Sabyl turned up the volume.

"Have the investigators ruled out that he might be a terrorist?"

Sabyl frowned. *What else would he be?*

"No, they're not ruling that out."

"So he might have been a sleeper."

"Maybe. We won't know for certain until we investigate further."

"Why the Secretary of State? Did the shooter mean to single him out or—"

"Again, we won't know the answers until we investigate further."

Nothing new was being reported so she turned off the TV, got up and put Beau's leash on him. Grabbing her keys, she headed for the elevator to the lower level of the massive condominium complex.

They got off the elevator and Sabyl unlocked her SUV. Two short beeps echoed across the cavernous concrete parking garage. Beau jumped in the back seat and they headed for the office. The agonizing crawl of traffic was the usual nightmare, but she had grown accustomed to it, and used that time to pray. Prayer had been an important part of Sabyl's life since she was a child. The only good memories she could recall were early in her childhood when she, her parents, and her brother Phillip attended a small gray stone church a few blocks from their house in Fairview, Pennsylvania. Sabyl loved Sundays more than any day of the week. The pastor seemed kind and always bent down to look her in the eyes and say hello. She remembered that he seemed to have one ear tuned to her and one tuned to heaven. Her fondest memory was sitting next to her mother and marveling at what a pretty voice she had when they sang the hymns. Sabyl would stop singing to listen to her sweet voice. It was the only time she could remember that her mother seemed to be at peace. She hadn't allowed herself to think about her for a long time. It was just too painful.

She entered the traffic flow on Rock Creek Parkway. It never ceased to amaze her how such a large, beautiful park could be right in the middle of a vast, bustling city like Washington.

As beautiful as D.C. was, it could also be inhospitable at times, with meter maids eyeing parked cars like a hunter eyes a deer, the constant howl of sirens, the yellow boots on cars whose owners undoubtedly had a glove box full of ignored parking tickets, and of course, the ever-present potholes. But this morning the sun laid its rays across the city, brushing the white marble monuments with a touch of pink edged with yellow, granting a captivating, almost pastoral setting, a welcome sight after last night's madness. She pulled into her private parking space and opened the door for Beau. He jumped down and headed for the front office door.

It was a delight to enter her new office near the Washington Harbor. After occupying a building for nine years that had no garage and was in a less-than-convenient area of D.C., she was elated to find such a perfect location. It was pricey, but the two-level garage alone was worth it to house all twenty-five sedans, six stretches, four mini-buses, and two luggage vans for heads of state and security, all outfitted with the latest GPS technology. The garage area included a spacious lounge area for the drivers with a small kitchen where the coffeepot simmered perpetually until it turned into something akin to tannic acid, two bathrooms, and an area to wash, wax, and vacuum the cars. In front, a canopy arched over a handsome brick circle drive to easily turn the sprawling stretches and sedans. Best of all, it was near the main arteries that connected the capital city.

She started her business with one car, one driver (Rudy), and one telephone. Now fourteen years later, things ran smoothly, for the most part, with two dispatchers, an accountant, two reservationists, and a small army of drivers. Through hard work and sheer determination, she had landed some major accounts over the years plus countless government contracts and Washington dignitaries.

Rudy greeted her with his fading accent and usual warm smile. Born in Al-Kosheh, near Luxor in Upper Egypt, he was a large man with black hair, copper-colored skin, and large brown eyes. He and his wife came to the U.S. eighteen years ago and had obtained their citizenship five years later. His father was a minister, who, at age seventy-four, was still preaching in Al-Kosheh. It was getting more and more dangerous to preach the gospel in Egypt. His life had been threatened more than once, but not wanting to worry his son, he didn't tell him these things.

Rudy's mother died when he was twelve, and he still carried her worn picture in his wallet along with those of his lovely doe-eyed wife, Layla, and their son, David, a medical student on a full scholarship at Johns Hopkins University in nearby Baltimore. No father was more proud of his son. He loved to show his picture and to talk about him to anyone who would listen. While the other drivers stood around smoking and trading jokes, Rudy would often be found sitting in his limo reading the little Bible he kept tucked away in the glove compartment or listening to the latest tape of his father's sermon on a small battery-operated tape player that he bought on eBay.

Sabyl looked to Rudy's quiet strength, and on more than one occasion, had asked him to pray for her, especially through her battle with breast cancer two years ago. Rudy was family.

Frank Lauriette, the head dispatcher, was in his glass-enclosed office talking on his headset and squinting at the computer monitor. He was forty-four, black, and wore glasses; his closely cropped hair was graying around the temples. He waved as Sabyl entered the small entryway. The usual background chatter of the reservationists hummed in the background. She waved back, walked into her office, dropped the heavy leather pocketbook, and took off her coat.

A computer monitor perched on the corner of her desk piled with neat stacks of files and contracts. Lining the front of her desk, enshrined in small silver frames, were pictures of Gary and Mike. Behind her chair was a massive bookshelf that held dozens of mementos given to her by grateful clients. On the east wall were photos of the last two Presidents graciously posing with Sabyl. She sat down, took off Beau's leash and patted his soft velvety nose. He fell at her feet with a grunt, laid his head on her shoe, and let out a big sigh.

Frank came in, handed her a handful of memos. "Boy, that was something last night, huh?"

"I'll say."

"I mean, you were right there on the scene. How did *that* feel?"

She opened her middle drawer looking for a pen. "Weird, scary, frustrating because I couldn't get to our clients."

"It's all the drivers have been talking about."

"I'm sure. It's all everyone is talking about."

"What time did you guys get out of there?"

"Around eleven. The shooting took place right after the party started. We were told to get in our cars and stay put. It was a long wait."

"Sure would like to know how the shooter got that gun in there with all the security."

Sabyl nodded. "Heads will roll for that, I'm sure."

He plopped his six-foot frame down in one of the two leather chairs across from her desk and drummed his fingers on his broad chest.

Frank pulled out a huge handkerchief and blew his nose, trumpeting like an elephant. Beau lifted his head and looked at him curiously. Frank was a recovering alcoholic. Sabyl had fetched him out of the drunk tank more than once. He was one of the few people who was bailed out of jail and driven away in a limousine. She kept him on even when he screwed up jobs, which happened more than once. On one occasion, Frank was so hung over he sent a limo to the wrong airport and kept the Prince of Liechtenstein sitting on the tarmac at Dulles for two hours. Sabyl took full responsibility and got a proper tongue lashing from his highness. When Frank saw that his drinking was causing her embarrassment and possibly costing him his marriage, he joined AA. He'd been sober for three years. "Heard anything new?"

"Only what's on the news channels."

"I'm keeping the TV in my office on mute in case there are some new developments."

"Let me know if you see anything." Sabyl moved her feet and Beau snorted, got up and moved over by the wall, dropped to the floor and went back to sleep. "So what's going on around here?"

"Not much. The usual runs. George has a two o'clock pickup at National. Lawrence, Burt, and Ricko have a wedding at three at All Saints Catholic, and Rudy just got back from Dulles. Went to collect somebody from overseas. Said he didn't get much sleep."

"Poor guy. Probably didn't get to bed 'til late."

Frank yawned loudly, "Me neither. Barbara and I stayed up half the night watching the news channels. Too bad about Fredericks. Hope he makes it."

"I hope so too." She began looking through the memos.

"When's Dotty coming back? I'm tired of playing secretary."

"Just a couple of more days, Frank. Karen's been doing a pretty good job helping out." Karen was one of her reservationists, a twenty-year-old with fire-red hair, brown lipstick and long acrylic fingernails. She was trying hard to fill in for Dotty Stevens, Sabyl's trusted secretary of nine years.

"Well, she's not here."

Sabyl looked at her watch. "It's not like Karen to be late. I'll give her a call."

"Call Dotty," he said with a half-smile.

"Dotty's on a well-deserved vacation and we're not going to disturb her." Sabyl looked through the stack of phone calls.

"A lot of those calls are just friends wanting to know if you were okay."

She smiled. "That's nice."

He heaved himself out of the chair. "You gonna call Karen?"

"Yeah." She picked up the phone. "I'll bet she and Jeff talked on the phone half the night. Did I tell you he was there last night? Drove the ambulance that took away the shooter."

"Jeff? No kidding. Well, tell her to get her sorry carcass outa bed." He grinned and sauntered back to his office.

Sabyl punched in the number. Karen answered a sleepy, "Hello."

"Rise and shine, girl. Get yourself down here pronto or you'll be looking at the want ads tomorrow."

"Oh, wow, what time is it?"

"It's nearly nine. What's your story?"

The voice answered, "Nine! Omagosh! I'm sorry, Sabyl. I'll be there in a few."

Sabyl hung up and smiled, shaking her head. Karen had never been late before. She wasn't about to fire her. Good workers were hard to find these days.

She continued looking through the stack of phone messages. Among them was a call from her oncologist, Dr. Solomon. The note said to call immediately. The urgency of it startled her. She thought she had detected a slight look of concern on Frank's face. She punched in the numbers. "Hi, Rita, this is Sabyl Martin."

"Oh, yes, Ms. Martin. We would like to schedule you for an ultrasound as soon as possible."

Her jaw stiffened. "Why?"

"Your last mammogram, well, we need to take a closer look. Can you come in this afternoon?"

"*Today?*"

"Of course with your history…"

"No, I can't come today. Maybe Thursday. What time?"

"Nine?"

"Okay, fine." She hung up the phone and looked at it as though it had suddenly become her enemy. This couldn't be happening to her again. *Lord, please, no!*

Frank stood in her door looking worried. "Was that the doctor's office?"

Rudy came in behind him. "What's wrong?" His large frame filled the door.

"Nothing. Just have to go in for an ultrasound Thursday morning, so I'll be late coming in."

Rudy looked stricken. "Not again…"

"It's probably nothing," she said, hoping her face looked more assured than she felt.

Rudy stood looking doleful. "Do you want me to go with you?"

"I'll be *fine.*" She smiled and shooed him out with the back of her hand.

Frank sat down and laid some papers on her desk. They went over the items at hand and as they finished up, Frank brought up the doctor's appointment.

The heavy glass front door opened. A tall man wearing a dark suit, his black hair slicked straight back, came in. He stood waiting quietly and could hear the man and woman in the office talking.

"Rudy will worry himself sick about this all day."

Sabyl's expression was perplexed and glum. "Just keep this to yourself, Frank. No one else needs to know. It'll just cause…you know…"

He agreed, stood up and turned to go into his office, nearly running into the man who stood listening to their conversation. "Oh! Sorry, sir. I didn't hear you come in." The man nodded politely. Frank's phone was ringing and he excused himself and ran to answer it.

Sabyl stepped out of her office to greet the visitor. "Good morning, sir, I'm Sabyl Martin. How may I help you?"

"I am John Endicott," he said in a stately British accent. "I wish to hire a car."

"Certainly. Step into my office and I'll fix you up." He walked in behind her and stood stiffly. "Please sit down. May I get you some coffee?"

"No, thank you." He sat down across from her. His expensive black suit smelled of a mixture of body odor and strong cleaners' chemicals. He rested a perfectly manicured hand on his knee. "Your driver, I believe his name is Rudy, picked me up at Dulles airport this morning and took me to the Lafayette House Hotel. I would like to hire this same car again…and the same driver."

"Of course. For when?"

"Now."

"Now?" She looked at him puzzled. "May I ask how you got here?"

"I called a taxi."

"We would have been happy to have picked you up at your hotel."

"I wanted to be sure I got the same car and the same driver."

"I see. I believe Rudy is still here. Let me buzz the garage." She punched the number. "George, is Rudy down there?" She waited a moment. "Rudy, can you come to my office?" She hung up the phone and smiled at the stone-faced man. "Are you from England? You have a lovely accent."

"Yes." He seemed tense and offered no conversation.

Sabyl reached in her desk drawer and pulled out a contract.

His dark eyes studied her every move. "Will the driver be available for several days?" he asked impatiently.

Sabyl turned to her computer and clattered on the keys. "Let's see. How many days do you suppose—?"

Rudy walked in and held out his hand. "Mr. Endicott."

The man stood and shook it. "I wish to hire you for two weeks…perhaps longer. I would like for you to be available to me exclusively, if that is possible. I will pay your fees and tip you generously."

Rudy looked at Sabyl and shrugged one shoulder. She turned from the computer. "As far as I know we're not that tied up. We'll just check with Frank to be sure."

The man looked at his watch.

Still thinking about the doctor's appointment, Rudy looked somberly at Sabyl like a concerned parent. Noticing the look, she frowned and shook her head as though to say, "Stop worrying."

Endicott watched them closely.

When Frank's phone light went off, she buzzed him. "Would you please check to see if Rudy has anything scheduled for the next couple of weeks?"

"We have that Kennedy Center event, but we have plenty of drivers—and we—uh," he lowered his voice. "I hate to say it, but we might have Secretary Frederick's funeral."

"We'll cross that bridge if and when we come to it."

"Okay, then, I think he's clear."

Sabyl put the phone down and smiled. "He's all yours. You understand that it's the law that he cannot drive more than twelve hours a day."

The man stood and bowed slightly. "I'll keep that in mind. May we leave now? I have an important meeting."

Sabyl handed him the contract. "I need some information first. If you'll just fill this out—and I'll need a credit card number."

He pulled out a wad of money and dropped several hundred dollars bills on her desk. "I would prefer to pay cash."

"I still need a credit card number, Mr. Endicott. And we need some kind of identification—for our own protection—you understand."

He grabbed the contract. "I'll take it with me and fill it out later. I don't want to be late for my meeting." Beau's head popped up and he eyed Endicott.

Sabyl hesitated, but let it go. "Certainly. Just leave the contract with Rudy."

"I'll bring the car around," Rudy said.

"It's the same car that I rode in this morning?"

"Yes, sir. The same one. Stay here where it's warm and I'll bring the car around."

Endicott nodded curtly, followed him to the door, and clasped his hands behind his back.

Sabyl stood and joined him in the entryway. The door opened and cold air swept through as Karen walked in looking fairly disheveled, wearing tight black pants and a pea jacket. A bulky pocketbook hung off her shoulder. She excused herself as she stepped past Endicott. "Hi, Sabyl. Sorry I'm late."

"Hi, Karen. Frank's waiting for you in his office."

Endicott eyed her curiously and then looked at his watch again.

Sabyl said goodbye to Endicott, closed her office door and sat down at her desk. Looking through the stack of phone memos, she saw that two were from Scott. She thought, *I'll bet Frank is wondering about that!*

Endicott watched her through the window with cold eyes, like a snake eyes a mouse. When the limousine pulled up, he stepped out of the front door. Rudy got out, opened the door for his passenger, made sure he was settled in and closed it.

⚔

Coffee urns and an assortment of donuts on trays were neatly arranged on a long, skirted table by the back wall. Eight of Sabyl's drivers were attending the Combating Terrorism Course (C.T.C.) at the Holiday Inn in Winchester, Virginia. Stubby brushed the white residue of a powdered donut off his tie and chatted with Maurice DeLorian. The drivers had watched the news of the shooting and wondered if their time at the course would be cut short. They gathered in the meeting room with eighteen other drivers from various companies and a handful of security people hired by large corporations to drive their executives.

A thunderstorm rumbled noisily overhead as the instructor called the class to be seated. The students tossed their Styrofoam coffee cups into the green plastic trash bin as they found their seats.

The attendees listened intently as the instructor spoke: "I'm sure you've all heard the news that the Secretary of State has been shot, which brings to bear even more precisely the reason we are here. It's quite possible that someone in this room will come face to face with a situation that will involve such an attack." Stubby leaned forward with his forearms on his thighs and listened intently.

"When you are assigned a primary, it is your job to get them to and from their destination as safely as you can. This takes time, effort, and study. You must familiarize yourself with all possible routes to and from their destination. Never travel the same route twice in a row. Be aware of anything unusual all along the route, especially at choke points. Always remember that people are creatures of habit; you will see the same people along your route, the same vehicles, people walking their dogs, and so on. If you see a vehicle you are not familiar with, or someone sitting in a car eyeballing you or after you go by they get in a car and leave, report it. Especially at choke points."

A young man in the back put his hand up. "Excuse me. What's a choke point?"

"Any area where there could be problems; where the road narrows, or where there is impenetrable congestion; where there's a lot of pedestrian activity or where there is construction. Of course, that sounds like just about anywhere in D.C." They all laughed.

"There are also situations that can arise that may force you to stop your vehicle. Let's say you're coming down the street and a lady pushing a baby carriage steps out in front of you. What do you do? Is this a legitimate carriage—or has she got an AK 47 in there? Are people standing around? She reaches in and pulls out something. Find an escape route, now!"

Stubby leaned back and crossed his arms.

The instructor continued. "While you're here, you'll learn maneuvers that will get you out of a tight spot in a hurry." Thunder rolled across the skies. "And, by the way, you'll be happy to know that the weather forecast for the rest of the week promises to be perfect for the outdoor course a few miles from here."

The guys smiled and nodded to each other. Even the veteran driver Maurice, who didn't think he needed to take the course, grinned with excitement.

⚔

John Endicott gave Rudy an address, told him he had some important phone calls to make, and ordered him to close the divider. Rudy pushed the button and the glass slowly glided up. Endicott immediately shoved his hand behind the back seat cushion and felt around. He searched for several minutes and finally got on his knees on the floor and pulled the back seat out. It wasn't there! He put the seat back, sat back down and rubbed his temples, his mind reeling with frustration. He looked at Rudy's face in the rearview mirror and observed that he did not have the same pleasant countenance he'd had this morning when he picked him up at Dulles. He leaned forward and tapped on the divider. Rudy pushed the button and the glass whirred as it came down. Endicott asked as calmly as he could, "I've lost a small black book and I had hoped I would find it in your car, but I have searched and it is not here."

"Oh, yes sir. I found a small black book and put it in my lost box at the office."

"You found it? Why didn't you tell me? Stop the car at once!" Rudy pulled over and looked in the rearview mirror at his passenger in the back seat. His eyes were wild. "Did you look in it?"

"Only to see if it had a name in it. I did not see one, so I put it in the lost and found box."

"But that is all you saw?"

Rudy felt uncomfortable with his question. "I saw that it was written in Arabic."

"You understand Arabic, do you not?"

"Yes, sir," he frowned. "I am originally from Egypt."

"Did anyone else see it?"

"No, sir. I just put it in the lost box."

"Turn the car around. I'll need it for my meeting."

"Yes, sir." Rudy circled the block and headed back to the office, feeling this was not going to be a pleasant two weeks.

Endicott sat back in his seat, peered through the darkened window and brooded. He didn't believe Rudy. The peculiar looks that passed between him and the Martin woman disturbed him. He would have to deal with both of them. He could take no chances.

᛭

At 7:05 that evening, Sabyl's keys clunked noisily on the glass coffee table. She sank down on the sofa, kicked off her shoes, put her cell phone on the charger on the end table next to her, and turned on the TV. Beau sat down beside her and leaned against her leg. The words "News Bulletin" came across the screen. Secretary of Homeland Security John Killian with a somber face announced sadly, *"The Secretary of State, Douglas Allen Fredericks, passed away just an hour ago at 5:58 Eastern Standard Time in Bethesda Naval Hospital."*

"Oh, no!" Beau looked at her startled. She gave him a reassuring pat, leaned forward and listened.

"His wife, Joan and their twin sons, Doug and Daniel, were at his side."

Sabyl's phone rang. It was Frank. "Sabe, did you hear?"

"Yes, I'm watching it now."

"John said to tell you calls are already coming in about the funeral."

"Tell him to hold them off until we hear from the State Department."

"Gotcha."

She hung up and unmuted the TV. *"We will now turn to a news conference at Bethesda Naval Hospital."* A middle-aged man in a white medical coat was being introduced. Cameras flashed as Secretary Killian introduced Dr. Barry Overland, Chief Surgeon at Bethesda. He stepped up to a large cluster of microphones. Clearly uncomfortable with the attention, he read his brief statement and gave his condolences to the family. He politely answered questions from the media and then stepped away. Killian stated that funeral arrangements would be announced at a later time.

᛭

At precisely 8 p.m., the President of the United States, Byron William Anderson, came on the screen and made his somber statement, vowing to get to the bottom of this heinous crime, declaring that DHS, DIA and the

FBI were working around the clock with the investigation. He announced that Secretary Frederick's body would lie in state at the Capitol rotunda on Thursday and Friday and that a funeral service would be held at the National Cathedral on Saturday. He would be buried at Arlington Cemetery.

⋏

Flowers began to gather at a makeshift memorial near the entrance of the Grande Continental Hotel. Dozens of tiny American flags jutted out from among the flowers. Candles flickered in the cold January air. The press camped out across from the hotel, using the memorial as a backdrop during their news coverage. Photojournalists took pictures of the somber faces of those who came by to pay their respects. Flags flew at half-mast in the nation's capital and across the America.

Phone calls from all over the world began to come in to the White House and the State Department offering condolences, calling Secretary Fredericks a great statesman. Some of the same callers had secretly cursed him behind his back when he would press them hard to give more cooperation in the war on terror. Many of the heads of state began making arrangements to fly to America to attend the funeral.

DAY 3

WEDNESDAY, JANUARY 7

The azure skies over Washington were awash with sunshine. The cold front had passed and the temperatures rose to the high fifties. Joggers were wearing shorts instead of sweats; bicycles were back on the trails, and street vendors were out in full force.

Rudy saw Endicott coming out of the historic Lafayette House Hotel near the White House overlooking Lafayette Square. He pulled up to the entrance, got out and opened the door. "Good morning, sir. Beautiful day, isn't it?"

Endicott nodded curtly and got in the car. "Take me to Union Station. I will be meeting a train."

"Yes, sir."

Endicott seldom spoke to Rudy. He and the men with whom he met in various odd places around town seemed intensely focused, which was nothing unusual for the types of important people Rudy usually drove. Yesterday, four men rode in his back seat, engrossed in deeply concentrated and sometimes greatly animated discussion. Rudy often noticed Endicott looking at him with an acid stare in the rearview mirror. It gave him a feeling of strange uneasiness. At one point he flipped it to night vision so that he wouldn't have to look at his cold eyes.

He pulled up to the front of the massive railway transportation building. Endicott got out and straightened his coat. "Wait for me here," he said, and headed toward the doors.

While waiting, Rudy finished listening to the tape of his father's sermon that he sent him weekly from Egypt: "And finally, my children, remember that you can never earn God's love. It is His gift. So many seem to be working hard to impress God with their good works, their benevolence, or their self-deprecating penance. But God is not impressed with anything after the Cross." Rudy could hear the smile in his father's voice. "He has already paid the ultimate price for your sins and for your eternal future. Instead of ignoring it and attempting to work your way into heaven, why not just receive the gift he has already provided? God loves you and wants that none should perish. Give him your heart today and be at peace in your souls. Amen."

Rudy smiled at the encouraging words his father had spoken. He could picture him standing at his simple, hand-hewn pulpit, his kind eyes searching the faces of his flock, genuinely loving each one. How he missed his father. It had been five years since he had gone back to Egypt to see his family. Perhaps one day he would persuade his father to fly to America for a visit. Smiling at the thought, he ejected the tape and carefully placed it back in its case and returned it to the glove compartment.

His long legs feeling cramped, Rudy got out to stretch and gave a friendly two-fingered salute to one of the Park Police standing nearby. It was someone he knew, so he would most likely let him remain parked there—at least for a while.

One of his favorite monuments was there. The gurgling water flowed from the fountains around the magnificent fifteen-foot-tall statue of Christopher Columbus with his cloak drawn tightly around him, his eyes looking toward the Capitol. Passersby stopped to gaze and to take pictures of the marble figure with two lions resting at the famous explorer's feet. Rudy offered to take a picture of a young couple together after they had taken each other's picture in front of the grand monument and attempted a few selfies. They looked to be in their early twenties. Rudy guessed they were on their honeymoon. He looked at his watch. Forty minutes had passed since Endicott entered Union Station. His cell phone rang. "Rudy here."

"Rudy, it's Sabyl. What do you want to do about this client of yours? I haven't seen a contract yet, and we've got the Fredericks funeral Saturday."

"I have the contract, boss. I just have not been able to bring it by. This guy keeps me pretty busy."

"So he signed the contract then?"

"Yes. He seemed reluctant to do so, but yes."

"Did he put down a credit card number?"

"I'm not sure."

"Okay, I guess you're stuck, dear. How's it going?"

"Alright, I suppose."

"Do you think there's any way he would let you do the funeral and then return to his service after?"

"I don't know, I'll ask. I'm at Union Station now. He has gone to meet a train. I'll ask him when he comes out."

"Okay, if he's not cool with it, don't worry about it, okay?"

"Yes, okay."

"Let me know."

"Okay, boss."

Endicott came walking out with a slender man with thinning hair, wearing a gray trench coat. A large leather camera case hung from his shoulder and he was pulling a huge suitcase. Endicott was carrying a long, narrow package. Rudy got out and helped the man put his luggage in the trunk. They got in the car and Endicott gave Rudy an address on E Street. The two men rode in silence in the dark, luxurious car to a brownstone house with an iron fence in front. A jagged hemlock overshadowed the house. The homes there had seen better days. Most had iron bars over the doors and windows. Children played in the street; many stopped and stared at the fine black car.

As the men got out, Rudy approached Endicott. "Sir, I wondered if you could spare me on Saturday so that I may cover the Fredericks funeral. After it is over I would be available to you again."

Endicott's eyes flashed. "I have a contract with you, do I not? You are driving for me Saturday and every day until I no longer need you!"

Somewhat startled by his reaction, Rudy lowered his eyes, cocked his head slightly and nodded. "As you wish, sir."

The other man walked over to them. "I need my package out of the trunk and my suitcase."

"Yes, sir, I'll get them for you."

Endicott's eyes narrowed into slits and drilled into Rudy's. A vein stuck out on his forehead. He spoke in a low hissing voice, "I have important business here and I hired you to serve me for at least two weeks, perhaps more." Bits of spit hit Rudy's face. "I will give you more money if that's what you want, but I must know that you will be available to me for that amount of time."

"I don't want extra money, sir. The contract says two weeks. I'm not sure that I can drive you any longer than that."

Endicott pulled his head back and studied Rudy. "Fine then. Now, let's take Mr. Fathid's luggage inside. We will call you in a couple of hours."

Rudy nodded. "You have my cell number."

The reservationists' voices droned softly in the background. They were inundated with calls regarding the funeral.

Sabyl hung up the phone and went into Frank's office. "Just spoke with the State Department. They want sixty-five limos total. We'll have to subcontract thirty-five more sedans. Call PDC and Vassette."

"Okay." Frank leaned back in his chair. "What about Rudy?"

"Just spoke with him a few minutes ago. He doesn't know if Endicott will let him off. I'm expecting him to call me back any minute."

Just then Rudy drove up, parked, and came in the office.

"Rudy! What'd you find out?" Sabyl asked.

"I guess I won't be doing the funeral. Here's the contract."

They went into her office and she sat down and put on her readers. "Yeah, he's written in the starting date, but left it sort of open-ended. I think we can remedy that if you want to be released from him at the end of two weeks."

Rudy fell into one of the chairs across from her. "I'll let you know then."

"I see he didn't put in a credit card number."

Rudy's large frame unfolded out of the chair. "I'm going to wash the car. Endicott said he would need me in a couple of hours."

"Okay, see you later." Sabyl buzzed Karen. "Come in here, please." Her office line rang. She instinctively answered, "Sabyl Martin."

"Sabyl, it's Scott."

She was taken off guard. "Scott. I really can't…"

"Guess you'll be busy with the Fredericks funeral."

"Very."

"Do you think we could have dinner after everything dies down?"

"No."

"I really need to talk to you."

"No, Scott. Please don't call again." She hung up the phone quickly and stood up and took a deep breath. Subterranean emotions were beginning to unearth. *Why does he still affect me? I hate this!*

Karen tapped on the door and stepped into her office. "Hey, Sabe…uh, you okay? You look kinda—like—weird."

Sabyl quickly gathered herself. "I'm fine. I need you to radio all the drivers that are out and find out if there are any changes on their ID's—you know—if they've renewed their 31-C's or whatever. I'll talk to the guys in the garage."

"What for?"

"Because State is very strict about the drivers after Nine-Eleven. We have to give them every bit of information each time they use us."

"I thought they all had—like—clearance."

"They do, but if any of our info has changed, it flags their computers, they freak and that driver is out." She sat back down. "Especially check with the Premiere DC and Vassette drivers. Our guys are pretty much up to date, but I'm not sure about them."

Sabyl handed her a large file. "Also, check and make sure all the descriptions of the cars, license plates, makes, models, and each of the driver's cell numbers haven't changed since the last State contract."

"You mean you have to supply descriptions of the cars too? They're all—like—black limos for crying out loud."

"Just do it, okay?"

"Sure." Karen closed the door behind her and walked away hugging the file, her red ponytail bouncing.

Sabyl picked up the phone and punched in the number of her pet sitter. "Conrad, can you do me a favor? I've got some major meetings today that may take all afternoon and perhaps into the evening and then I have an ultrasound tomorrow morning."

"An ultrasound? Not again!"

"It's probably nothing. Can you take Beau to the groomer and keep him overnight and then bring him by my place tomorrow evening?"

"No problem. Want me to come by the office and get him?"

"That would be great. Thanks, Conrad."

Sabyl headed out the door, her heels echoing in the wide corridor that led to the garage. Lawrence and Burt were watching the morning talk shows, George's least favorite thing. He sounded off regularly that morning talk shows were two minutes of news and fifty-eight minutes of drivel. Jamal and Ricko were helping Rudy wipe down his car.

Jamal al Hamid, a Jordanian, who had worked for Sabyl for three years, was intense, studious, and the quietest one among them. He often pulled his sedan over in front of the Islamic Mosque on Mass Avenue at certain times of the day to pray, as did many taxi drivers in D.C. He and Rudy had gotten into a couple of heated debates about religion, but decided to agree to disagree and let it go. Ricko Garcia, the chef of the bunch, was always bringing in spicy creations for everyone to try. They happily accommodated him, and then passed around the antacids.

Sabyl sat down next to Lawrence, crossed her legs and clasped her long fingers around her knee. Rudy continued wiping down his car. The other drivers ambled over. She began, "We got the contract for the Fredericks funeral. Give Karen any information that has changed. You know the routine. I have a meeting with State this afternoon. I'll get the info on the funeral line-up and then we need to have a meeting Friday night at seven o'clock to go over it. Anyone who can't be here?"

They looked at each other and shrugged.

Jamal folded his arms. "What about the drivers at the C.T.C. course?"

George stood jingling the change in his trouser pocket. "When we took the course, it lasted to Friday noon. Winchester's not that far away. They'll be back in time."

Sabyl stood. "Okay, great. Gotta run."

Lawrence headed for a limo. "Me too. I've got a transfer at National. See ya guys." He got in, started it up, and pulled out.

Sabyl stood aside as the long, shiny car passed her. As she walked away, she overheard Ricko ask, "What about you, Rudy? You doing the funeral?"

Rudy put the wet towels in the large hamper. "No, I cannot. I'm tied up."

"Bummer."

Rudy sighed, "Yes. Bummer."

⋏

Conrad parked his yellow PT Cruiser in the center of the circle drive and went inside. His long blond hair was combed to one side and the beginning of a goatee was manifesting on his thin face. He was a Howard Law School dropout who ran out of money and put an ad in the *Washington Post* advertising himself as a "Critter Sitter." He was making such good money taking care of peoples' pets, he decided that he needn't bother with law school.

Frank was talking on the speakerphone when Conrad came in. He was getting an earful from Burt who had just gotten a ticket for parking near the Smithsonian. "Take it easy, Burt."

Burt had a perfect driving record until he came to Washington. He had a hard time getting used to the erratic traffic patterns and orbiting the numerous traffic circles. After five years, he was finally beginning to get used to it. Parking was another matter altogether. "I thought you guys cleared that up. Didn't you tell us that we could park there? And now another ticket! How the heck do the cops in this town think we're supposed to make a living around here? We're just doing our job and they're all over us like ants on road kill!"

"We'll take care of it, Burt. We've got lawyers on retainer for this very reason." Frank hung up and waved at Conrad. "You can go on in to Sabyl's office and get Beau. She's already left for her meetings."

"Is she having problems again? I mean..."

"Aw, I think it's just a precautionary measure. You know, with her medical history and all."

Conrad nodded. "I hope that's all it is."

⚓

Rudy pulled up in front of the brownstone on E Street. Endicott came out with Fathid, who was carrying the large camera case and something rolled up in a blanket. Rudy got out and started to open the trunk. Fathid quickly said, "No, I will carry them in the car with me."

Endicott walked over to Rudy. "Take Mr. Fathid wherever he wishes to go. Then when he's finished, bring him back here, and await further instructions."

"Yes, sir," he said and opened the back door.

Fathid got in. "Take me to the Lincoln Memorial." Rudy nodded, closed the door, settled in behind the steering wheel, and they headed for the famous monument. He parked and Fathid asked Rudy to open the sunroof. He pushed the button and it slowly yawned opened. Fathid unrolled the blanket, stood and poked his head up through the opening, and spread the blanket over the top of the car. Rudy got out and eyed him carefully as Fathid opened a short aluminum tripod and set it on top of the blanket. He grinned at Rudy as he mounted his high-powered camera on the tripod.

"You see? I will not scratch your car."

Rudy smiled weakly, nodded and got back in the car while his passenger took pictures for several minutes then told him to drive to the Capitol where he repeated the same scenario. He photographed every angle of the imposing building, and then on to the Washington Monument. Rudy parked across from the Ellipse. Fathid seemed to be intrigued by the famous monument. Around the famous obelisk, the circle of fifty flags representing the fifty states, all at half-staff, fluttered and snapped in the cold January wind. He took several pictures and then instructed Rudy to drive to various points around it so he could get photos from every possible angle. When he was finished, he turned his attention to the White House. Rudy returned to the parking area across from the Ellipse and pulled up next to one of the familiar U.S. Park Police vehicles. Fathid took the camera off the tripod and walked across the street to get a closer view. The Park Police eyed him closely as he took several pictures of the White House. Rudy got out and leaned against his car and chatted for a few minutes with Louis Jones and Bill Shanklin, better known as "Shank."

"Hey, Rudy. Your man here a professional photographer?"

Rudy shrugged. "I suppose."

"How's your boy doing? Does he like it in Baltimore?"

Rudy's face lit up. "He likes it very much. He is carrying a heavy load of classes, but doing quite well. Thank you for asking."

Shank smiled kindly and nodded, "So he's going to be a doctor."

Rudy beamed, "Yes, he will be a fine physician." He saw Fathid heading back towards them, camera in tow. Fathid ignored the men and carefully folded up the tripod and rolled it back up in the blanket.

Rudy said goodbye to the officers and got in the car. They drove back to the brownstone and parked. Fathid went inside and Endicott came out with another man Rudy had not seen before named Talib Sahba. He ordered Rudy to drive them to a park in McLean, Virginia. Sahba was bald with small squinting eyes, eyebrows that knit together and a bulbous nose. His jaw protruded, set in a permanent scowl. Endicott stared at Rudy. It was beginning to unnerve him.

⚔

While idling on the marked up pavement strewn with old tires and orange traffic cones, Stubby listened as the instructor sitting next to him in the white four-door sedan went over the maneuver once again. "Okay, remember, these guys chasing you are pros. They're going to put you through some hairy situations. Just listen to me and you'll be fine. I want you to get comfortable doing high speeds—even ninety to a hundred miles an hour. Okay, head up that track, get up to about fifty-five."

Stubby accelerated and went around the long, winding course. Just as he reached cruising speed of seventy, a car came out of nowhere, pulled up beside him and tried to run him off the road. The instructor sat silently. Stubby floored it and got it up to eighty—then ninety. He was able to pull away from them for a few seconds. Just as the chaser started to approach them again, the instructor said, "See that switch right there? Slam on your brakes, hit that switch, and turn the wheel a quarter turn to the left."

Stubby gritted his teeth, hit the brakes, and flipped the switch. The back brakes locked, he turned the wheel, and before he knew what was happening, they were going in the opposite direction.

"Now, *gun* it!"

Stubby laughed and hit the pedal. He had just completed his first J-Turn, leaving behind the chaser and the skid marks of a perfect "J" on the pavement.

Scott leaned back and folded his arms. "What do you make of it?"

Scott's boss, SAIC Ron Keefer, a veteran of the Protective Division, forty-two, black, athletic, dressed in a gray wool-blend suit, wire-rimmed glasses, and sporting a well-groomed mustache, sat behind his desk and shook his head. "The guy had no priors, kept his nose clean, worked hard."

Agent Lou Martz, Scott's partner, stood with his hands in his pockets. "You got any ideas, Scott?"

"Sounds like a sleeper to me, but it's way too early to tell. He didn't have any ties to Al Qaeda or any terrorist organization that we know of."

"That's just it," Keefer said, scratching his cheek. "These guys come in as students, no previous background—get recruited overseas because they have a clean background. We can't always trace them to anybody."

"Or they're recruited at their mosque or online."

"Right." Scott stared at the photograph of Ja'bar al-Mansur, the man who had assassinated their Secretary of State. "Hope he's a loner."

Keefer nodded, "You got that right."

Just as Sabyl was unlocking her door she heard the phone ringing. Jerking the key out of the door, she dropped her handbag and grabbed the phone. "Sabyl Martin."

"Sabyl, dear!"

"Rebecca! How *are* you?" It was her longtime friend, Rebecca Carriere, a former columnist for the *Washington Times* now writing her third novel. "Grinding away, dear. And you?"

"The same. What's going on?"

"Oh, just thought we should get together soon. It's been entirely too long."

"It certainly has. Way too long. When?"

"How about Friday night for dinner?"

"I've got a meeting with my drivers Friday night."

"What time?"

"Seven."

"How long will it last?"

"Not long. I just have to go over the funeral directives with them."

"Oh, the funeral," she whispered. "How awful, huh?"

"Yeah. Still can't believe it. All my cars are going out, plus thirty-five I've subcontracted."

"I guess lots of heads of state will be there."

"From all over the world."

"So, after your meeting, could we meet at, say, eight-thirty? Will that give you enough time?"

"Definitely. Where?"

"How about that little pub in Georgetown on Wisconsin I was telling you about. I've been there a couple of times. It's a great place to unwind and talk—they have booths—usually not too crowded, and great pizza."

"Sounds perfect."

"The only problem might be parking—you know, Georgetown on a weekend night."

"I'll find one. See you then, Bec. I've got something I want to talk to you about."

"Great. I want to hear all about what you've been up to."

She hung up and smiled. Sabyl hadn't seen her friend since they met for High Tea at the *Hay-Adams Hotel* just before Christmas. It was an annual event for them, and celebrating their birthdays together, which were both in the same week in December.

Sabyl hit the remote and a blaze sprang to life in the gas-log fireplace. She made some herb tea and settled down deeply into the lush cream-colored sofa and took a sip. It warmed and comforted her. The tenseness of the day began to fade. Orange flames leapt and danced in the hearth. The very atmosphere of her home seemed to reach out and hug her. It was arrayed with treasures she had bought while living in Italy. A hand-painted armoire held her TV, chairs sat at angles in the corners of the plush Oriental rug in front of an elegant stone fireplace. A Florentine sideboard with a marble top squatted between two arched windows that overlooked a hedged courtyard seven stories below. She looked around at the things she had collected over the years: gifts from friends and grateful clients and treasures she picked up in the friendly little antique shops around her hometown of Fairview, Pennsylvania. She was tired of dusting them all, but couldn't bear to part with any of them.

She picked up the remote and turned on a local news station. A young blonde meteorologist wearing a smart fitted suit pointed to a red line pushing upward from the south. An unusual warm front was moving in. Showers were not ruled out for Friday and possibly Saturday. Sabyl frowned and hoped the rain would be gone by the time the funeral was over and they headed for Arlington Cemetery for the burial. She flipped it to Fox News. Deputy Secretary of State Marvin Dougherty was being sworn in, taking the place of his boss and good friend, Douglas Fredericks. Dougherty's wife was by his side, their somber faces revealing their grief. *How sad,* Sabyl thought, remembering her own grief when her husband and son died. Her thumb hit the off button and the TV screen went blank.

Laying her head back, she contemplated the ultrasound the next morning. She realized her emotions were leaning toward anger. *Am I mad at God,* she wondered? She shook her head and rubbed her eyes with her forefingers. *I'm not going that route. That's a real nowhere road.* The face of Joan Fredericks hung in her mind. She said a little prayer for her and found it made her feel better. Determined not to worry about tomorrow, she thought about Rebecca and how she was looking forward to seeing her. She was such a good listener. Maybe it was time to talk about Scott. She sighed and closed her eyes again. Beau was sorely missed.

DAY 4

THURSDAY, JANUARY 8TH

Sabyl put on the familiar gray-green cotton gown and followed the technician to the ultrasound room. "Just climb up on the table and cover up with this and I'll be right back," she said, handing her a paper sheet.

The room was chilly and the padded table felt cold to her bare skin. She lay with the flimsy paper sheet over her. The tech came in, pulling on rubber gloves. She smiled down at Sabyl. "Okay, put your right arm above your head. I'm gonna slime you. It might be a little cold." She squirted the ultrasound gel on her breast.

"Whoa!"

"Sorry." Her skilled fingers moved the probe over her breast, spreading the gel. She peered intently at the screen at strange images that looked like an aerial view of a troubled sea. Occasionally, she would stop and clack a few keys on the computer to record a particular area she thought was significant.

Forty minutes later, Sabyl was back in the dressing room buttoning her blouse. Two years had passed with no reoccurrence. She took a deep breath and whispered, "Please, God, let it be nothing." She stepped out into the waiting room. A half-dozen women sat watching with glum faces the sad events on the wall-mounted TV. The unblinking C-SPAN cameras were set on the flag-draped casket of the assassinated Secretary of State in the capitol rotunda. Hundreds of mourners slowly passed by to pay their respects.

Sabyl stepped up to the receptionist window. The dark-haired girl looked up and smiled. "Okay, Ms. Martin. You're done for the day. We'll call you with the results as soon as we get them."

Sabyl walked out of the medical building and looked at her watch. Almost eleven o'clock. The skies were bright and sunny. Washington went about its normal routine. Pedestrians walked purposefully, many carrying briefcases on their way to and from meetings. People of every complexion moved about the city. Women dressed in warm clothing and carrying department store bags window-shopped. Couriers on bicycles darted in and out of traffic, none realizing there was a frothy brew of terrorism boiling in their midst. Sabyl climbed into her Nissan Murano and headed for the office.

⅄

Rudy paid little attention to his clients' activities. His only concern was to make sure they got where they wanted to go and returned safely and reasonably happy. But his curiosity leaned hard on him as he watched the activities of his passenger for the past two days. Endicott had met other men on several occasions and had Rudy drive them to different locations, often to the Washington mall to meet with other men. They would walk the length of it, talking, pointing, and sometimes arguing. Sahba accompanied Endicott on his treks around D.C. during the hours that Fathid was not photographing the monuments.

Rudy drove them to a park in McLean a couple of times a day. He parked under a long line of leafless trees and waited. Each time, Sahba would sit on a park bench and watch the passersby. Joggers sprinted by and nannies pushed the latest high-tech strollers along the wide, curved sidewalks. And each time, Sahba approached a man walking his black Labrador retriever. He and the man would sit on the park bench and converse at length then the man with the dog would get up and walk away, the dog wagging his tail contentedly.

Sahba returned to the car and got in. Endicott ordered Rudy to drive to Hains Point at East Potomac Park. It was the second time they'd gone there. On the way, Endicott told Rudy to stop at a convenience store by the Key Bridge for copies of several newspapers, and once again, ordered him to close the divider window. Rudy parked, opened his glove box where he kept a roll of quarters, got out and scanned the headlines of the major newspapers locked in their various cases. All the headlines were about the shooting. He bought four. Getting back in the car, Rudy handed Endicott *the Washington Post, The Baltimore Sun, The Wall Street Journal,* and *The New York Times.* When they arrived at Hains Point, another man waited in a white Subaru. Sahba got out and met with him. After talking for a few minutes, the man became irritated at something Sahba said. Endicott stayed in the limo and read the papers and talked on his cell phone.

A little flotilla of ducks swam happily in the frigid water and a small group of birders watched hopefully for a pied-billed grebe or an elusive red-throated loon. A tiny grebe hid from the intruders by sinking until only its head showed. Rudy wished he could do the same.

Rudy watched with great interest as the two men quarreled. Finally Sahba returned to the limousine, and instructed Rudy to take him to the University of the District of Columbia (UDC), where he exited. Endicott remained in the car. "Take me to the Pentagon," he said in a low tone. "I want to see where the airplane hit the building."

Rudy was surprised and felt a strange uneasiness at his request. "I cannot park in there, sir, but I can drive near enough to where you can see where it was hit."

"Yes, fine."

Rudy drove south on I-385, exited, crossed over and turned left to get on the ramp and came back north. He took the Memorial Bridge Exit, and coming around the curve, the side of the Pentagon that was hit was directly in front of them. "There it is," Rudy said. "You cannot tell it was ever hit."

"So I see, "Endicott mumbled. "So I see."

⚓

"So what about this John Endicott?" Floyd Crabb, Sabyl's accountant asked. "I see he paid in cash—enough for Rudy to drive him for the next six weeks. How long will he—"

"He says two weeks. We can reimburse whatever is left over."

"I can't make out his address. The contract he filled out is one big scrawl."

Sabyl frowned, "Yeah, I know. I'll ask Rudy to get him to clarify his information if he expects a reimbursement." Sabyl completed her meeting with

Floyd and headed back toward the front offices. She paused to look in to Frank's office. "Have you talked to Stubby?"

"Yeah. I got the idea they hated to leave, they're having such a good time at the course."

Sabyl smiled, "Almost makes me want to sign up."

Frank tossed some papers in the trash. "Oh, and the lawyer called and said Burt's ticket has been taken care of."

"That's good. Have you told him?"

"Naw, he's been out with the World Globe security guys. He'll be driving the lead car for them and they want to see the lay of the land. He just pulled in a few minutes ago."

She nodded. "Sounds like everything is running smoothly. What about PDC and Vassette? Do we have enough cars for the funeral?"

Frank took off his headset and rubbed his neck. "Yep."

"Has Rudy come by or called?"

"No. Haven't heard a peep out of him."

"That's not like him. Hope that Endicott guy isn't running him ragged."

"He can take care of himself."

The front door burst open. "Hi, everybody, I'm back!" It was Dotty, Sabyl's secretary, a middle-aged woman, with a head full of thick, curly dyed-brown hair, a pleasant smile and twinkling blue eyes. She was as loyal as a pit bull and shaped amazingly like one.

"Dotty!" Frank got up from his desk and ran over to her and hugged her so hard he lifted her off the floor. "Am I glad to see you!"

"Umph! Frank, you're gonna break my ribs!"

He put her down, stepped back and looked at her. "You look great! Must've done you some good to get away."

"It was wonderful, but I'm ready to be back."

Sabyl came out of her office. "Dotty! You were sorely missed, dear."

She smiled gratefully and hugged Sabyl. "That's very nice to hear. Boy! The weather in Florida was great! Now I see why all the snowbirds go there. Hey, sounds like you've had quite a time of it. I can't believe what happened. I purposely tried not to watch TV while on my trip, but couldn't help but hear about Fredericks. Everybody and his dog was talking about it. I thought about coming home early, but that would have gone over like a screen door in a submarine with Mary. And I knew what you'd say, so..."

Sabyl smiled and rubbed her shoulder. "No, I'm glad you stayed, dear. You deserved your vacation, and I know Mary would have been terribly upset if you had cut it off."

"Upset? She'd have had a ring-tailed hissy fit!"

Dotty was a fighter—a real trooper—as Frank called her. She had overcome cancer three times, as well as an abusive husband who had beaten her so badly when she was pregnant that it put her in the hospital. As a result, her baby girl was born severely mentally handicapped. Dotty got a good lawyer, divorced him, got the house and a good settlement, and after agonizing over Mary's need for special care, placed her in a wonderful facility on Maryland's Eastern Shore. She had grown into a lovely twenty-year-old young woman who had the mental capacity of a seven-year-old. Mary loved Sabyl and the feeling was mutual. Sabyl always made sure they did something special when Mary came to her mom's for a visit. The last time, the three of them went for pedicures in a fancy salon in downtown D.C. Mary loved it and decided that should be a regular thing to do when she came to visit.

"Is Mary okay? Did she have a good time?"

"Oh! The best! She loved seeing Mickey and Minnie, but Sea World was her favorite. She's probably jabbering about it to everyone at the school." She pulled off her brown tweed overcoat.

Sabyl hugged her again. "I am *so* glad you're back."

"Yeah, me too. Actually looking forward to getting back to work. Guess you guys are swamped, huh?"

"Uhhh, yeah, we're swamped." Frank smiled at Sabyl and winked.

"Oh, yes! Everything is complete chaos. Thank God, you're here!"

"That's what I figured. Okay, fill me in."

Frank took her into his office and buzzed Karen. "Get in here, Sunshine. Your replacement has arrived."

⋏

Marty held onto the steering wheel of the blue four-door sedan and swallowed hard. Her instructor fastened his shoulder harness and said, "Okay, we showed you on the blackboard in class, now you're going to do it for real."

"Okay, "she said weakly.

"You did great on the J-Turn yesterday, Marty; this isn't that much different. The only thing you have to remember is if the car dies you'll have to stop, put it in park, and restart it. You *don't* want to have to do that. That can mean the difference between life and death to your primary. If you'll put a little gas to it, it won't die, most likely."

Her huge brown eyes grew wide and looked at him sideways. "Most likely? Oh, Lord!"

"Now turn up that street on the right."

Marty made the turn and scanned everything carefully, watching for anything unusual. Suddenly a woman with a large pocketbook stepped in front of her. Marty put on the brakes and when the woman reached into her pocketbook, the instructor yelled, "Bootleg!"

Marty slammed it in reverse and gunned it.

"Get it up to 40!"

"Oooh, Loorrd!" Marty fought to keep it from swerving.

"Now!"

She cut the steering wheel as fast and far as she could. The car began sliding around and she started to put it in drive.

"No! Not yet!" When it was three-fourths the way around, he said, "Now!"

She shifted quickly from reverse to drive and crammed her foot down on the accelerator so hard it fishtailed for fifty feet.

"Yes!" she yelled, beating on the steering wheel. "Yes! Yes! Yesssss!"

"You did it, girl!"

"Can we do it again?"

"Go for it."

"This'll be wild in a stretch!"

⚓

Scott leaned his elbow on the desk and stared at his phone. He took a deep breath and punched in Sabyl's number. Dotty answered, "Martin Transportation."

"Dotty, is that you?"

"Scott? Scott Terhune?"

"Yeah, how are you, you old war horse?"

"Hey, watch who you're calling a horse. I guess you want to talk to the boss. She talking to you?"

"Dotty, I do need to talk to her, but she's not taking my calls. Can you help me out?"

"I don't know, dude. She's got every right to nail your rear end to the wall."

"I know, but..."

"Don't think I'd try to call anytime soon. She's pretty loaded up with this Fredericks funeral, you know."

"I know. But do me a favor, will you? Tell her to please call me. I've got to talk to her. It's really important."

"I'll tell her. Not sure how she'll react, but yeah, I'll tell her."

"Thanks, Dotty. You're a real lady."

"Yeah, not bad for an old equine. Later."

Sabyl walked in and went through the mail. "Who was that?"

Dotty dropped her hand in her lap and crossed her fingers. "Uhhh, nobody."

⚔

Following Endicott's orders he had given him over his cell phone, Rudy picked up Fathid at the brownstone, who once again brought out his camera equipment; they headed for the Lincoln Memorial and then to the Washington Monument. Had it not been for the fact that the Park Police had known Rudy for fourteen years, he would not have been able to get near some of the monuments for Fathid to do his incessant photography. At one point, officer Shanklin asked to see some ID, which Fathid produced immediately, along with a brochure of his specialty work.

Rudy parked, opened the sunroof, got out of the car and looked up at Fathid. Once again, he stood up in the opening, spread the blanket on the car top, set up the tripod, mounted the camera and peered intently through the camera lens.

The Park Police pulled up beside the car and got out. Rudy got out of his car to greet them. "Hi, Shank, Louis."

Fathid looked down at him. "Please either remain in the car or stay out. You are moving the camera."

Shanklin looked at Fathid curiously, smiled and shook his head. "Hey, Rudy. You're getting to be a regular fixture around here."

"So it seems."

"You going to drive for the funeral Saturday?"

"No," he sighed. "I will probably be right here."

The policeman leaned closer to Rudy and whispered, "How many pictures can you take of the Washington Monument?"

Rudy smiled and shrugged one shoulder.

"The skies change each day making interesting backdrops, if you must know," Fathid said dryly.

"Well, take it easy, Rudy, and give Ms. Martin our regards."

"Thank you, I will."

They got in their car and drove away. Fathid pulled his camera off the tripod and handed it to Rudy. He then folded the tripod, kneeled down and pulled it down into the cabin of the limousine, and carefully rolled it up in the blanket. Rudy opened the back door and handed him the camera, got in the driver's seat and asked if he was ready to leave.

Fathid smiled coldly. "Yes. I believe I got what I came for."

⅄

A deep sadness etched in his face and still stinging from the pain of knowing that they had provided protection for thousands of National Special Security Events (NSSEs), including both Democratic and Republican Conventions, hundreds of Summits all over the world, all without incident, and now, in their own town, in their own back yard, the top diplomat of the United States of America is gunned down right before their very eyes. How could it have happened? That was the question on everyone's minds, especially Special Agent in Charge Ron Keefer.

Several glum looking agents were seated in the conference room next to Keefer's office when Scott arrived and took his place at the table.

All the agents were waiting for the proverbial butt chewing. But it never came. It was unnerving. It was as if Keefer was taking the blame completely on his own. The SAIC handed each one a file.

"Before you open that, I want to bring you up to speed from the BITA, which, as you know, is the crossing point between the State Department and the U.S. intelligence community on all terrorism matters, both domestic and international, especially those leveled against Americans and U.S. diplomats, and in particular threats against the Secretary of State"

The Bureau of Intelligence and Threat Analysis researches, monitors, and analyzes all intelligence and chatter on terrorist activities and threats, against senior U.S. officials, visiting foreign dignitaries, resident foreign diplomats, and foreign operations in the U.S. for whom the State Department has a security concern and responsibility.

"They had no intelligence on this attack of the Secretary of State."

The agents sat in stunned silence. Finally, Scott said, "So there was no chatter on this at all?"

"None. There was some residual chatter because of the previous week's café bombing in Sweden, but nothing concerning the SecState or anything remotely related to this attack. That's got a lot of people worried, gentlemen. However, we did get this. Take a look at your files."

Scott, sitting next to his partner, Lou Martz, opened his file and asked, "What is this?" Reminiscent of a ransom note, there were letters that had been cut out and pasted on a single sheet of paper.

"The Director got it this morning. They sent copies to the DHS, CIA, DIA, FBI and NSA as well."

Scott read it aloud: HOW ABOUT A GAME OF FIVE-CARD DRAW? FREDERICKS WAS EASY. WHAT WILL WE DEAL OUT NEXT?

Lou frowned, "How do we know it's not some prank?"

Keefer took his glasses off and rubbed his eyes and put them back on. "We don't. But we've got to take it all seriously. Forensics has the original."

Scott sat quietly and stared at the words.

"Take these copies and etch them in your brains. Call me if you come up with anything."

One of the agents asked, "When are you going to say it?"

"Say what?"

"How did this happen…how did the shooter get through?"

Keefer looked at them thoughtfully. "I've already talked with the advance team. They're taking full responsibility for the breach. I can tell you this: it won't happen again."

The doorbell rang. Sabyl padded over in her bare feet, looked through the peephole, and opened the door. Beau jumped up and down, his tail wagging like a windshield wiper in a heavy rain, and did his funny little sneezing thing that seemed to be part of his greeting. He jumped up to greet her and licked her face as she bent down to let him give her his wet kisses. She smiled and thought of something her pastor had said once: "Dogs are a study in worship."

"Hi, Conrad. Thanks so much for bringing him home."

"No problem. How'd your appointment go?"

"Okay." She rubbed Beau's ears. "Heeeey, how's my boy…oh, you smell so good. Did you get all prettied up at the groomer?"

"He's always good there, but very glad to leave."

She walked over to her purse and pulled out her wallet. "Here's your check. You're a life saver, Conrad."

"No prob. Anytime."

"Thanks. I'm sure I'll be calling you soon."

"Okay. Bye. See ya, Beau."

The handsome dog headed for his water bowl and lapped happily. Sabyl sat back down on the sofa and picked up the paper she had been reading and stared at the headline,

TERRORIST CONNECTION SOUGHT IN FREDERICKS
KILLING

Washington, D.C., January 8—Secretary of Homeland Security John Killian said today that the assassin, Ja'bar al-Mansur, had all the earmarks of a terrorist sleeper and that there were "probably several more in our country, perhaps right here in the District."

Beau came over to her, panting and wagging his tail. "Hey, boy. You ready to go for a walk?" She put her shoes back on and got up. "Go get your leash!"

Beau ran into the hallway, carefully picked up his green leash and brought it to her. She snapped the leash on his collar, put on her overcoat, and grabbed her keys. They got on the wood-paneled elevator. She pushed the "L" button; they got off and walked through the lobby, Beau's nails clicking on the shiny marble floor. The doorman greeted her and Beau warmly as did the two smiling women behind the massive front desk. "Good afternoon, Ms. Martin. How are you and Beau today?"

"Wonderful, and you?"

"Oh, praise God, we are happy that the sun is shining and all is well," the one on the right said in her warm Jamaican accent.

"Can't ask for more than that," she smiled with a wave, and walked out the front door. Sabyl smiled at the friendly greeting and thought, *those gals are true Christians and are so open about it. I think I need to work on my attitude. I've gotten a bit surly lately. Lord, please help me to show more kindness to others like that.*

Beau pulled at his leash, happy to be going for a walk. They passed the ivy-bordered fountain in front of the stately, eleven-story building, and turned left on the wide sidewalk and headed toward Rock Creek Park. She passed a white Subaru that was parallel parked along the street. The man inside watched her closely.

DAY 5

FRIDAY, JANUARY 9

Dotty buzzed Sabyl's office. "Dr. Solomon's office on line one," she said with concern.

Sabyl took a deep breath and answered, "Sabyl Martin."

"Ms. Martin, we need you to come in for a needle-guided biopsy. There's a tumor that we need to take a closer look at. Can you come right in?"

The words hit hard. Sabyl closed her eyes and rubbed her forehead.

"Ms. Martin?"

"You mean now?"

"Yes."

"I suppose," she sighed. "I'll be there in a few minutes." She slammed down the phone in frustration and grabbed her coat.

"Where you going?" Dotty asked, worried.

"Dr. Solomon's office. I'll be back."

She drove nervously to the clinic, parked and walked resolutely to the automatic glass doors and went inside. They sent her back to the familiar ultrasound department where the same technician once again ran the probe over her breast, located the tumor, and then called the radiologist in. The young Puerto Rican doctor greeted Sabyl warmly. "You've been here before, haven't you?"

"Oh, yes," Sabyl replied.

"Good, then you know what to expect." He administered a local anesthetic and carefully inserted a core biopsy needle straight into the tumor guided by the high-resolution ultrasound images. A small sample of tissue was collected and the procedure was over within minutes. "Okay, that's it."

Sabyl dressed and went back up to Dr. Solomon's office. The nurse behind the desk smiled, "Okay, you're done. We'll call you in a few days as soon as we get the results."

Sabyl bristled. "Look, the last time I had a biopsy, I had to wait nine days to get the results, and I'm not about to go through that again! I can't sit around wondering about the results. I've got a business to run."

The nurse smiled sympathetically. "I'll make sure the doctor calls you himself as soon as he gets the results. Does he have your cell number?"

"Yes, I think so. Thanks." She left and drove back to the office.

Dotty poured her a cup of coffee. "Just made it fresh. So how did your biopsy go?"

"Okay. Not much to it. I'll get the results in a few days."

"Hope it doesn't turn out like last time—you having to have radiation and all."

"Yeah, me too. I had enough last time to suit me. I probably still glow in the dark."

"We'll keep our fingers crossed."

"A lot of good that'll do. I'd rather you'd pray!" She immediately felt a stab of guilt for having been so short with the nurse and now with her friend and remembered the little prayer she had whispered earlier about showing kindness to others.

Dotty looked stricken. She picked up some papers and put them in a file. "Yeah, guess that would be better."

Sabyl pulled her coat off and hung it over her arm. "I'm sorry, Dotty, I had no right to talk to you like that."

"That's okay. I've been through the same thing and I know exactly how you feel." She beamed, "You prayed me through mine and I'm gonna pray you through yours."

Sabyl hung up her coat, walked around Dotty's desk and hugged her. "Thanks, dear. I knew I could count on you."

⚔

Rudy watched Endicott and Sahba in the rearview mirror behind the glass divider as they argued vehemently about something. It unnerved Rudy, who was a peaceful man. He felt he was chauffeuring a keg of dynamite with a very short fuse. Thinking it might calm them, he put on some soft classical music. Endicott immediately banged on the divider. Rudy pushed the button to let it down and his client bellowed at him to turn it off, then continued to rail against Sahba. Rudy pushed the button again to put the divider back up. Before it closed completely, he heard him say, "Your absurd addiction has no place in our business here. This isn't a game. How dare you to take it upon yourself to send..."

Rudy hoped he wasn't driving a drug dealer or anyone involved in anything illegal. He kept his eyes straight ahead and decided the less he knew the better.

⚔

Dressed in a camel-colored sweater and pants with matching jacket and black low-heeled shoes, Sabyl welcomed the drivers from PDC and Vassette to the meeting, joining her drivers who had come in late that afternoon from the Counter Terrorism Driving Course. Seeing their excitement, she let them tell about their newly acquired driving prowess. Maurice talked about his J-Turn, and Marty told about her first Bootleg, which brought peals of laughter and hoots from the other drivers. It was good to see them laughing. Sabyl wished that Rudy could be there. Lately, he looked like he could use a good laugh.

She handed out sheets of paper to all the drivers that contained the funeral procession line-up. The drivers looked at them and listened intently as she explained the process. "With this many heads of state in one place, the feds are really sensitive about security, so we are to meet two hours early at the Capitol to be swept. So just be ready for that." She then admonished them to arrive with absolutely spotless cars. "I don't even want to see a windshield wiper streak. Is there anyone here who has not given us their updated ID sheet?" Her eyes scanned them carefully. Relieved that no one's hand went up, she took questions and afterwards, treated them all to pizza. "I'm sorry I can't join you, but I'm meeting a friend for dinner, so I'll see you guys in the morning. Thanks for coming." She left and headed for Georgetown.

D.C. traffic was a wall of humanity wrapped in metal and fiberglass. Drivers grinded their teeth at the delays, anxious to get home or out of town and wanted to put the workweek behind them. Pedestrians dressed in wool overcoats and nylon parkas crowded the sidewalks. Sabyl drove round and round the cobblestone streets of Georgetown until she finally found a parking place big enough for her SUV. She parked snugly and headed to meet Rebecca.

The small, cozy pub was crowded and smelled of beer and pizza. The bartender chatted amiably with the customers at the bar like they were old friends. Rebecca saw Sabyl come in and waved cheerfully, "Over here!"

They hugged the way old friends do. Sabyl removed her coat and slid into the booth. "I can't tell you how happy I am to see you," she said with a warm smile. She pulled off her leather gloves and put them in her purse.

Rebecca reached over and took her hand. "You look wonderful, dear." She wore a plum colored cashmere sweater and pants with matching suede boots. Her slender wrists were loaded with rows of bracelets that clunked together each time she moved her arm. Her blond hair fell softly around her classic face framing her sapphire blue eyes. "You have any trouble finding a parking place?"

"Not really." She saw no point in going on about how many times she had to circle around Georgetown to find one. She rubbed her arms and shivered. "It is so cold out there."

Rebecca waved the server over. Turning back to Sabyl, she asked, "You hungry? We could go ahead and order."

"Yeah, I'm starved. Pizza's good, huh?"

"The best."

"Wanna split one?"

"The white cheese and sun-dried tomato is great."

"Sounds perfect."

The server asked if they wanted salads. They said yes, she took their pizza order and left.

"So, Miss Limo Lady, what have you been up to lately?"

"Not much. Well, that's not exactly true. I'm still dealing with that French driver, Claude Bagot. He drove for me a couple of years ago, had a minor fender bender, faked a neck injury and is suing me."

"I remember you talking about that ages ago. You're still dealing with that? My goodness, how much is he suing you for?"

"Millions."

"Yikes!"

"Yeah. His lawyer smelled money and has dragged the case out for two years. It's a royal pain, but I'm hoping it'll be over soon."

"Is your lawyer optimistic?"

"He thinks we'll win. If not, it's going to be really, really bad."

"Good grief, girl. That's awful. It must be hard to break in good drivers."

"It's one of the toughest parts of the business. I've seen all kinds come and go over the years. Some were lazy, some were troublemakers, and some didn't like having a woman for a boss. I had to fire one simply because he had terrible body odor."

Rebecca laughed, "You're kidding!"

"Nope. Imagine being cooped up in a car with someone who smells like a goat? No amount of entreating helped. He just refused to take a bath."

Rebecca laughed, "So what else is going on?"

Sabyl sighed, "They found another tumor. I just had a needle biopsy."

"Oh, honey, I'm so sorry!"

"Thanks. Had the biopsy this morning. Now I'll just wait for the results."

"How long has it been since the last...?"

"Two years." Sabyl smiled weakly, "I'm just full of good news, aren't I? So tell me how you are and what's going on with you."

Their server brought their salads and left.

Rebecca caught her up on the latest. "I talked with Audrey Aberholdt today."

"Really? Poor dear. Is she devastated that her party was crashed by a terrorist?"

Rebecca laughed, "She's already organizing her next party!"

"Good for her!"

Rebecca poured dressing on her salad. "Now tell me what you wanted to talk about."

Sabyl hesitated and then said, "Scott."

"Scott Terhune? Are you kidding? Is he back in your life?"

"No, but he wants to be."

"Really?"

"I ran into him the other night while doing an event. In fact it was at the Grande Continental the night Fredericks was shot."

"You were there?"

"Yeah. He was protecting Brassfield. Just as I was leaving, he came over to talk to me. Said he wanted to talk...to explain..."

"So, what are you going to do?"

"I don't know. I feel like I need to hear him out...and then again..."

Rebecca dabbed her mouth with her napkin. "So let him explain and if it holds water, then take it from there."

"So, you think I should?"

Rebecca shrugged, "Sure, but it had better be good."

"You're right. What's it going to cost me to listen?"

"Nothing. In fact, if you're anything like me, you're sort of curious, right?"

Sabyl chuckled, "I really am."

"Then there you are."

The server brought the pizza. Sabyl ate one piece and Rebecca ate three. "What's the matter with you? You usually scarf up half a pizza!"

Sabyl smiled weakly. "Not as hungry as I thought. Just trying to sort things out."

"You need some time off to unwind, dear."

"Time off?" she chuckled. "What's that? No, you're right. This has been one tough week."

"I guess it has. Let's see, you practically witnessed an assassination..."

"Well, not really..."

"Then Scott shows up and wants back in your life, you're being sued, you have a needle biopsy, then you do the meeting for the Secretary of State's funeral—you have a right to be uptight!"

"I suppose."

They looked at the table thoughtfully. Sabyl perked up. "I've got a great idea. Why don't you come to my house in Pennsylvania this weekend? I've just got to get away and I can't think of anyone I'd rather hang out with than you."

Rebecca sat up straight and smiled, "Sounds wonderful. I've always wanted to see your country place. But what about the funeral tomorrow?"

"We can leave right after. The funeral's at nine—then the burial at Arlington. I think we could be out of here by one o'clock at the latest."

"Are you sure you want company? You've been under so much..."

"Absolutely. I really want you to come." She grinned, "I'll tell you all about my little house and even give you the latest dirt on my neighbors."

Rebecca laughed, "Sounds delicious."

The two friends talked for another hour and a half. The server took up the plates and asked if there would be anything else, hoping they would leave. Sabyl looked at her watch. "Oh my, I had no idea it was so late! We'd better go. We have a big day ahead of us."

"You mean, *you've* got a big day. All I'm doing is packing and going to the country."

Sabyl smiled warmly. "Doesn't that sound just wonderful?" She slid out of the booth and put her coat on.

"Where did you park? Want me to take you to your car?"

"No, no. It's not far. I need to walk."

"You sure?"

"Yes."

Rebecca insisted on paying the bill and hugged Sabyl goodbye. "Okay, dear. See you tomorrow."

Sabyl plunged out into the cold air. It hit her like a slap, burning her cheeks. She walked down the hill to the corner of Wisconsin and Volta and turned right. Since it was Friday night, she expected to see people still out on the streets but there were none. The further she got from well-lit Wisconsin Avenue, the darker it got. She could not remember the streets of Georgetown being this dark—ever. Her eyes darted back and forth as she walked down the silent street. It was complete blackness. *Do they turn out the streetlights at a certain hour like they do the floods that light up the monuments?* She remembered when she first moved to D.C., she came in late from an out-of-town trip, and just as she crossed Memorial Bridge, the lights on the Lincoln Memorial went out. It was spooky then, but this was creepy.

Stopping for a moment to get her bearings, she thought she heard something. Footsteps? She stood silent—listening. *It's probably someone walking their dog.* She moved on deeper into the darkness. It was a narrow street, but then they all were. She remembered circling around several times to find a parking place and had grabbed the first one she saw in front of one of the many townhouses in Georgetown, but which one? So many of them looked alike.

Finally, a light! A dim lamp over a small liquor store barely lit up one corner, but even a little light was enough to give her some comfort. She listened hard, thinking she still heard footsteps. If only she had followed the advice she had been given on the first day she moved to Washington fourteen years ago. Never walk *anywhere* in D.C. at night alone.

She stopped again at the corner. Why hadn't she let Rebecca give her a ride to her car like she offered? *Because I couldn't have told her where my stupid car is that's why, you idiot!* She turned left on 34th Street. For the first time Sabyl began to feel panicky. Her father used to call her "Bird Dog" because she had such a good sense of direction, but not tonight. She was hopelessly lost in a maze of posh townhouses neatly lined on cobblestone streets, with BMWs and Mercedes parked bumper to bumper, and an occasional SUV towering above them.

She remembered seeing a red Lincoln Town Car, an old one, about an '88, parked behind her. She had bumped it a couple of times while parallel parking, something she still had not gotten down after all these years.

Footsteps! This time she heard them clearly. They were behind her less than a half a block. Her heart pounded as she quickened her steps. *God, help me!* She fumbled in her purse for her keys and punched the "unlock" button, hoping to hear it beep, but heard nothing. *Where is my car?* She turned another corner onto P Street. Had she gone this way? Why hadn't she paid more attention? The footsteps behind her seemed closer and moving faster! *Oh God! Help me! Where is my car?*

There was a faint light in the distance. She hoped it was in a window and not a closed storefront. She was desperate enough now to beat on someone's door and make some noise. *Why weren't people still up? It's a weekend in Georgetown!*

Suddenly, she felt something brush her arm. She let out a little scream. It was a shrub that overhung the sidewalk. She ran toward the light. She saw the bulky squared form of a red Town car. Punching the "unlock" button again, she heard the two short beeps. *Thank God! Just a few more yards. Jesus, help me!*

The footsteps were closing in behind her. She broke into a full run, not an easy feat on cobblestones. As she passed the cars on the street she slammed her hand against each one and alarms began going off. She could no longer hear the footsteps because of the noise. Porch lights began to come on; people opened their doors and yelled, "Hey! Get away from my car!"

She thought she felt a presence close behind her. She screamed, "Get away from me!" and jumped in her car and quickly closed the door and locked it. A man ran out of his apartment and screamed something at her. She started the car and began maneuvering to get free from between the two cars, bumping the Town Car and the Camry in front of her, setting off its alarm. Finally clear, she fishtailed wildly up the cobblestone street. "Lord, thank you! Thank you!"

She told herself she was safe but her body didn't believe it yet. Her heart thudded in her chest and the adrenaline pumped like a fire hydrant. Finally, she was out onto well-lit Wisconsin Avenue. She knew it was illogical that whoever was chasing her could be following her, but she kept looking in the rearview mirror. Did she dare go straight home? She turned onto Mass Avenue and then onto 39th to the Second Precinct police station. *If I go there, what can they do for me? There has been no crime; no one was hurt.* She decided to go anyway, just in case she was being followed. Sabyl stepped inside feeling awkward and foolish.

The desk sergeant, rotund and gap-toothed, scolded her for walking alone in the dark late at night. A young black woman officer sitting in front of a computer gave her a sympathetic look as the desk sergeant spoke coldly to Sabyl. "A woman was raped and murdered just a few nights ago right around where you were."

She looked at him sideways. "Did you catch him?"

"No."

"I'm an idiot."

"There have been several such incidents in that area."

"I think I remember seeing that on TV."

"We can't do anything about what happened to you tonight. No crime has been committed."

"No, except maybe disturbing the peace by setting off alarms."

"I have to admit that was quick thinking, lady."

"Thanks."

"Just be careful from here on, okay? How long you been in D.C.?"

"Fourteen years."

"Long enough to know that you don't ever—*ever* walk alone in D.C. Not even in the wealthy areas. It's just plain stupid."

"Clearly. Thanks, officers." She turned to leave and hesitated.

"Something else?"

"Yeah." She screwed up her face sheepishly. Could one of you walk me to my car?"

He sighed and grunted as he got up, "Sure. No problem."

"Thanks."

"Where do you live?"

"Not far. Over by UDC."

"Okay. Keep your doors locked. You live in an apartment or a house?"

"Condo."

"Parking garage?"

"Definitely."

"Good. You don't have to park on the street then."

"No."

They walked out of the wide glass doors.

She realized she missed Scott more than ever. He always made her feel safe. But could she ever be safe with him again? She was going to find out.

DAY 6

Saturday, January 10

The horse-drawn caisson carrying the flag-draped casket of Secretary of State Douglas Allen Fredericks proceeded up the hill in Arlington Cemetery. The family walked silently behind, their eyes cast down. Following were dozens of heads of state from all over the world. The caisson came to a stop and the bodybearers carefully lifted the casket. With precision steps the six-man Honor Guard moved to the open grave under a canopy and placed it upon the steel lowering device. The family was seated on folding chairs beside it. The rain had let up and was now reduced to a light sprinkle. Sabyl stood on the perimeter of the scene holding an umbrella and watching as the quiet service proceeded.

The robed minister stepped back at the end of the brief service and stood beside the family. The crack of three volleys by seven riflemen in a twenty-one-gun salute echoed throughout the burial ground. The mournful sound of "Taps" tugged at Sabyl's heart. She said a silent prayer for the Secretary's family as she dug around in her pocket for a tissue. The chaplain received the folded flag from one of the bodybearers and remained in place at attention until the music stopped. He then stepped up to Joan Fredericks, bent down and presented the flag to her, and said softly, "On behalf of a grateful nation." He then stepped back and rendered a final salute to the flag.

A uniformed man standing on the perimeter spoke quietly into a radio, an aviator assigned out of Andrews Air Force Base to be the ground controller for the approaching Missing Man formation. Four McDonnell-Douglas F/A-18C Hornets, with their distinctive swept-back wings, approached the famous cemetery; one of the planes trailed off just as they flew over the former Navy pilot's casket now being lowered in the ground. The high-pitched whine of the planes thrilled the onlookers as they watched with moist eyes. To avoid Reagan National's air space, they pulled up sharply and climbed into the heavens within seconds. The service over, several people gently offered their final condolences to the Fredericks family, as did Sabyl. Within a half-hour, her cars were moving. She wondered about Rudy.

A

Another poker riddle had come in that kept Scott and his colleagues up half the night trying to decipher it. He took a break, left the conference room, went back to his office and sat down. Rubbing his forehead, he tried Sabyl's office again. Frank answered.

"Frank, this is Scott. Is Sabyl there yet?"

"No, she's still at the funeral, and then she's going out of town."

"Frank, I really need to talk to her."

"Can't help you, pal."

"Look, please give me her cell phone number. I really need to get in touch with her."

"I don't think she's going to want to talk to you."

"You know I can get her cell number, don't you?"

The dispatcher rubbed the back of his neck. "Yeah, I suppose you can."

"I don't want to have to go that route. Will she be calling in or coming by before she leaves town?"

"I'm sure she'll check in."

"Then just tell her it's urgent, will you?"

Frank smiled and rolled his eyes. "Urgent?"

"Yes."

"I'll tell her. Your number?"

Scott gave the number and they hung up.

A

Sabyl parked in the circle drive in front of her office, grabbed her handbag and came inside.

Frank heaved out of his desk chair, stood up straight, and stretched his shoulders wide. "Hey. How'd it go?"

"It went well. How are things here?"

"Fine. The drivers for tonight's Kennedy Center event are all set."

"Good."

"Oh, and…uh, Scott called."

"Oh, pleeease."

"He said it's urgent."

"That's very interesting. Nice try."

"Sabyl, the guy sounded…"

"Pitiful?"

"No, but—why don't you give him a call. It might be important."

"Oh, all right. Give me his number. Has Rudy called?"

"No. Haven't heard from him."

"Okay, thanks." She sat down at her desk, took a deep breath and punched in Scott's number. She cleared her throat, crossed her leg and pumped it up and down nervously.

"Scott Terhune."

"It's Sabyl."

"Sabyl! Thank you for calling me. I really need to talk to you. Can we meet?"

"You're talking to me now. What's the big urgent thing you need to discuss?"

"Sabyl, please let me explain…why I…"

"Scott, don't…"

"I owe you an explanation. Please, it's the least I can do."

"Scott, this isn't the time. I'm trying to leave town. I'll…call you when I get back and…we'll talk."

She hung up and rubbed her eyes with her fingers and wondered why she said what she said.

George came in with Beau. The beagle jumped up and down when he saw Sabyl as though she'd been gone for a year.

She grabbed her pocketbook. "Okay, guys, I'm outa here. Frank, you can go on home. Just forward the calls to my cell."

"Naw, I'll forward them to my house. You go and relax and I'll see you Monday."

"Thank you. Have a great weekend."

⋏

The scenery changed as they pulled off the four-lane highway onto the gray ribbon of a country road that wound through batches of leafless trees overhanging the highway, up and down hills and over small wooden bridges. They laughed and talked, letting off city-life steam and seemed to take on an entirely different disposition. Coming into Fairview, they passed a little brick church set back from the road with an ancient-looking cemetery to one side, where its faithful departed members were laid to rest.

They climbed a steep hill and turned right onto a country road. The tires crunched on the gravel driveway that wound back through trees in a park-like setting; there stood a lovely old white two-story farmhouse. Dark green velvety Leyland cypresses lined the front yard.

Rebecca unbuckled her seat belt. "It's exactly as you described it!"

The engine was turned off; they gathered their pocketbooks and stepped out. Sabyl pointed and said, "From there over to where that window ends was the old house. I added the rest and had it resurfaced and a new roof put on."

"It's charming! And what a wonderful yard! How on earth do you keep it up?"

"I have a couple who take care of it. Jerry and Kate. They're wonderful."

"Lucky you!"

She opened the back and let Beau out. They grabbed their suitcases and headed up the curved flagstone walkway. She called Beau, who had just watered a tree. He came bounding toward them.

They stepped through the heavy wooden door. Beau's nails clicked on the Italian tile in the wide entryway, which gave way to polished hardwood floors. The room was ablaze with reflected light pouring through the west windows.

They stepped down through beveled French doors into a large room with a stone fireplace. Two sofas faced each other in front of it. Between them was a large coffee table on which books from Italy were stacked. Hearty plants were all around the room. There were so many windows that the room seemed glass-enclosed. "This is my favorite spot. I had it added two years ago."

"I love the openness of the room, yet the trees give plenty of privacy."

"I wanted to feel like I was outdoors. Let's take our things upstairs and I'll start dinner."

They each put their luggage away, freshened up, and went back downstairs and resumed the tour.

"Sabyl, this is wonderful. You must love coming here to get away from work."

"It's nice and quiet here. With my business, I'm seldom able to escape my job, but sometimes I'll bring a briefcase full of work up here and I can get a lot done without the usual interruptions."

They walked into the kitchen. "This is my mother's old stove," she said, pointing to an ancient gas range. "I splurged and had it resurfaced in red."

"I love it! It's so bright and cheery!"

"I replaced the refrigerator, but the stove works fine. I had these cabinets put in and added the pantry. Now let me put some music on and I'll feed Beau and then we'll have dinner. Kate shopped for me this afternoon."

"May I help?"

"No, just relax or walk around in the yard if you want. There's a dear little kitty that has adopted me. She comes around when I'm here. Her name is Miss Piti."

Rebecca laughed, "Miss Piti? How'd she get that name?"

"I hadn't been in this house for years. After my mother died, I knew I was going to have to do something with it. I didn't want the house. When I walked up to the back porch and started to open the door, this little cat came toward me, arched her back and leaned against my leg. She had the most pitiful meow I've ever heard, so I named her Miss Pitiful—Miss Piti for short."

"I'm going to see if I can find her." Rebecca stepped out the back door and turned, "Call me if I can help with dinner."

Sabyl fed Beau and let him out the door into the fenced-in half-acre back yard where he began sniffing around, following all sorts of interesting scents.

The rich tones of Andrea Bocelli soon filled the house, as did the aroma of garlic, herbs, and spices. Rebecca sat on the back porch swing listening to the music and watching the squirrels playfully chase one another. Miss Piti lay in her lap, purring like a well-oiled machine.

Sabyl hummed along in the kitchen and soon called Rebecca in and served dinner in the den.

The fire crackled and warmed them. Miss Piti draped herself lazily across the back of the sofa and purred steadily. Her eyes were closed as she dozed with her noble head upright. Beau looked from Sabyl to Rebecca and back to Sabyl, hoping for a morsel to drop on the floor. Giving up, he finally dropped with a grunt and listened to their talk and laughter. The little black and white cat yawned and stood up, unsheathed her claws and began doing her nails on the sofa.

"Miss Piti! No!" Sabyl stood up and headed for the sliding glass door. With a scratchy meow of protest, the little cat's dainty steps followed her, and she slipped out through the door. Sabyl closed the door and smiled. "She hasn't learned her indoor manners yet. I got her a nice scratching post and she ignores it."

Rebecca wiped the corners of her mouth with her napkin and said, "Sabyl that was wonderful! You're a fabulous cook!"

"Thanks, dear. I took some cooking classes in Italy on one of my trips."

Rebecca picked up a picture on the coffee table. "Are these your husband and son you told me about?"

"Yes."

"How long has it been?"

"Sixteen years."

"Does the pain ever go away?"

"Not really. But...we go on..."

Rebecca put it back, sat up straight and said, "Okay, so tell me the latest dirt on your neighbors."

Sabyl laughed, "You remember when I pointed out the junky yard about a quarter mile down the road?"

"Yeah, pretty awful."

"Two men live there. Brothers. Last name is Oswald. Major rednecks. The older is the more dominant one. The younger—well, not the sharpest knife in the drawer."

"What's with all the junk?"

"They've got old refrigerators, washing machines—you name it—piled everywhere over there. They're breaking every ordinance there is, and still get away with it."

"Why don't the police do something?"

"They were afraid of them, I think. They're pretty volatile. I got really fed up with it so I got up a petition and the police finally realized the town was behind them, so they've given them a month to clean the place up, or they'll be fined—maybe arrested."

"You think they'll comply?"

"Not sure. The police have never really gone after them, so we'll see what happens."

"When did they serve them the notice?"

"A couple of weeks ago, I think. I haven't seen any change so far, but who knows?" She placed her empty plate on the tray.

Rebecca folded her napkin. "You said you would tell me about your house. I'm dying to hear."

Sabyl sat up straight. "I was born in this house."

"You're kidding!"

"Nope." She pointed up and to the left. "Right up there in the corner bedroom. My mother was...unstable."

Rebecca lowered her eyes and shook her head slowly. "You don't have to tell me."

"No, I want to talk about it."

Settling back on the sofa, she put a throw pillow over her stomach. "Okay, tell me about it."

"Until I was eight or nine, life was pretty good. My parents for the most part got along okay. But then my mother began to change. I watched my parents drift apart. I always wondered what was wrong. My mother even started to look different. There was a sort of darkness about her. Sometimes I could hear her talking to herself, lashing out at the—I guess—demons in her head. She caught me watching her in the doorway one day, and screamed at me, 'What are you looking at?' I ran and hid under my bed and she chased me, dragged me out by my ankle and beat me until my legs bled. Then she walked away, clomped down the stairs and resumed her strange conversations."

Rebecca swallowed hard. "Oh, Sabyl, how awful."

"But you know, I think God protected my heart somehow, because I've never been bitter. I just felt she was to be pitied. I would walk away from the beatings thinking, "I'll be okay."

Rebecca leaned forward and looked intently at Sabyl. "And you are. If that had happened to anyone else, they'd probably be pretty messed up."

"It's God's grace, for sure."

"So what happened?"

"My brother Phillip despised Dad for not being stronger and taking up for us." She reached over and picked up a small, framed picture and handed it to Rebecca. "This is Phillip."

Rebecca looked at it plaintively. "He's nice looking. You look alike...especially around the eyes." She handed it back.

"When he was sixteen, after mother had beaten me badly, he went out to Dad's woodworking shop and beat him until he was unconscious. Then he left and never came back."

"Where is he now?"

"In Arizona—married—keeps to himself. We talk a couple of times a year. That's about it."

"How could you return here? I mean—the memories..."

"When I first came into the house, the gloom that I always remembered hung in the air mingled with—I guess nostalgia. I had mixed emotions at seeing the place that I had called home, yet without the peace and sanctity a home should offer. I remember looking out the window at the weatherworn picket fence and wondered whether to paint it or replace it. I was surprised at the thought because I had not planned to keep the house. A strange excitement came over me and I decided I would restore the house and make it into a home—a real home. I would fill it with things that make me happy and I would love it to life and make it into the home it should have always been."

Rebecca studied Sabyl and realized that even though she had known her for seven years, she didn't really know her at all.

Sabyl stood up. "Come with me. There's a room I haven't shown you yet." She led her into a small sitting room with an old upright piano by a window, a small sofa against the wall, and a wing-backed chair next to it. Across from the sofa was a wall-to-wall, floor-to-ceiling bookcase filled with old books, a half-dozen hat boxes, a wedding picture of Sabyl's mother and father, a picture of Phillip as a toddler, and one of Beau when he was a puppy.

"Before Mother died, I'd heard that she had gone berserk and ripped up her own underwear and all of her prettiest clothes. The only things she didn't destroy were her gloves and hats. She had stacks of these hatboxes in the attic and drawers full of gloves. 'A young lady should wear a hat and gloves when she goes out in public,' she would always say. One of these days I'm going to go through all of these hatboxes and her journals. I just haven't had time."

"Sabyl, you've come out so triumphantly. A lesser person would be a complete wreck."

"Thanks, Bec. Let's go back into the den."

The two of them sat in silence staring at the fire for a few moments. Finally, Rebecca broke the silence. "So, what's your next dragon to kill?"

"The whys of it all."

"The whys?"

"Why did she beat me every day? Why did she make life miserable for my brother and me and my father?"

"You think you'll find the answer? Here?"

"Yes—somehow, someday."

"And when you do?"

"I'll be free."

"You're not free now? You've overcome a horrendous childhood; you've made a great life for yourself—"

"I have all the material things and I'm not ungrateful for them, but those are outward things. This is an inward thing."

"You have a shrink—what does he say?"

"He has theories—he has prescriptions—I want neither. I want the truth—then I'll be free."

Rebecca sighed. "I hope you find it. Maybe we're all looking for truth deep inside."

"A couple of months ago, I flew to L.A. to meet with a client. They took me out to dinner and then took me back to my hotel room and I was alone again. You know how that can be—you meet yourself when you're alone."

Rebecca took a deep breath. "How well I know."

"I got ready for bed. TV was boring, so I turned it off and looked around for something to read. I opened the drawer by my bed and there was a Bible."

Rebecca felt her face flush. She didn't want Sabyl to continue, but she wasn't sure why. "Yeah, I've seen those. The Gideons, right?"

"Yes. I shut the drawer and decided I would just go to sleep. But I kept seeing that Bible. It was like it was calling to me. So I opened it and you know what it opened to?"

"What?"

"And you shall know the truth and the truth shall set you free."

"Oh, my goodness!"

"Out of that whole book—and it's a pretty big book—that particular verse is where it opened. I didn't really understand what that meant then but I believed it."

Rebecca's expression was a meld of wonder and skepticism. "So what did you do?"

"I closed the Bible and put it back in the drawer and decided I would just let God reveal the truth to me and that would set me free. I'm not looking anymore. I've cancelled all my appointments with my shrink and I'm just sort of...waiting."

Rebecca looked at her with a trace of envy. "Will you let me know when you find it?"

Sabyl smiled. "Yes, I will. Rebecca, I hope I haven't embarrassed you."

"No, I needed to hear it. All of it."

Sabyl cocked her head to one side. "You really mean that?"

"Yes. I think I need to rethink some things too. I feel so empty sometimes. I try to reach for the big gold ring—a bestseller—a new romance—whatever—but it's all so empty. I've had the bestseller—I've had men but I always wind up feeling empty. It's like there's a big hole in my soul that I keep trying to fill with—something."

"I know. I've tried everything too, but I feel like I'm beginning to see the light—a little."

Rebecca smiled warmly. "Thank you for sharing that with me."

"You're welcome, Bec." She stood, gathered up the dishes and set them on the tray. "Now, how about a cup of decaf? And then let's head for bed. We've got a big day tomorrow."

"Sounds great." Rebecca thought, *I want to write about this search for the truth, but what would my friends or my editor think?* And then she realized much of her life had been shaped by what other people thought.

The grandfather clock in the dining room struck eleven chimes—bong, bong, and finally the last bong. As though on cue, the little clock in the kitchen whirred and cuckooed and played a tinny little tune and then receded back inside the tiny door to wait for the grand finale at twelve midnight.

"I'll shut the grandfather off so it won't disturb us," she said, as she opened its door and unlatched the pendulum. Beau suddenly jumped up and ran toward the sliding glass door, barking fiercely.

"Beau! What is it, boy?" Sabyl grabbed a flashlight and walked toward the door.

"Sabyl! What are you doing? Don't go out there!"

"Don't worry, if someone's out there, Beau will scare them off, if he hasn't already."

Sabyl slid the heavy door open. Beau ran out barking like he was on a fox hunt. Sabyl stepped out and followed him. He sniffed around the perimeter of the fence and then came back to his master, whining. "What is it, boy?" She shined the flashlight where Beau had been sniffing, then walked over to the fence and shined it on the gate. It was still locked from the inside.

"Come on, boy. Let's go back in." Beau came bounding through the door. Sabyl slid the door closed. "There's nothing out there. It was probably a possum or something."

Rebecca was trying to quiet her pounding heart. "Aren't you afraid your neighbors might try to get even with you somehow? I mean, they know you were responsible for that petition, right?"

"They know better. I've made it clear that if they mess with me, they're going to find themselves in court."

"Still, anyone who lives like that—might try something..."

"Don't worry, Bec. Now about that decaf."

Sunday, January 11

Finding her favorite mug, Sabyl poured it full of steaming coffee and headed for the den, her bedroom slippers gently snapping against her heels. She sat her mug down, flopped on the sofa and out of habit, picked up the remote and started to turn on the TV, but changed her mind and laid it back down. Sun rays slanted through the east windows, warming the room. She stood and walked over to the fireplace. Scrunching up some old newspapers she kept in a large vessel next to the hearth, Sabyl started a fire and sat back down on the sofa. She put her feet up on the coffee table and spread her toes and wiggled them pleasurably, glad to have them at home and in front of the fire. For the first time in days, she could feel her body truly relax. The usual stress headache was gone. It almost felt strange; it had been her companion for so long.

Beau scratched at the sliding glass door. She got up and let him in. He wagged his tail and began to whine. Sabyl heaved the heavy glass door closed. "You hungry, boy? Your breakfast is in your dish." He headed for the kitchen. She sat back down and sipped her coffee.

Wearing a white terry-cloth robe and matching slippers, Rebecca yawned, "Morning."

"Good morning! How did you sleep?"

"Great. What time is it?"

"Nine-thirty."

"Nine-thirty! I thought it was at least eleven! How long have you been up?"

"Not long. It was wonderful to sleep in for a change. Want some coffee?"

"Definitely."

Rebecca followed her into the kitchen. Sabyl poured her a mug and stepped aside. "Fix it like you want—cream's over here. Sugar or sweetener?"

"Sugar, please."

"Now, you go on into the den and enjoy the sunlight. I'm going to fix us a good country breakfast."

"Sounds heavenly. What can I do to help?"

"Nothing." She shooed her with the back of her hand. "Out—out—."

"Okay," Rebecca grinned. She walked into the den, sat down on the far sofa and sipped her coffee. Beau stood at the glass door and peered out, whining. Rebecca hollered, "How about some Bocelli?"

"Absolutely!"

The sweet strains of Andrea Bocelli's rendition of *Time to Say Goodbye* soon filled the air. The scent of coffee was soon overridden by the aroma of sautéed onions and tomatoes, cheddar cheese in omelets, and toast. Sabyl carefully filled a large white wicker tray and headed for the den.

"Sabyl, you're spoiling me rotten!"

"I want to! Here's your napkin and your orange juice." They ate a leisurely breakfast and debated whether or not to try to find a flea market. Beau kept whining. Sabyl stood up. "What's the matter, boy? You need to go out again already?" She opened the door and he went out and began sniffing all around the back door and by the back fence. Sabyl slid the door closed. "He's probably still looking for that possum."

Rebecca loaded her plate onto the tray. "Let me help you with these dishes."

"No, dear, I'm only going to put them in the dishwasher. You relax. The CD just finished. You want to hear it again?"

Rebecca picked up the remote. "Do you mind if I turn on the TV?"

"No, go ahead." Sabyl turned off the sound system and finished putting the dishes on the tray and headed for the kitchen.

The TV came to life. Pictures of a charred automobile came on the screen. Reporters talked over a picture of an ambulance leaving the scene. Aerial views came from a news helicopter.

"*...National Security Advisor's car slowed in traffic and then exploded...*"

"What on earth—Sabyl! Come look at this!"

"What is it?"

"I don't know—it looks like a car was bombed! They said something about National Security Advisor Brassfield..."

Sabyl sat down with a dishtowel in her hand and leaned forward. They watched live along with millions of other stunned Americans.

"*National Security Advisor Wayne Brassfield and his wife Gloria were on their way to attend morning services. As they approached National Presbyterian Church on Nebraska Avenue, a basketball rolled into the street toward the car, witnesses said. The driver slowed, obviously thinking there may be a child following it. The ball caught under the front bumper and exploded. Brassfield and the driver were killed instantly. His wife, Gloria, is in critical condition.*"

Rebecca gasped, "Oh, no! Not another one!"

The news anchor touched his earpiece, looked at a monitor in front of him and said, "*We turn now to Secretary of Homeland Security, John Killian.*"

The broad-shouldered ex-marine stepped up to the microphones. "*This morning at 8:50 AM Eastern Standard Time, National Security Advisor Wayne Brassfield and his wife Gloria were en route to the National Presbyterian Church to attend the early service, when an explosion occurred. Mr. Brassfield and his driver were killed instantly, along with the Secret Service agent accompanying them.*"

"Oh, my God! That's who Scott was protecting!"

"Oh, Sabyl, no!"

"Listen..."

"*Mrs. Brassfield has been taken to Georgetown University Hospital. As of yet, we have no report of her condition. The Secret Service agent's name is being withheld until his family can be notified.*"

Sabyl sat on the edge of the sofa, her stomach in a knot and her fingers pressed to her mouth.

"*This is the second attack on our nation's top leaders. We are asking every citizen to be calm but to be aware of any suspicious activities, conversations, or unusual behavior. I will take a few questions.*"

The press threw questions at him. "*Andy Garth, Fox News. Sir, what caused the explosion? Was it a bomb?*"

"*Looks like it.*"

Another reporter asked, *"Any suspects yet?"*

Sabyl turned off the TV. "Bec, I'm so sorry, I've got to get back."

"I understand."

They got dressed, packed and headed for the car. Rebecca offered to drive, but Sabyl seldom would abdicate the driver's seat. She was used to being in control, although, at the moment, she was feeling very much out of control. Frost glittered on the hood of her Nissan Murano. Snow threatened. They hoped it wouldn't start before they got to D.C.

Beau usually ran for the car when he saw Sabyl's luggage, but he ran out the front door barking like a bloodhound on the scent of a criminal. Sabyl and Rebecca finished putting their things in the back of the SUV.

"Beau, come on, let's go!"

She walked over to the side of the house by the gate and found Beau whining and looking at something. She walked over for a closer look and there she found Miss Piti with her throat slashed in a dark pool of blood.

Frank walked into the garage and found George, Ricko, Burt, and Stubby watching a ballgame on ESPN, the only channel not covering the bombing, on the big screen TV Sabyl had bought for the lounge area. Jamal sat on the bench, leaning against the wall, working a crossword puzzle.

The familiar smell of scorched coffee filled the air. "Hey, Frank. What're you doing here on a Sunday?" George asked.

"Aw, Barb's at her mom's in Lorton and I got bored. What're you watching?"

"Playoffs. Giants and Steelers."

"Not the news about Brassfield?"

"Nah. Watched that all morning."

"Who's winning?"

"Nobody. It's a tie. Ten - ten."

"What quarter?"

"It's halftime."

"Oh." He poured a cup of coffee and sat down at one of the tables.

"Ricko made some kind of chili with meatballs."

"No, thanks."

Burt smiled wryly. "Don't blame you. Blasted things oughta be called Gut Grenades."

Frank took a sip of coffee and made a face. "Man! This stuff tastes like melted doorknobs."

Just then a newsbreak interrupted the program. The face of a man with piercing dark eyes filled the screen. "Here's the latest on this morning's car bombing in which National Security Adviser Wayne Brassfield was killed."

George shifted in his seat and turned up the volume.

"We believe that it was the work of this man, Yasar al-Afdal, who has been on our Most Wanted list for some time. An eye witness saw him near the location where the incident happened and another said he saw him roll a basketball toward the vehicle in which Brassfield and his wife and the Secret Service agent were riding."

Stubby shook his head.

"Who would've thought anything like this could happen in America," George said, frowning at the screen and sounding philosophic.

"Who would have thought Nine-Eleven would have ever happened?" Burt said.

George got up and poured himself another mug of coffee and sat down at Frank's table. "Yeah. Nine-Eleven. How can any human being believe that it's okay to take the lives of thousands—?"

"Or even one?" Stubby added.

"Yeah—even one. Look at this guy's face. What makes a guy like that tick?"

"It's what they're taught," George said. "These terrorists are taught that God wants them to kill innocent people. If this same guy was born in America, and was taken to church every Sunday and was taught that God hates murder—"

"He'd believe that and he wouldn't be a terrorist," offered Burt.

"Yeah, but even if you are taught that it's okay to kill for the sake of religion—or whatever—isn't there something inside a man that says, 'This can't be right?'"

"Guess not," Burt said. "I mean look at Hitler and all the people that followed his orders without batting an eye."

"Wouldn't you have batted an eye?"

Burt shrugged his shoulders, "Sure."

Frank sipped his coffee and listened.

George continued. "I cannot believe that a man can plot to kill thousands of innocent lives and can't have something inside here" — he tapped his chest over his heart — "that says, 'This is wrong — this can't be right.'"

"What about prejudice? Isn't that what is at the core of this?" Stubby said. "One person hates another because they either don't believe like they do, don't look like they do, don't act or think like they do?"

Burt got up and put his plate in the sink.

"It's a taught thing, George," Stubby said. "You put a little black kid and a little white kid in the same playpen together; they're going to get along fine. They might fight over the toys, but they won't fight over what they look like. That's where the parents come in."

"And grandparents," offered Maurice.

"Yeah, and grandparents. They say, 'Oh, no! We don't play with little black kids—or little white kids,'—they're different. See—their skin is different. So, we don't like them.' Hatred and prejudice are taught things."

Stubby leaned back on his chair and balanced it on the back two legs. "You see this guy here?" he continued, nodding to the picture of the alleged assassin on the screen. "He was taught from day one to hate us. But if he had been born an American—"

The newsbreak was over and the game returned. The camera scanned the crowd and moved in on a close up of fans whose faces were painted with their team colors.

"Look at those idiots, "Burt said.

Frank looked at them thoughtfully. "Yeah. That's their belief system."

"Huh?"

"They've been taught probably since childhood to be Steelers or Giants fans."

"I guess if you took one of those Steelers fans and he was born in the home of Giants fans, he'd be a Giants fan."

The drivers looked at him thoughtfully. "Wow. That's deep, Frank."

"Yeah, deep."

Stubby folded his arms and tucked his hands under his armpits. "My point exactly. No different with these terrorists. They were born in it. It's all they know. You couldn't talk them out of it if you tried. They think they're right and everybody else is wrong." He brought his chair down on all fours. "They don't listen to their conscience because they're listening to their teachers, their leaders, their parents—but not their hearts."

George leaned forward on the table. "How do you know they even have a heart?"

Stubby hesitated. "I don't know. I wish I did, but I just can't help but believe that there is a place deep inside all of us, unless, I guess, they're, I don't know...insane..."

Jamal listened closely. He frowned deeply as they talked.

Noticing, George asked, "What do you think, Jamal?"

He put down his crossword puzzle and said stoically, "There's an old saying, 'One man's terrorist is another man's freedom fighter.'"

Stubby grew red in the face. "Tell me how plowing into buildings and killing three thousand innocent people brings freedom to anybody's cause!"

George looked at him intently. "Which is it for you, Jamal? Are these guys terrorists or freedom fighters?" Jamal didn't answer. And went back to his crossword puzzle. He had said too much already.

With the assassination of Wayne Brassfield, it was now conceded that the killings were the work of terrorists. Chaos was beginning to be the norm. Wall Street was reacting nervously.

Several terrorist organizations applauded the attacks that had been taking place in America's capital, but so far none had taken responsibility for them.

DHS's hotlines were scrambling to pull qualified people in to take the calls. They tightened security at airports, mass transits, borders, ports, convention centers, monuments, bridges, and gas stations. The churches called for prayer, emails and twitters flew through cyberspace, and the citizens talked about it non-stop. Once again, small flags proudly fluttered from the windows and antennas of America's automobiles, and were displayed with gusto on front porches, mailboxes and tee shirts.

A

John Endicott stood looking out of his window of the top floor of the Lafayette House Hotel. He could see the teams of uniformed Secret Service Countersniper Team, the best in the world, atop the White House roof, armed with specially built rifles, scanning every angle with binoculars as though an attack were imminent. Each one must qualify every month hitting targets accurately at 1,000 yards. They were always on high alert, but now more than ever, looking for any possible threat to the President of the United States (POTUS) and his family.

Endicott looked down at them. *I could take out any one of them if I so desired,* he mused with a smirk. His trigger finger twitched at the thought of it.

He was responsible for hundreds of assassinations. Those were the ones he had executed himself. There were many more that he had masterminded in twelve countries ranging from high-ranking military officers to prime ministers. The assassin felt nothing for his victims. It was business, pure and simple.

It was well known that he had connections with terrorist organizations, most of which were Al Qaeda wannabes. He had learned early on that large sums of money could be made through an association with them.

Having been born to a Croatian mother and a British-Arab father, he was raised and educated in London until his mother and father were killed in an automobile accident. His maternal grandmother brought him to live with her in Croatia. A year later, she died of cancer. Having no other known relatives, he wound up in an orphanage and within weeks, he ran away and lived on the streets until he was taken in by the Croatian Mafia. At the age of eleven, they taught him how to use a gun. He liked the power he felt when he handled them, and his mafia benefactors found he had a real knack for getting in and out of places without being noticed. At the ripe old age of fifteen, he became their number one assassin and now forty years later, he was known as the most wanted international hit man in the world. With his many aliases and an uncanny ability to change his appearance, the face the FBI had on their list looked nothing like the one he wore now. He was older, had gained a few pounds, had his nose reduced, a chin implant put in, his hair dyed black and slicked straight back. Even biometric cameras would not easily recognize him.

Pleased with how well the Frederick's assassination had gone, he walked over and sat on the bed. He enjoyed watching the news of the attacks, and flipped back and forth between CNN and Fox News. It disturbed him that Yasar al-Afdal had been identified so quickly. He had little use for the men he had recruited. Money was no object and much of it had gone to the families of the religious fanatics who were willing to die for their cause. Endicott smiled wickedly. *They're the perfect weapon. They don't mind dying; in fact they welcome it.*

He opened his wallet and took out a picture of his wife and son and looked at their faces longingly. It was fitting that his last assignment was the most important one of his career. After much meticulous planning, he made certain that he could not be connected to any of the killings. Coordination is much better than the chance of being caught. This would be his final contract. He was going to retire and had bought a villa in southern Italy where he would live out his days with his beautiful wife and son who already showed promise of becoming a fine soccer player.

He tucked away the worn photo back in his wallet and picked up the remote. Leaning back against the pillows, he turned up the volume and listened to President Byron Anderson' videoed address condemning in the strongest terms the assassinations and vowing that they would find the perpetrators and bring them to justice and they would do it swiftly. Endicott sneered at the President's image and changed the channel back to CNN. Felicia Gomez, Senator from New Mexico, said she deplored the assassinations, but raised questions about why hadn't the Secret Service done their job, why had the FBI not been able to find who was behind the killings, and why hadn't Homeland Security worked? She was working hard at trying to blame somebody.

He flipped it back to Fox News. The pensive face of DHS Secretary Killian appeared on the screen. "*Our number one mission is to protect our leaders, our citizens, our children, our cities, and our borders. We have increased security at the schools.*

They will remain open, but there is heightened security." He went on to say that they were looking into every lead, but had nothing that they could disclose at this time. Endicott folded his hands, smiled and nodded off to sleep.

⋏

While en route to Washington, Sabyl tried once again to call Scott from her cell phone, but got no answer. After dropping Rebecca off, she arrived at her condo and quickly checked her voice mail. Still nothing. She couldn't help but think of Gary and Mike and how she had received the dreaded word of their deaths. If anything happened to Scott, would anyone call her? Her throat constricted as she tried to shake off the thought. She spent the afternoon unpacking, doing laundry—anything to keep her mind busy. The news commentators droned in the background as she went on with her household tasks.

After dinner and a long walk with Beau, she sat on the sofa and rubbed her forehead as though trying to sort out the scattered thoughts that were flitting about in her mind like birds caught in a storm. Beau looked up at her, his intelligent eyes shining. She was exhausted and emotionally drained. She turned on the TV and punched in the numbers for CNN. One of the news panel's guests was Audrey Aberholdt. *"Tell us how you felt having your party crashed by a terrorist."*

"Oh, darling it was ghastly."

Beau began his gentle little growling bit, letting Sabyl know he was ready for bed. "Okay, okay", she whispered. She listened a few more minutes and then turned off the TV and headed to her room. Just as she sat on the bed to take off her slippers, her phone rang. She picked it up without looking at the Caller ID.

"This is Sabyl."

"Sabyl, it's Scott." He was smiling broadly, seeing on his caller ID that she had called several times.

"Scott! I—thought—"

"That I was dead?"

"I saw the news. You were protecting Brassfield the other night. I didn't know..."

"That was temporary duty. It happens sometimes." He cleared his throat nervously. "Thanks for your concern," he said quietly.

"Good," she said, trying to flatten her voice. "I'm glad."

"I'll probably be pretty busy from here on out. I'll call you when I can."

"Uh, sure, okay. Guess I'll be pretty busy too."

"More funerals?"

"Yes, unfortunately, more funerals."

DAY 8

MONDAY, JANUARY 12

D HS Secretary Killian required all top government leaders, including members of the House and Senate who might be considered potential targets, to have Secret Service protection. Hundreds of agents were pulled in from field offices all over the country to help protect the nation's leaders, on and off duty. He considered having the Speaker of the House, Laura Fielding, taken to an undisclosed place, but she resisted vehemently, so he decided to just keep more agents with her twenty-four/seven.

Scott had finished his six years in the field office in Richmond, eight years on protective detail with former President Stanton, and four years at Headquarters in D.C. For the last three years, he had been a part of the *Electronic Crime Special Agent Program (ECSA),* training agents in computer networking and digital forensics. He worked with local law enforcement on computer crime investigations handling internet fraud, network intrusion and destruction, and identity theft. With the greater need for protection, he now found himself back and forth between the office and temporary protective details.

Today, his charge was Senator Tucker Shelton, Chairman of the *Taskforce to Combat Domestic and International Terrorism (TCDIT),* who worked hand-in-hand with the FBI and DHS to develop proactive strategies to enhance law enforcement efforts in all fifty states in the war on domestic and international terrorism. Shelton, known as "The Warlord of Capitol Hill, was a workaholic and was in and out of his office constantly, keeping his protectors hopping.

The Senator's car pulled up to the side entrance of the Dirksen Senate Office Building, named after Minority Leader Everett Dirksen from Illinois in 1972. Scott walked alongside him, scrutinizing everyone and everything around him. He whisked him inside the car and then got in the front seat. Senator Shelton had an appointment at the White House at nine o'clock sharp to meet with the President and the Directors of the FBI, CIA, DIA and Secretary of Homeland Security. President Anderson was a stickler for being on time.

The sedan pulled into the southwest gate at eight forty-seven. Agents of the Uniformed Division of the Secret Service, known as the White House Police Force, met them at the gate and politely ordered everybody out. The driver popped the trunk and a small Belgian Malanois, a shorthaired canine, a breed known for their protective and hardworking characteristics, sniffed for explosives. IDs were produced and they checked the vehicle's tag number against their lists, then scanned them with metal detectors and finally let them pass. The driver pulled up to the entrance of the west basement. Scott got out and opened the door for the Senator and walked to the entrance with him, then returned to the car. The driver, an agent named Mason Thundercloud, a Native American from Anadarko, Oklahoma, moved the car to the side and the two of them stood at the ready, waiting for the Senator to text them when he was ready to leave.

Scott studied Thundercloud's noble features. His thick neck revealed he had been pumping iron. "How long have you been in D.C., Mason?"

"One week today. Came in from the field office in Oklahoma City."

"Oklahoma City? Nice town. Bigger than I had expected."

"Yeah. City limit to city limit, it's the largest city in America."

"No kidding? Were you there when the Murrah Building was bombed?"

"Yeah, that was right after I joined the Agency. I was just a young pup then. After the bombing, agents had to do a lot of work out in the field—literally. Farmers can't buy more than 20,000 pounds of fertilizer without being checked out and made to prove they're utilizing it for its intended use. We had to keep tabs on large shipments to make sure they weren't being used for terrorist activities. So we went out to the farms and made sure the owners were using it for their fields."

"Never know what kind of assignment you'll get."

"I enjoyed it, though. You know, talking to the farmers and all. My father was a farmer."

"Wheat?"

"Alfalfa."

The two agents continued to scan their surroundings as they talked. "How do you like it here?"

"It's okay. I was here for twelve weeks of training after my time at the Center in Glynco. Then they sent me back to Oklahoma City. That town's easy to learn; everything's on a simple grid. You always know whether you're going north, south, east, or west. Not here. You ever get used to this town? I mean, this place could confuse a compass. But it's pretty cool."

"You'll get used to it."

He looked up at the pillared splendor of the White House. "And seeing the President and coming inside these gates and all..."

Scott smiled. "It's still pretty awesome."

"You ever work Presidential protection?"

"Eight years."

"Pretty competitive, I hear."

"It's the highest honor, so, yeah."

"I'll never forget how I felt the first time I met him. The President, I mean. I felt like I did when I first saw the Grand Canyon—kinda small and insignificant."

Scott nodded thoughtfully.

Mason folded his arms. "What do you think about these killings? I mean, doesn't it seem strange that nobody has claimed responsibility? Some terrorist organization has got to be behind this."

"Could be."

"But a terrorist organization has to be paying for it, right? It takes millions to fund something like what these guys have been doing. I mean, Mansur was a student at AU. That means some serious tuition, an apartment; he had a car."

"Pretty brazen, I'd say, taking on our leaders like this."

"Reminds me a little of how we went after the leaders in Iraq."

Scott nodded thoughtfully.

◤

Dotty greeted Sabyl cheerfully. "Morning! How was your weekend in the country?"

Sabyl unleashed Beau. "Not great. My cat was murdered. Any calls?"

Dotty's penciled eyebrows shot up. "What? How…?"

Sabyl held her hand up, signaling she didn't want to talk about it.

Dotty had a ton of questions, but knew she'd better wait. "Yes. Betty Zimmerman at the State Department called. Guess you heard about Brassfield."

"Unbelievable. This world has gone completely mad. I'm sure she wants to talk about cars for another funeral. I'll call Betty now. By the way, I need to talk to Maurice. I want him to pick me up tomorrow night at eight and take me to the Australian Embassy."

"Oh, a hoity-toity thing, huh?"

"Yes. Not much in the mood to go."

"Oh, go and have a good time. You deserve it. What are you wearing?"

Sabyl's face relaxed a little. "I bought a new gown while I was in Italy. A *Giorgio Armani*. It's gorgeous. Blue and sparkly. I just hope I can still get into it."

"You'll knock 'em dead."

"Yeah, right," she smiled.

"Oh, and there was a call from our lawyer."

"Good. It looks like we're getting close to winding up this court case with Claude."

"Finally," Dotty said, disgusted. "Dragging it out like this for so long. That's just the pigs. Let me know when it is. I want to be there to see him cry."

"We *hope* he's the one doing the crying."

"Didn't the lawyer say he thought we'd win?"

"Yeah, I'm optimistic."

Dotty smiled, "You always are, boss."

Sabyl sighed, "Maybe not always, but thanks, dear. Okay, I'm going to call State." She walked into her office and sat down behind her desk.

Frank walked into Sabyl's office and excused himself when he saw she was on the phone. She motioned to him to have a seat. He plopped down on the leather chair. After hanging up, she pulled her hair back and held it there for a moment. Frank looked at her and cocked his head to one side. "You look awful."

"Thanks."

"I heard about your little cat. I'm really sorry."

"Thanks."

"So what did you do?"

"I called the police and buried her in the back yard."

"What happened? Dotty said your cat was murdered. How'd that happen?"

"Somebody slit her throat."

Frank sat up straight, his eyes blazing. "Who would do such a rotten thing? Your crazy neighbors, I'll bet."

She shrugged slightly. "Don't know yet."

"What are the police going to do about it?"

"They took my statement—agreed it's probably my neighbors, but can't prove it—you know the bit."

"So did you get any rest?"

"Sort of. My friend Rebecca Carriere came up for the weekend. We were going to relax and just hang out—"

"Rebecca Carriere? The writer?"

"Yes."

"Man! You know her?"

"For years."

"You're kidding!"

"Nope."

"How come I didn't know that?"

"I don't tell you everything, Frank. Anyhow, when I heard the news of the Brassfield attack, I thought—the agent that was killed—"

"You thought it was Scott?"

She sat back and folded her arms. "Yeah, anyhow, it wasn't him."

"You guys getting back together?"

"No."

"Was that him on the phone?"

Sabyl leaned her head to one side and smiled. "No, Mr. Nosey. That was State. We're doing the Brassfield funeral."

"At National Cathedral?"

"No, National Presbyterian."

"National Prez? Why there?"

"Because that's what their children want."

"Parking will be a nightmare."

"With that many cars, it'll be a problem anywhere. But it'll work out. It always does."

"How many cars?"

"State's figuring thirty for us. Of course their own cars and the White House and the military fleets will be there." She picked up some papers and looked at them. "Everything go okay while I was gone?"

"Yeah. The Worldglobe Bank thing went off without a hitch. And Roberto Enrique's agent called to confirm."

She turned to her computer. "Yeah. I've got him down for theeee—" She clattered on her keyboard and peered at her flat screen monitor, "—the fifteenth."

"Wants his usual treatment."

"Right. That would be a stretch limo, Ricko to drive him, champagne in the car bar, a security van for his bodyguards and me personally directing everything. Set it up with Ricko. And get Burt to drive the security van."

He leaned forward. "Okay, boss. You got it."

"Stay on top of this, Frank. You know how crazy entertainers' schedules can be. Somehow they always manage to have a ton of last-minute changes."

"Will do. We're set for the Kennedy Center event tonight. Eight cars."

"That's great. So what about Rudy? Heard anything from him?"

"Haven't seen or heard from him at all."

Sabyl frowned, "That's not like Rudy."

"I know. As Dotty would say, 'That's the pigs.' Guess that British guy is really keeping him hopping."

"Hope he's keeping a log. He'd better not be overworking him."

"Right. You know Rudy found a little black book in the back seat of his car after he picked up this Endicott character at the airport last week. He told me about it. It was written in Arabic. I thought that was kind of strange since he's from England, don't you?"

"Rudy knows Arabic. Did he read any of it?"

"He said it contained some kind of list—names, phone numbers, and what looked like directions—but he only glanced at it. You know Rudy, didn't want to snoop."

"Yeah."

"The guy seemed relieved to get it back."

"Probably a list of his girlfriends."

"Yeah, probably," Frank chuckled.

Sabyl frowned, "I wonder why it was in Arabic, though. You don't suppose he's—"

"Don't let your imagination run away with you, boss," Frank grinned. "Half of Washington speaks Arabic."

"Well, maybe not half, but I get your point. I just don't want Rudy stuck with some character that might be giving him a hard time."

Dotty buzzed Sabyl, "Rebecca on line two."

Frank grinned, "Rebecca Carriere?"

Sabyl smiled, "Yes, Frank."

He got up and went back to his office.

"Hi, Rebecca."

"Sabyl, are you okay?"

"Yes, I'm fine. I'm so sorry we had to cut our time short."

"That's alright, dear. There'll be other times, hopefully."

"Definitely."

"Just wanted to check on you. I want you to know that the weekend wasn't a total loss. I've thought a lot about what we talked about. It really helped."

"Oh, Rebecca, I'm so glad. If that was all we were supposed to accomplish for the weekend, it was worth it."

"I went out and bought a Bible."

"You did?"

"Yeah, I figured if it could give you some answers, it can give me some too."

"Bec, that's wonderful!"

"I definitely need some direction. And Sabyl, I'm so sorry about Miss Piti."

"Thank you. And thanks for putting up with my little makeshift funeral. I just had to—"

"I know. It was so sad, but you gave her a good sendoff. Wasn't it just so perfect when the church bells pealed just as it ended?"

"It gave me goose bumps!" Just then Rudy drove into the driveway. "Bec, I've gotta go. I'll call you later this week."

She sat there a few moments to see if Rudy would come in. Dotty stood at her door. "Rudy just drove in."

"Yeah, I saw."

Frank yelled at the two of them. "Sabyl! Dotty! Come here!"

They quickly went into his office. He turned up the volume on the TV. Secretary Killian was holding a press conference. *"Gloria Louise Brassfield died this morning at 8:17 AM Eastern Standard Time from injuries sustained in a terrorist attack in which her husband, National Security Advisor Wayne Brassfield, died."*

Sabyl gasped. "Oh, no!"

"I thought she was doing better," Frank said quietly.

Killian turned it over to the Brassfields' doctor. *"Her death was not the direct result of the injuries sustained from the explosion. A blood clot formed due to the trauma to her shoulder and lungs and moved to her heart, causing acute pulmonary embolism."*

"Isn't that the same thing that killed that nice reporter several years ago in Iraq?" Frank asked.

"David Bloom. Yeah. So sad."

The Secretary moved back to the microphones. *"The Brassfield children were with their mother when she passed away. They will be making a statement later on."*

Sabyl shook her head. "Those poor kids."

Dotty pulled out a tissue from a box on Frank's desk and blew her nose. "Yeah, and one little grandkid. A girl, I think."

Sabyl unfolded her arms and shook her head sadly. "Looks like there'll be a double funeral this time." She turned and walked toward the garage.

George was watching the news along with Lawrence, Stubby, and Burt. George stood up when he saw Sabyl. "Boss! Did you hear?"

"Yes, I just saw it." She sat down next to Stubby.

George shoved his hands deep into his pockets and dropped his head. "Terrible. Just terrible."

Burt put his cigarette out. "Who would have ever thought such things would happen on our soil?"

Rudy came out of the men's room. His face lit up when he saw Sabyl. "Hi, boss."

"Rudy!" She stood and gave him a big hug. He sat down and fingered his cap.

Sabyl sat down beside him. "We haven't heard from you. How's it going with your client?"

"Okay, I suppose. I'll be glad when it's over."

"Is he treating you okay?" Sabyl asked.

"It's okay. I don't wish to complain."

Sabyl patted him on his massive shoulder. "You've never been a complainer, Rudy. That's what makes you so special."

George spoke up. "We miss you around here, buddy."

Rudy looked down at Sabyl. "I really wanted to be with you for the Fredericks funeral. How did it go?"

"It went fine—no problems at all," Sabyl sighed. "Now there will be another. A double."

Rudy looked perplexed. "A double?"

"Yeah," George answered. "Mrs. Brassfield just died."

Rudy shook his head. "We live in perilous times."

"Yes, we do," Sabyl agreed.

"Hey y'all, listen to this." Burt nodded toward the TV.

A tall, thin gentleman with gray hair, wearing a brown suit, stepped up to the cluster of microphones and cleared his throat. *"The Brassfield children have requested that their parents' bodies be flown to their home state tomorrow. The funeral will be held at the First Presbyterian Church in Omaha, Nebraska, at 10:00 AM Central Standard Time on Saturday, the seventeenth of January."*

He stepped back and the news anchor added, *"Simultaneously, at 11:00 AM Eastern Standard Time, there will be a memorial service held for Wayne and Gloria Brassfield at the National Presbyterian Church here in Washington."*

Sabyl stood. "That changes things a bit for us, but not much. We'll still have the memorial service but not the burial. I'd better go call State. Talk to you guys later. Rudy, I need to talk to you." He walked back to the office with her.

Dotty met them at the door. "Rudy! We never see you around here anymore!"

"I know. Just a few more days."

Sabyl went into her office and fell into her large desk chair. Rudy sat down on the leather chair opposite her. "So, Rudy, tell me about this Endicott guy. He's from England, yet he speaks Arabic?"

"Yes, he speaks it perfectly with his friends."

"What friends?"

"He has four or five friends that I drive as well."

"Really? And what do they talk about?"

"I don't know. They insist that the divider remains closed." He looked at his watch. "I must be going. I'm supposed to pick him up at his hotel."

She looked at him seriously. "Look, keep in touch, okay?"

Rudy nodded sadly and left.

Sabyl called Betty Zimmerman at State and confirmed that she would need as many cars as she contracted for the Fredericks funeral. Sabyl thanked her and buzzed Dotty.

"You rang?"

"Can you come in here for a minute?"

Dotty came in, sat down, poised her pen over her pad and said, "Shoot."

"Call PDC and Vassette and tell them we need the same number of cars as last Saturday. Do the usual security bit. Also, send them a note thanking them for a job well done for the Fredericks funeral."

She jotted it down, "Got it." She cocked her head to one side. "You okay?"

"Yeah. Look, I'm sorry I cut you short this morning. I was just upset about my kitty—and—well, this whole terrorist thing—"

"I know. It's scarier than when the D.C. snipers were on the loose."

🅰

Mason Thundercloud's pager went off. The two agents jumped in the car and retrieved Senator Shelton. "Where to, sir?"

"S.O.B."

Thundercloud looked at Scott and then at Shelton in the rearview mirror. "Sir?"

Scott smiled. "Senate Office Building." He turned back to Shelton, "Which one, sir?"

"R.S.O.B."

"I guess that would be the Russell Senate Office Building."

"Correct."

He headed toward the newly renovated office building where they had recently completed the physical security and telecommunications upgrades. Shelton settled into his seat, fastened his seat belt and announced, "Killian got another poker riddle this morning." The agents looked at him and waited for more. He reached inside his briefcase and handed Scott two memos. "Give one to—what's your name again, son?"

"Mason Thundercloud, sir."

"Right. Great name."

"Thank you, sir. What does it say?"

"It says, 'TWO OF A KIND ARE GOOD CONNECTORS, AND BABY MAKES THREE.'"

"Any idea what it means, sir?"

"No, but we'll figure it out. You guys wrap your brains around it. Let us know what you think."

"We will, sir."

Thundercloud took him to the Russell Senate Office Building north of the Capitol and parked. Scott walked him inside and waited outside the office of Katherine Todd, a powerful Senator who formerly co-chaired the Federal

Advisory Committee of the U.S. Commission on National Security/21st Century, the predecessor to Homeland Security. The agent protecting her stood next to Scott in the corridor in front of the heavy door that led to her office. The two agents nodded to one another and began their silent surveillance.

A few minutes later, earsplitting alarms went off all over the building. Scott and the other agent quickly went inside the senator's office. Scott grabbed Shelton and shoved him through the door. Right behind him was the other agent nearly carrying Senator Todd down the wide corridor. Scott led Shelton down the stairs into the waiting car. Shielding him, he shoved him in, dived in and shouted. "Go, go, go!"

Thundercloud took off, burning rubber.

"It was just a drill!" the Senator protested.

"Can't take any chances, sir."

"Aren't you guys being a little paranoid?"

"We get paid to be paranoid, sir."

"Where are you taking me?"

Thundercloud shouted, "A.B.H., sir."

Scott looked at him. "What the heck is that?"

"Anywhere but here!"

Scott smiled and shook his head as if saying, "That is so lame." After getting the all-clear, they dropped Shelton back at his office and turned his protection over to two more agents. Scott and Mason then drove to Alexandria and attended the quiet funeral of Agent Dodson who was killed in the Brassfield bombing. The agents noticed that media attention was almost nonexistent for the fallen agent. After the burial, Scott and Mason headed back to the office. They rode in silence through the winding streets of Washington. Finally Scott said, "Dodson was a good man."

"Yeah."

"Any leads on this 'Basketball Bomber' Afdal character?"

"Not yet."

"We'll find him."

"You got that right."

That night in his apartment Scott worked on the poker riddle until his head throbbed. After two hours, he stood up, stretched and rubbed his neck. He had run word sequences through his computer to see what came up; nothing that seemed significant. He sat back down and punched in "Poker Terminology." Up came a screen full of terms. He thought out loud, "Two of a kind, obviously that must mean the two they've already killed. Connectors—what does that mean?" He squinted at the screen. "Oh, wow." He sat back in his chair and then quickly called Keefer's office. "I may have the first part of the riddle."

"Get down here now."

⋏

Scott tapped on his boss's door.

"It's open!"

Scott walked in his boss's office and sat down next to his partner.

Keefer leaned back in his chair. "I called Martz in. I want him to hear this. So, what have you got?"

Scott opened his file and reread the riddle. "The part that says, 'Two of a Kind'—I figure that means the two they've already played. "Connectors" is a poker term for consecutive cards that could make a straight."

"So they're going for a straight—like five consecutive—executives?"

"Yeah, looks like they're going after our top five leaders."

"But they're not following the order of succession according to our government setup. Those would be the President, Vice President, Speaker of the House, the President Pro tem of the Senate, and then the cabinet officers in designated order, SecState, Secretaries of Treasury, Defense, Attorney General, and on down the line."

Scott slightly shrugged. "Maybe they're going after the ones they view as the most dangerous or the most powerful—"

"That would certainly fit." Keefer clasped his hands. "What I don't understand is, why these riddles? Why the poker jargon? It doesn't sound like your run-of-the-mill terrorist."

Martz said, "I didn't know these guys knew anything about cards."

Scott replied, "Could be the Iraqi thing with their leader's faces on a deck of cards."

Lou Martz looked at him sideways. "Man! I hadn't thought of that! That makes perfect sense. I remember that it really ticked them off. Said it was offensive to their religion."

Keefer leaned forward. "I think you've got something there, Scott. Retaliation?"

"Maybe it's payback time."

Martz asked, "But didn't we have fifty-something people on the deck of cards we were seeking to kill or capture?"

Keefer nodded, "Yeah, but my guess is that they're going after five, not fifty. I doubt they're that well-coordinated."

"Let's hope not."

The SAIC closed the file. "As always, keep this under wraps."

Scott nodded. "Of course. Until it leaks."

"If it does, this town will go ballistic," Martz said.

"You got that right." Keefer stood up. "We've got work to do, gentlemen. By the way, Scott, what about the rest of the riddle? AND BABY MAKES THREE?"

"Not a clue."

TUESDAY, JANUARY 13

The maitre'd' escorted Scott to the table where his old college buddy, Neil Harper, a reporter for *Reuters,* was waiting. He was seated against the window in the Revival Restaurant on the top floor of the Key Bridge Marriott, overlooking the Potomac. Neil stood and grabbed his hand and shook it with gusto. "Scott! Good to see you, man!"

Scott pounded him soundly on the shoulder and they sat down. "How are you, Neil? How's Crystal?"

"She's fine. We're pregnant, you know."

"Wow, that's great! Congratulations! When's the blessed event?"

"In June. How's Sabyl?"

"Uh, fine. She's fine."

"Been a long time, man."

"Over two years. Glad you called me. Sorry I haven't been in touch. I've been really busy."

"Yeah, me too. You know how it is, you get married and nothing's the same. I'm not complaining, mind you. It's just different."

"You happy? I mean, you got a great gal."

"Never been happier. So did you and Sabyl, I mean we never heard—"

"No. We—uh—we didn't. But, who knows, eh?" They picked up the long, narrow menus and perused them. Soft piano music played in the background. The server took their orders and the conversation turned to the assassinations.

"You're an agent, Scott," Neil said in a low voice. "So, what's going on with this thing? Off the record, of course."

"Can't really talk about it."

"Yeah, I know. Sorry. Old habit, I guess, trying to get the inside story. But that's not why I wanted to talk to you." He lowered the menu and leaned forward. "Scott, I saw a guy the other day that I would swear I've seen before. It's one of those *déjà vu* things, you know?"

Scott took a sip of water. "Yeah?"

"I think he's someone I wrote about a long time ago when I was in Afghanistan, around 2005."

"What about him?"

Neil shook his head slowly. "I'm not even certain he's the same guy." Scott frowned with interest and waited for more. "If it's him, he's bad news. A chemist. The kind of guy we don't want in our country."

"What's his name?"

"Ahmad al Shatir."

"Never heard of him."

"Probably has a ton of aliases."

"Where did you see him?"

"On Van Ness, over near UDC. I met with one of the professors there, an old friend of mine. I'm helping him with some background for a book he's writing."

Scott looked at him intently. "That's near the Israeli Embassy."

"Yeah, and a lot more embassies."

Scott thought, *And just a few blocks from Sabyl's condo.* "Was he in a car or walking or what?"

"He was walking, but he may have parked around there somewhere, not sure."

"What day was this?"

"Last Thursday."

"You say you wrote about him. You got a copy of that story?"

"No, but I'm pretty sure I can get one. And the photographer I worked with, Royce Bradford, might have a picture. Shatir wouldn't let us photograph him, so Royce did it without his knowledge. But they never ran it with the story."

"Where is Royce?"

"I heard he and his wife moved to Maryland near Baltimore. I'll make some calls and track him down and let you know."

"You say this Shatir is a chemist? What else do you remember about him?"

"The guy loves gambling."

Scott's eyebrows shot up. "Poker?"

"Yeah, his favorite is Five Card Draw."

Rudy parked as instructed in the usual place at the park in McLean. The men in the back seat sat in silence for several minutes as though waiting for someone. A white Subaru pulled into a nearby parking space. Endicott and Sahba got out and walked over to it. A man opened the car door, stood up and stretched, then opened the back door and let out a black Labrador retriever. Rudy had seen him several times before. They talked for a few minutes and Sahba handed a small package to him. The recipient looked at it closely and nodded. Endicott gave him a thick envelope. They shook hands and he went back to his car. Endicott and Sahba returned to the limousine and ordered Rudy to drive them back to the brownstone.

Keefer and Martz listened closely as Scott gave them the information Neil had just given him. Keefer leaned back in his chair. "A chemist, huh? That name isn't coming up in our database."

"Probably an alias."

"You say you can get your hands on a photo?"

"Possibly."

"Go for it."

Scott went back to his office and called Neil who said he was already working on trying to locate his photographer friend and would get back to him.

▲

Dotty rinsed out the coffeepot and placed a new filter in it, scooped coffee out of the tin, dumped it in the basket, and poured the water in the opening at the top. Within minutes it was hissing and dripping and filling the office with the aroma of fresh coffee.

Karen was squinting hard trying to decipher the thick accent of a Korean client who spoke very little English. She finally handed it over to the reservationist next to her, Jenny Wong, who managed to get the information down.

Frank hung up from talking to their mechanic. He got up and walked into Sabyl's office. "That commuter bus that broke down—the Number Three Bus?"

"Yeah?"

"George will pick it up after lunch."

"Good. What was the problem?"

"It was the oil pressure sensor."

"Do you want me to follow him over there?"

"Nah, Ricko's going to."

Sabyl looked at Frank intently. "An oil pressure sensor can shut down an entire bus?"

"Yeah. The oil pressure has to stay high enough—around seventy pounds—and if the sensor goes bad and it registers, say, forty pounds, it shuts off to save the engine."

She nodded, impressed at such clever technology. "How much did it cost?"

"A hundred bucks."

"Good. I'm glad that's all it was. We've got to keep those commuters happy. That's a huge contract and it's time to renew."

"Think they will?"

"I don't see why not. That one little breakdown is the only problem we've had all year. And we had another bus there within five minutes."

"You gonna up the price?"

She smiled and leaned back. "I'm going to bid. Maybe we'll get lucky."

"You know Vassette would love to have that contract."

"Like I said, I'll bid and we'll see who gets it." Sabyl loved to outbid the competition and she was good at it. "I've got an appointment with them after lunch."

Frank grinned, "You go, girl." He headed back to his office.

Dotty came in with a fresh cup of coffee and set it on her desk. "Just the way you like it."

"Thanks, dear." Sabyl sipped the steaming liquid. "It's perfect as always." Dotty smiled approvingly and went back to her office. Sabyl sat her mug down and clattered on the keyboard, looking for a client she needed to call whose company's check had bounced. Her accountant had no luck with them. She was going to have to deal with it herself. Not her favorite thing to do.

Dotty buzzed Sabyl. "Scott on line one."

Sabyl hesitated and then picked up the phone. "Hello, Scott."

"Hi. You busy?"

"Sort of," she said, glad for the brief reprieve from playing bill collector. "What's up?"

Scott was encouraged by the amiable sound in her voice. "Just thought you'd like to know I saw Neil Harper."

Sabyl remembered him and Crystal fondly. "Oh, really? How are they?"

"They're good. Neil asked about you."

She leaned back in her chair and smiled sideways. "And what did you tell him?"

"That you were fine. They're expecting a baby in June. Said they want to invite you to a shower."

"That would be nice." There was an awkward pause. "Uh, Scott, I've got to run. I've got a phone call to make."

Scott went for it. "Will you have dinner with me tonight?"

"I can't. I'm going to the Australian Embassy."

"Alone?"

Sabyl bristled. "Yes, alone."

"Let me take you—"

"No, Maurice is picking me up in his limo—"

"Let me pick you up after—"

"No, Scott. Besides," she said playfully, "I might meet some dashing young Aussie—"

"How about Friday night?" He held his breath.

She hesitated. "Okay, Friday night."

Scott couldn't believe his ears. "Okay! I'll talk to you before then and we'll set a time."

"Okay."

He hung up smiling and whispered, "Yesssss!"

Sabyl hung up, her face burning. She wondered why she agreed to have dinner with him. Maybe it was time to let him explain.

⚜

Sabyl looked at her image in the bathroom mirror, fluffed her hair and checked her teeth for lipstick. She thought about how fortunate she was to have such good straight teeth, never having had the benefit of a dentist when she was a child. After a spritz of perfume, she walked into the bedroom and looked at herself in the full-length mirror on the back of her closet door. She turned from side to side inspecting her new *Armani* gown. It fell over her body like a lovely cascading waterfall, blue and sparkling. The low neckline lay across the rounded upper curve of her breasts. She looked at the slight cleavage and frowned, knowing that to some it might appear to be lovely and inviting, but beneath the surface was a battleground, an unseen adversary that seemed bent on taking her life. She lifted one eyebrow and said to the lurking enemy, "I'm not afraid of you. No weapon formed against me will prosper!" She felt a strength rise up in her at the declaration of that scripture. After dousing her hands with lotion, she put on her rings. Her lipstick and cell phone were all that would fit in the tiny designer beaded evening bag she had found on sale at Nordstrom's in Crystal City.

Tonight would be different for Sabyl. Instead of commanding a fleet of limousines while others attended one of hundreds of Washington functions, she would be an attendee herself at the elegant Australian Embassy. Her good friend, Ambassador Hawthorne, had invited her to a formal dinner honoring the Prime Minister of Australia. He was in town to meet with DHS Secretary Killian to get briefed on some new ideas on how to keep his country safe, which had recently been under attack by terrorists.

Beau's bark erupted at the sound of the doorbell. He looked at the door and back to Sabyl, barking and growling and doing his job as her protector. She shushed him to no avail until a familiar face appeared at the door and then barks were exchanged for wags and the funny little sideways dance he always did when greeting someone he knew. Maurice, wearing his chauffeur's hat, whistled when she opened the door. "Boss! You're gorgeous!"

Sabyl smiled, "Looking for a raise, Maurice?"

"Of course!"

He helped her on with her evening coat and escorted her to the car he had just washed and vacuumed. He opened the door and helped her in, carefully tucking the shimmering gown inside, and closed the door ceremoniously. He felt honored that she had chosen him to drive her. Maurice had a light touch when he drove and handled a car like a French pastry chef handles dough. He knew every street in Washington and every possible place where a limo could be parked and not be harassed by the tenacious D.C. Metro police.

Sabyl was seldom seen in her own limousines, preferring instead her rugged SUV, her dog, her bottled water in the cup holder, and a CD of Bocelli or Jonas Kaufmann playing softly in the background. The richly upholstered cabin filled with her perfume. The immaculate car was warm inside. Maurice knew she hated to be cold. He got into the driver's seat, pulled the door closed, and headed for the Australian Embassy on Massachusetts Avenue, better known as Mass Ave.

As they rode silently, Sabyl suddenly felt very much alone. She almost allowed herself to miss Scott, but quickly fortified her emotions, not granting them any leeway and tried to forge her thoughts ahead to the anticipated evening of gaiety. Still, she could hear his words echoing in her mind, "I've changed...I know I hurt you." And then today over the phone, "Let me take you..."

It would have been nice to have the strong, handsome Scott Terhune at her side tonight, but something had opened the earth beneath their feet, she on one side and he on the other. The gap had receded into a rumbling crevice that grew so wide neither of them could cross it; a deep gorge with no bridge—yet he had offered a bridge. It seemed flimsy, like one of those hanging bridges seen in B movies with ropes frayed and slats missing. She was terrified of it and dared not step out on it. Not yet. It had need of much repair. In fact, the bridge would have to be so strong and so wide you could drive a limousine over it.

The party was well under way when she arrived. Maurice got out and opened the door for her with flair. She stepped out and thanked him. "I'll text you when I'm ready to leave." He smiled and kissed her on the cheek. "Knock 'em dead, boss."

It was a rare occasion for Sabyl to attend parties such as this one. Invitations came to her almost daily to everything inside the beltway: embassy parties, Kennedy Center events, and concerts. She seldom attended the functions, but politely declined, content to finish a good day's work and head home with Beau for a long walk in Rock Creek Park. Though she was well able to master the formality of grand dinner parties and to bring a rare genuineness to the conversations, she was unimpressed with Washington wealth. She found it boring to put on appearances and could spot a phony at twenty paces. But the ambassador was not one of them. She found him to sincerely care for his country and for people. The Honorable Mr. Roger Hawthorne had been in the United States for two years after serving in Paris, Moscow, and Oslo. He had occupied a number of positions in the Department of Foreign Affairs and Trade where he met his wife, Diana, who was then serving as Parliamentary Secretary.

The ambassador spotted Sabyl. She clutched her tiny handbag and walked toward him. The hem of her gown flowed behind her like glittering water tumbling over rocks in a stream. The ambassador came over to greet her. "Sabyl, my dear, you're the most ravishing creature here!" He was short, early fifties, handsome in his tux and known for his intelligence, charm and wit. Sabyl held out her hand. "How kind of you to say so, Mr. Ambassador. No wonder you were appointed as a diplomat." He laughed loudly and offered his arm and took her around to meet the other guests; some she knew—most she did not. Several guests were holding little crystal plates of hors d'oeuvres that the chefs had spent the day creating; others were standing together in small clusters chatting. A few were attempting the tango that the orchestra was playing with enthusiasm. Sabyl hoped no one would ask her to dance. She had never quite gotten the hang of the tango, and certainly not in her new *Ferragamo* shoes.

The ambassador stopped a server passing by with a tray of sparkling glasses of champagne. He deftly lifted one off the tray and handed it to her. "Here you are, my dear," he said in his lilting accent. "Now, where the devil is my wife?" He looked to his right and saw her approaching. "Ah! There she is! Darling, you remember Sabyl Martin of Martin Transportation. She took such good care of our friends from Oslo when they came to visit."

"Oh, yes, Sabyl, how good of you to come." Her engaging birdlike features with large round eyes, a small beaked nose and a wide, thin mouth were framed in a cloud of blond hair that curled dramatically in every direction. "You are the envy of every woman here in that exquisite gown. Where ever did you find it?"

"Thank you, Mrs. Hawthorne."

"Call me Diana, darling."

"Thank you, Diana. I found it in Italy."

"It's absolutely divine. Now, let me introduce you to some of our other guests."

"Hold on, dear," the ambassador said as he played tug of war with Sabyl's arm. I want to introduce her to our guest of honor."

"Oh, of course, dear. Sabyl, don't let him hog you all night. There are some single men here who are dying to meet you."

Indeed, there were. They gazed in awe as she and the ambassador passed by. She smiled as she was introduced to each guest, and nodded to those who made eye contact with her as they made their way through the crowd. How would she get through the rest of the evening? Her new shoes were pinching already. The ambassador showed her off as though she were his personal trophy. "I want to introduce you to the Prime Minister, but he seems to be missing. Perhaps he has been kidnapped by one of the other guests—no doubt talking up a trade deal. You know, the U.S. is our largest foreign investor and largest single trading partner—ah! There he is."

Just as the ambassador was introducing her to the Prime Minister, her cell phone chirped. Aghast at the timing, she said contritely, "I'm terribly sorry, sir. Please excuse me." She turned away from them, and pulled it out of her beaded evening bag. She answered, "This had better be an emergency." Her face registered complete shock. "Oh, no," she whispered. The others watched closely as her eyes widened. "Thanks for letting me know, John." She closed the phone, stunned at the news. Turning back to the waiting diplomats, she said, "The Secretary of Defense has just been taken to the hospital along with his wife. They suspect ricin poisoning."

"Good grief! Not another one!" the Prime Minister said, horrified.

Cell phones began going off all over the room. Because of the gravity of the situation, the party broke up quickly. The wire services picked up the news and soon it was beamed clear around the world.

Sabyl called Maurice. He was there within minutes and drove her home in silence. As she got out, she quietly thanked him, handed him a handsome tip and went inside. Beau tried to jump on her when she came in, but she quickly grabbed his paws to keep him from ripping off a few hundred beads. Her shoes were the first to go. Then she walked into her bedroom in her stocking feet, reluctantly took off her beautiful gown and hung it on a blue satin padded hanger, pulled the plastic cover over it and hung it up, wondering if or when she would wear it again. She quickly put on her pajamas and robe and headed for the kitchen to find a bite to eat, first stopping to turn on the TV in the living room and increasing the volume.

After microwaving some leftover lasagna, she went to her bedroom, curled up on her massive antique bed, and turned on the TV that was nestled in a hand-carved armoire in the corner. The all-news cable channels were showing pictures of Secretary of Defense Carson Hodges and his wife Marion with their two prized black Labs. Word had it that someone other than Sergeant Maynard, who walked the dogs twice daily in a park near their home in McLean, Virginia, had handled the animals and had apparently, placed a small black pod resembling a large tick on the neck of one of the dogs.

The news anchor reported, *"Secretary Hodges, as shown in this footage, always rubbed his dogs' necks when petting them. Upon greeting the dogs when he arrived home, he apparently felt it, and when he pulled it off, it released ricin at a close proximity to Hodges' face."*

"Mrs. Hodges was next to him when it was released. The deadly poison is odorless and colorless, so it's doubtful they knew what had happened until their symptoms began to manifest. Secretary Hodges, who is extremely knowledgeable of weapons of mass destruction such as ricin, recognized the symptoms and managed to call 911."

"Oh, how awful!" Sabyl said, pulling her bedcovers over her legs. She prayed silently for them.

"Both have been taken to George Washington University Medical Center. No word as yet of their condition. Sergeant Maynard had already left the premises before the gas was released. Both animals died as a result of the ricin and have been moved to an undisclosed location for autopsy. The small pod has been taken to a laboratory for further investigation. The Secretary's children, Carson, Jr., a patent attorney in New York, and their daughter Amy, a student at UCLA are flying in, but will not be able to see their parents as they have been quarantined. Their home has been sealed off as well as the entire area surrounding the park where the dogs were walked."

The news media had to do their reporting a block from the scene, their voices professional with grave tones. Helicopters flew overhead, providing shots of the Secretary's home, now dark and empty.

Investigators asked for witnesses to come forth that may have seen the man who talked with Sergeant Maynard, the dogs' caretaker. They especially wanted to know if anyone had any information that could help in the investigation, and to please call the number on the screen. The Sergeant, of course, gave a description to the investigators and looked through hundreds of photographs. None matched the description of the man who, walking his own black Lab, had talked with him on several occasions in the park and had petted the Hodges' dogs.

The city's—indeed the nation's—atmosphere was that of a seething fury. Nine-Eleven was no longer lapsed from consciousness. America was once again under attack.

▲

Rudy sat watching the news with his wife, Layla. His face paled as he watched in disbelief the unfolding story. His stomach knotted up and his mouth went dry. *Surely not,* he thought. Just then the phone rang. He got up and went into the kitchen to answer it. His wife looked at him curiously, wondering who would be calling at that hour, but returned her thoughts to the unfolding news story.

Rudy sat in a heap at the kitchen table. "You cannot do this," he whispered. "Why are you doing this?"

Endicott's voice was cold as a glacier. "Do not tell anyone what I have just told you. Not even your wife. Or your son will die."

Rudy gritted his teeth, "If you harm one hair on his..."

"If you do what I tell you, he will live. If you do not, you will never see him alive again. You will pick me up tomorrow at the usual time."

Layla muted the TV. "Rudy! Who is that on the phone? Is that David?"

"No! It is not David. It's business."

She shook her head and unmuted the voices.

"My wife will know—"

"Put on a normal face and return to your wife. Remember, we have your son and we will not hesitate to kill him."

Rudy choked back tears. "How do I know you have him?"

"Listen."

A garbled tape played. The unmistakable, frightened voice of his son spoke. "Dad, it's me. I've been kidnapped, but I'm okay. Tell mom not to worry—" His voice cracked and trailed off.

"That is your son, correct?"

Rudy held his hand over his mouth and sobbed silently. He finally managed, "Yes."

"Be at my hotel tomorrow as usual." He hung up.

Rudy slowly hung up the phone and began to pray.

"Rudy, bring some more popcorn, please." He tried to answer but he could not. "Rudy, honey."

He went to the kitchen sink and splashed cold water on his face and dried it quickly. His shaking hand opened the cabinet door and took out a package of microwave popcorn and put it in the small oven. He stared at it as it popped and grew inside its package. His mind raced as he thought about David and the implications of what these people were doing and were capable of doing. He had been driving the very ones who had been doing the killings! Now they have his son, their only child. *God! Don't let them harm him, please!*

The microwave beeped and Rudy took it out, poured it in a bowl, took a deep breath and slowly walked into the small den. He would have to act normally and he would have to be convincing.

"Honey, who was that on the phone?"

"No one. A telemarketer."

"I thought you said it was business."

He was a terrible liar. How would he get through this?

Layla looked at him sideways. "Why is your face red?"

Rudy sat down beside his wife of thirty years. "Oh, it's probably your cooking. Don't worry about it." She jabbed him in the ribs with her elbow and took the bowl of popcorn, munching contentedly and happy to have her husband home for a change.

⅄

The air in the room was layered with cigarette smoke. Sahba and the others at the brownstone watched the news on their 32-inch TV they had bought so they could enjoy seeing the mayhem they were causing. The news analyst asked his guest, a chemistry professor at Georgetown University, to give his analysis of the pod that was placed on one of the Hodges' dogs.

"First off," the interviewer began, *"Don't you think that it is quite remarkable that the dogs didn't react at the first scent of the contents of the pod. Labrador retrievers are often trained and used by law enforcement because of their ability to sniff for, not only explosives, but specific deadly chemicals such as ricin and Sarin gas."*

The bearded professor answered, *"But you just said it. The canines you mentioned have been trained to sniff out such chemicals—these dogs had not. And let me add, even if the dogs were trained in such a way, whoever designed this pod had it so air tight that it went unnoticed by even the most highly sensitive noses, those of the dogs themselves."*

The news commentator said, *"Sergeant Maynard, the dogs' caretaker, did say that after he walked the dogs and then returned them to the Hodges home that, and I quote—both dogs seemed a bit agitated—end quote. He added, 'I thought it seemed unusual, since they're typically very tranquil animals.'"*

The professor agreed that it was amazing how anything so tiny could be engineered in such a way to be that airtight and yet so easily opened when pulled off the dog. *"You're looking for a highly trained chemist who has some sort of engineering skills or had help in that area."*

Sahba smiled and nodded as the others looked at him with a new respect.

⚔

Scott and Martz sat in Keefer's office watching the images that had become so familiar in the last few days. The late Secretary of State's smiling face, handsome in his tuxedo, the last photo taken of him at the Grande Continental Hotel to attend Audrey Aberholdt's soirée; the bronze casket draped with the American flag; the funeral service at the National Cathedral and the burial at Arlington; the picture of the shooter, flags flying at half mast, interviews with the Secretary of Homeland Security, and the swearing in of the new Secretary of State, Marvin Dougherty, the former deputy who had worked so well alongside his boss and friend, Douglas Fredericks. Then the Brassfield pictures—the charred limousine and the face of the terrorist they alleged to be the "Basketball Bomber." And now images of the smiling Hodges family along with their two beloved black Labs. The camera slowly zoomed in on the faces of Ja'bar al-Mansur and Yasar al-Afdal until they covered the screens of America.

They watched with horror mixed with anger the news of the Hodges attack. "You two get over to the—" Keefer's phone rang. "Hang on." He answered, "Keefer here." He listened stone-faced and then hung up. He looked somberly at the two agents. "That was DHS. The rest of the riddle, 'AND BABY MAKES THREE,' we know what it means."

Scott quickly leaned forward. "What?"

"The dog that carried the lethal pod—her name was Baby."

DAY 10

WEDNESDAY, JANUARY 14

O nce again, the State Department called on Martin Transportation to be available for yet another funeral. Marion Hodges had died in the night. The Secretary of Defense was not expected to live. Frank flipped from CNN to OAN News. It was a rehash of what he had just seen. He punched the numbers for Fox News just as his phone rang. Sabyl walked into his office with a thick folder held to her chest and sat on the edge of his desk and watched a bearded scientist talk about deadly ricin poison.

"The symptoms of inhaling ricin, especially in close proximity, would be respiratory distress, coughing, nausea, fever, tightness in the chest, heavy sweating, seizures and the skin would turn blue. Pulmonary edema...uh...fluid building up in the lungs, makes breathing extremely difficult. Finally, respiratory failure may occur, leading to death."

Sabyl winced. "What a horrible way to go."

The news commentator interrupted with a special announcement: *"Just a moment, ladies and gentlemen—we have breaking news..."* Sabyl turned up the volume.

Frank got off the phone and looked at the screen. "Now what?"

"Listen."

Attorney General Gordon Pruitt's somber face stepped up to a dozen microphones. *"The Secretary of Homeland Security will now make a statement."* He backed away and Killian walked up to the microphones. *"We have just received word that Secretary of Defense, Carson Hodges, died at 9:13 this morning."* Cameras clattered and flashed and little gasps wafted through the press. *"Funeral arrangements are not complete at this time, but will be announced later today."* Sabyl and Frank looked at one another in dismay.

Killian paused and then his demeanor changed. *"The Secretary of State, Douglas Fredericks, National Security Advisor Wayne Brassfield, and the Secretary of Defense, Carson Hodges, have been the targets of terrorists. These assassinations are considered to be the work of more than one or two people. We believe there may be several operatives working in and around the Washington, D.C. area and perhaps other cities. It is a possibility that they may be out to eliminate others. We hope not, but it is something we must take into account. We ask that you do not panic, but that you will keep your eyes open for anything—I repeat anything -- unusual. We are releasing photographs of some individuals who may be operating in the United States. At this particular time they are unaccounted for. These are the latest pictures that we have. It is, of course, possible that they could be wearing disguises. We have artists working on composites to show what they might look like without their beards and different, uh, appearances, if you will. We will be showing those later this afternoon. Please call the phone numbers on the bottom of the screen if you see anything unusual. Every call will be taken seriously. We will deal very severely with those who would attempt to misuse these phone numbers. This is extremely serious and we are calling upon the eyes and ears of America to help bring these people to justice. There is no such thing as perfect security when you're dealing with a network of cold-blooded terrorist killers. But we are committed to protect America's unique freedom and we need your help to do that."*

A seasoned reporter asked, *"Sir, are the agencies cooperating with each other?"*

Killian frowned," *I assure you we are in sync. We have a governing council that each agency answers to. And each agency is making its contribution, working as a coalition to bring an end to these killings. That's all I have for now."*

A young member of the press yelled, *"What about the Five Card Draw notes?"*

Killian's jaw unhinged. Someone had leaked the story. His face turned crimson. *"That's all we have for now."* He and Pruitt turned and quickly walked away. The press yelled out simultaneously for answers.

Frank muted the TV and frowned. "What the heck was he talking about, Five Card Draw?"

Sabyl shrugged her shoulders. "No idea."

"This whole thing is unbelievable."

"I know. Three of our top leaders have been assassinated. It's downright scary."

Frank leaned back in his chair. "So, has State called about Marion Hodges' funeral? Guess now there'll be a double—again."

"Yes," she said, shaking her head. "This is getting to be morbid." Sabyl stood and started out the door. She turned and smiled, "Hey, Frank. How about some good news for a change?"

"I could use it."

"We got the shuttle contract with GTI."

"Whoa! That's great!" he said, giving her two thumbs up. "You outbid Vassette, huh?"

"Yep. GTI doesn't want us to miss a beat. We go on just like always. Only change they want is to beef up security, meaning they'll have their own security guys aboard the buses, which really doesn't affect us one way or another."

"That's really great, Sabe. You the man! I mean...you the..."

"I get it, Frank."

He took off his glasses, laid them on the desk and looked at her carefully. "Any other news?"

"You mean about the biopsy? No, haven't heard yet."

"Why don't you call those turkeys? They shouldn't make you have to wonder about—"

Just then Rudy walked in, waved weakly and headed for the garage.

Sabyl grabbed him. "Whoa, buddy, not so fast!" With hands on her hips, she frowned. "My goodness, Rudy, you look like you just came out of a Turkish bath!"

Rudy gently pulled away and said, "I really have to go to the restroom." He hurried out to the garage, ignored the other drivers, went into the bathroom and locked the door.

Sabyl looked at Frank. "Buzz me if he comes back in." She went back to her desk and dialed the doctor's office. Rolling her eyes in frustration, she punched the unavoidable numbers the electronic menu dragged her through, amounting to exactly eight punches before getting to a human being. "Yes, hi. This is Sabyl Martin. I haven't heard back from your office regarding the results of my biopsy...yes, I'll hold."

Just then, she saw Rudy's car pull out of the driveway and speed away. "Blast! Uh, no, I wasn't talking to—no, never mind—yes, I'll hold."

Frank stood in her doorway. "Rudy just left."

Sabyl looked at him vacantly. "Yes, Rita? Sabyl Martin." Frank waited. She frowned, "Okay, fine," and hung up. "They still don't know anything. Dr. Solomon will call me himself as soon as he knows."

"Okay." He turned and walked back into his office, mumbling, "Buncha turkeys…"

↳

The question about the "Five Card Draw" notes and the subsequent non-answer from Secretary Killian poured fuel on the fire. Reporters' fingers flew over their keyboards all across America with every kind of twist to the story that could be imagined. Editorials filled pages of newspapers, and the talk shows had plenty of meat to chew up and spit out. The reporter who had initially asked the question was inundated with requests for appearances on radio and television talk shows, thoroughly enjoying the new attention he was getting. He managed to keep his source a secret just as his heroes, *Washington Post* reporters Bob Woodward and Carl Bernstein had done with "Deep Throat," the secret informant who provided information in 1972 about the involvement of President Richard Nixon's administration in the Watergate scandal.

Finally, under a great deal of pressure, a statement was released by the DHS, without disclosing the contents, that three notes had been received with references to a game of Five-Card Draw. It was not yet confirmed if the notes were genuine or if they were from some crank. He warned sternly that any such pranks would be dealt with severely.

Tourism was down, as well as the DOW and NASDAQ. Reporters were everywhere. They came from nearly every city in the U.S., compiling their "Eyewitness" news and then feeding it back to their hometowns. The major networks each had their own dramatic headline title opening and theme music for the top news story of the year. One called it TERRORISM IN THE CAPITAL. Another, ASSASSINATION ATTACKS, and still another, THE WAR ON OUR LEADERS.

A public outcry began for the Secret Service Agency to come under a congressional investigation. Why hadn't they protected our leaders? Were they doing all they could? Reporters questioned Homeland Security and the police about what they were doing to protect the citizens. One commuter asked, "If the terrorists are using chemical warfare, would they use something like Sarin gas?" Metro Police Chief Max Hawks was quoted in the *Washington Post* as saying, *"Even though it appears that they are targeting our top leaders, we are still on high alert to protect all of our citizens. Since a chemical was used, many people are concerned about their safety in the metro system. With hundreds of thousands of bus and subway commuters moving about each workday, we have a network of cameras and a highly visible police force in place, including our Metro Transit Police. Some officers carry portable chemical detectors. Our Metro stations are equipped with special devices that can detect chemical or biological weapons. After Nine-Eleven, all eighty-three rail stations removed their trash receptacles and replaced them with "explosion containment" cans. We have dozens of bomb-sniffing dogs and trained officers checking out suspicious or unattended packages or bags."*

It was related once again to go about their lives in a normal but cautious manner and to be aware of their surroundings and to always remember, "If you see something, say something."

Stubby finished his log sheet for the day and walked over and sat down with Burt and George. Burt lit a cigarette, turned his head and blew the smoke away from them. Stubby clicked his ballpoint pen closed and put it in his pocket. "So what do you think about what Jamal said the other day?"

"I wondered when you were going to ask that," George said with a smirk. "What did you think?"

Stubby took a deep breath. "I've thought about it. Seemed to me he was a little too sympathetic sounding—I mean that remark he made, 'One man's terrorist is another man's freedom fighter.' "

"Yeah. That was a sorry choice of words at a time like this," Burt said, his brows knit together in a knot. "I mean with all that's been going on. Kinda insensitive, in my opinion."

George frowned deeply, "I hate to say it, but I just don't trust the guy anymore."

"Think you should tell the boss?" Stubby asked.

"I don't know. You know how she feels about the drivers gossiping among themselves."

Burt blew a smoke ring. "We're not gossiping, just observing."

Stubby leveled his eyes at George. "You'd feel pretty bad if he turns out to be a sleeper and you never said anything."

"Yeah, I know."

"At least give her the option to make some sort of decision about him."

George shook his head. "It's more complicated than that."

"What do you mean?"

"You can't have a guy lose his job just because he's insensitive."

"No, but you sure as heck can make him wish he'd never said it."

"What do you mean?"

"We could scare him a little," Stubby said. "Let him know we're watching him."

"I imagine he knows that already. In fact, all Middle Easterners in D.C. are probably being scrutinized pretty closely by their coworkers and neighbors." He waved Burt's cigarette smoke away from his face. "We need to have more to go on than just a stupid comment."

"Why don't we follow him?" George said, leaning forward on his elbows.

Burt put out his cigarette. "Follow him? Where?"

"Just to see where he goes—after hours, I mean. Who he meets with—stuff like that."

Burt smirked, "Buncha gumshoes. How would you know what to look for? If he met up with some other guys, how would you know if they were just some friends or if they were up to something?"

George's head sunk down in his shoulders. "Guess we wouldn't."

"Still, it's worth a try," Stubby said.

George's head bobbed back up. "Okay, when?"

"He's off today—wanna go by his apartment?"

Burt pursed his lips into a look of suspicion. "And do what?"

"Wait. See if his car's there or if he goes out."

"And then what?"

"We'll follow him."

"When?"

"Tonight."

✦

It was six-thirty when Scott took his jacket off, hung it on the back of the kitchen chair, and looked through his mail. Just as he pulled off his tie, his cell rang. It was his boss. "Scott, I need you to come back down to my office. Now." Scott grabbed his jacket, and drove to the office. Traffic was slow but steady. He turned into the familiar parking garage, got out of his car, and took the elevator up to the seventh floor.

When Scott entered Keefer's office, he saw the disturbed look on his face. He took off his coat and hung on the back of a chair and sat down slowly as Ron shut the door. "Scott, you had lunch with a reporter yesterday."

"Yeah, an old college buddy. I told you about it and what we talked about."

"Somebody leaked the story about the poker notes."

"Aw, come on, Ron, you know me better than that!"

"I thought I did. Talk to me, Scott."

"I had lunch with an old college buddy, Neil Harper. He writes for *Reuters*. He called me. Told me about Shatir. I told you all that we discussed."

"All of it?"

"Blast it, Ron, I didn't leak it!"

"The Director wants you to take a hike for a few days."

"You've got to be kidding!"

"We've got to get to the bottom of this, and you're the scapegoat—for now."

"That's just great." He stood up and grabbed his coat. "Just what we need. A bunch of paranoid political posturing while some nutcase whacks our leaders!"

"Give me your gun, Scott."

"I don't believe this!" He handed him the .357 SigSauer.

"And your shield."

Scott's throat went dry. He laid down the symbols of his training, his career, his life. He turned and headed out the door. "See ya!"

"Hey, Scott. Here's another poker riddle. Take it home with you, will you?"

"I thought I was suspended."

"We can't suspend your brain."

Scott glared at him, grabbed the paper out of his hand, and drove home.

⚔

Due to the nature of their parents' deaths, and the threat on the nation's top leaders, the Hodges children made the painful decision that as soon as the bodies of Carson and Marion Hodges were released by the pathologists, a double funeral would be held at an undisclosed location; only family and close friends would attend. Sabyl's cars wouldn't be needed. The White House and military fleets would handle it. Frankly, Sabyl was relieved.

⚔

Scott called Neil Harper and told him what had happened. "They think I leaked it to you."

"To me? That's absurd. My guess is the assassins leaked it themselves."

"You're probably right, but nobody in the media is taking credit for it. Especially that young reporter that first asked about it."

"Could be the bad guys told them that if he did tell, they wouldn't get any more tips. Do you want me to call your boss?"

"No. When can we see that photographer friend of yours?"

"You want to be seen with me? That could jeopardize your job."

"It's already jeopardized."

"I'll pick you up in half an hour."

⚔

Neil and Scott drove to nearby Glen Burnie, Maryland, pulled into a sprawling brick apartment complex, and parked. They checked the address and walked up to building Number Three and found the name, Royce Bradford. Neil rang the button beside the name. A woman answered, "Yes?"

"Mrs. Bradford?"

"Yes?"

"It's Neil Harper. I called earlier?" The buzzer signaled that the door had been released. They went inside and walked up the steps to the third floor. Donna Bradford met them at the top of the stairs. She looked startled when she saw two men.

"This is my friend, Scott Terhune. He's a Secret Service agent investigating the assassinations in D.C." Scott hoped she wouldn't ask for his ID.

"Come in," she said weakly.

Donna Bradford wore a simple pair of tailored pants that hung on her lean body as though she had recently lost a lot of weight. A long-sleeved tan blouse covered her thin arms. She wore no makeup, her brown hair was streaked with gray and hung straight and slightly curled under at the ends. Her face was drawn and her eyes sad. It was obvious she had seen better days. Although she looked haggard, a bygone beauty still remained. She motioned for them to sit on the sofa. She sat across from them in a Queen Anne chair, pulled an afghan over her legs, sat with her feet together, her bony hands in her lap, clinging to a handkerchief. "You knew that Royce died right after Thanksgiving."

Neil was shocked. "No, Ma'am, I didn't know." He leaned forward. "What happened?"

"Brain tumor. It grew very rapidly. Thankfully, he didn't suffer long." She took in a labored breath and continued. "And now I have stomach cancer."

Neil leaned forward. "Oh, no! Mrs. Bradford, I'm so sorry!"

Scott's expression was troubled. "What's your prognosis—I mean—"

"They told me I have three, maybe four months. I'm trying to get my affairs in order." She tried to look brave. "My children will live with my sister in Van Nuys." She put her handkerchief over her mouth and wept silently.

Neil looked at her intently. "If there is anything at all I can do..." His voice trailed off. He felt his words sounded lame.

She blew her nose. "There is one thing."

"Anything."

"If you will take that box over there." She pointed to a large cardboard box in the corner of the dining room. "It's Royce's photos—and his stories that were never published."

"Stories?"

"He wanted to be a writer. He submitted several articles, but they were never accepted."

"I'll be happy to take it. Is there anything else I can do?"

"No. I'll keep his scrapbooks and cameras. The children may want them someday."

Neil told her about the story he had written about Shatir. "I know that Royce took a photo of him without Shatir knowing it, but they never ran the picture."

"It would be in that box. He labeled everything..." She pushed herself up out of the chair. "I must rest now." She shook their hands. "Thank you for coming."

"No, ma'am, thank you."

Scott felt like there was an anvil on his chest. Neil picked up the heavy box and walked to the door. "Mrs. Bradford..."

"Please, call me Donna."

"Donna, my wife and I will be praying for you. May we call you sometime? We'd like to know how you're doing."

She smiled weakly, "That would be nice. And thank you for your prayers."

They said their goodbyes. The two men walked heavily down the stairs in silence.

⼈

Burt, Stubby, and George sat in Burt's wife's car, a 2008 Toyota Corolla with a Clemson tiger-paw decal on the back window. They figured Jamal wouldn't recognize it. They saw his car parked in front of his apartment complex near the mall in Alexandria. After waiting an hour, Burt said, "Aw, this is stupid. Let's go home."

"Just a few more minutes."

"He ain't going nowhere. I wanna go home and watch the game," Burt lamented.

"Hey! There he is."

Burt scrunched down in the driver's seat. "Sure is. Look! He's getting in his car."

"Stay far enough behind him that he won't notice."

Jamal got on I-395 and headed north toward D.C. The three sleuths followed, turning with him and watching closely. He got off at the Memorial Bridge exit, headed up Delaware, turned onto Mass Ave and passed Union Station. He turned right and parked in front of a house and went inside.

Burt stopped and wondered whether to park or not. "Okay, so we followed him to a house. What does that prove?"

Stubby sat back. "I don't know. Maybe nothing."

"What would a sleeper be doing working for Sabyl anyhow?"

"Maybe he's gathering information," George offered.

"About what?"

"About...I don't know. Let's head back." They took down the address and drove away.

$$\lambda$$

Rudy's limousine pulled up in front of the brownstone and let out Fathid and Sahba. He pulled away from the curb and turned onto Mass Ave and pulled up behind Burt's car. They saw a limo in the rearview mirror but the overhead streetlights gleamed on the windshield, preventing them from seeing who was driving it. At the next light, they pulled up alongside Rudy and honked. He rolled down his window.

"Hey, Rudy!" Burt shouted. "Where you been? We never see you anymore."

"I've been very busy." The light changed and he pulled ahead of them and turned off Mass Avenue onto North Capital, hoping they wouldn't follow. Another light. They pulled alongside again. "Hey, Rudy, roll down your window!"

Reluctantly, he pushed the button and it silently slid down.

"We're heading back to the garage. You coming in?"

"No, I have an early pick-up in the morning." The light changed and he drove away heading for home. His heart was so heavy he could hardly breathe. He just wanted it all to end.

$$\lambda$$

Scott stared at the poker riddle again. FOR OLD TIME'S SAKE, WE'LL TAKE A CARD UPSIDE DOWN. He ran it through the computer and searched for anything that would give him a clue. Nothing. He couldn't seem to concentrate for thinking about the assassinations, about his suspension, about Mrs. Bradford and about Sabyl. And he could do nothing about any of it. He finally gave up and went to bed.

Thursday, January 15

Rudy pulled up to the brownstone on E Street for the third time that day. Knowing he was chauffeuring terrorists was unnerving enough, but knowing that they held in their hands the life of his only child was staggering. He got out and reluctantly opened the back door of the limo. Endicott got out and ordered Rudy to come inside with them. This was a first. He looked at the aged house and wondered if David could be inside. Hope rose in his heart.

The door opened on the other side and Sahba got out. The three of them walked up the steps to the iron gate. Endicott opened it and went up on the sagging porch and unlocked the heavy wooden door. They went inside and Rudy followed the two men into a hallway, through a door and up the stairs to the second floor apartment. Endicott held the door and told them to go in.

The blinds were drawn on the two front double windows. There were several pallets on the floor; one of them was occupied. The place smelled of body odor. A small desk sat in the corner with a computer on it. Rudy's eyes took in everything, wondering if David was in one of the other rooms, or perhaps there would be at least a hint of where he was being held. A stack of newspapers was on the floor beside a worn-out recliner. Its footrest was stuck in the open position and sagged sideways. Fathid's camera equipment lay on a table with the tripod rolled up in the blanket that he had seen on so many occasions.

Something that looked like a toolbox sat in a corner along with cardboard boxes that were sealed and looked to be unopened. Some clippings of the Secretary of State, the Secretary of Defense and photographs of Hodges and his dogs were taped to the wall. More photos were strewn around on the table next to the camera.

Endicott spoke in Arabic to the others. They argued heatedly, and the one who had been sleeping on the floor glared at them, stood up, dragged his pallet into the other room and slammed the door. A fifth person came out of another room. Rudy recognized him as the man he had seen at Hains Point.

Endicott pointed to a kitchen chair by the window. "Sit down."

"Why am I here? Where have you taken my son?"

"He is not in this city, but nearby. If you do exactly as we tell you, he will not be harmed, nor will you or your wife."

Rudy's eyes widened. He was now threatening his wife as well. "What do you want?"

"Nothing more than what you have been doing. When we are finished with our tasks, we will release your son and we will leave the country the same way we came in."

"Why would you let me live? I've seen your faces. I know you are the assassins. I could identify you."

Fathid spoke up. "You won't, because we know where your son lives and we know where you live. We have operatives all over the U.S., and all we have to do is make a phone call and your son and wife are dead. You won't talk. Besides, you are a brother. We have no quarrel with you. Only the leaders of this degenerate country."

Fathid said, "You can be a part of us, Rudy. You know that we are in a holy war and the infidels must die!"

Rudy was silent. He felt a glimmer of hope. Perhaps if he pretended to be one of them, they would spare his family. He would choose his words carefully. "Yes, I have been here many years, but I cannot forget my roots, my history..."

Fathid's eyes widened. "You wish to join us then?"

Rudy couldn't bring himself to say anything more. He knew he could not deny his Lord.

They moved closer to him and started to talk excitedly. Endicott watched them with cold eyes. He wasn't interested in their cause. He was a mercenary, a cold-blooded hit man who had recruited the others under the guise of doing it for their religion.

Endicott walked over and slapped Rudy across the mouth. "You're lying." His lip bled and began to swell immediately. The others backed off and began to chatter excitedly in Arabic.

"Shut up!" They fell silent instantly. "There is no need to tell him anything. He is needed only to follow our instructions as we reveal them each hour. Don't trust him to suddenly become one of you. His father is a Christian minister!"

Their faces suddenly changed to hatred. Fathid spat in his face. Rudy balled up his huge fist and then slowly released it. He took out his handkerchief and wiped his face.

"Besides, he already knows more than you think. He knows about the list, and so does his employer, the Martin woman."

Endicott's words cut into Rudy's heart like shards of glass. "My boss knows nothing. No one saw the book but me. And I did not read—"

"You're lying!"

"Sir, I do not lie."

"Everyone lies, Rudy. You are no exception. What did you see in the book?"

"Nothing!"

"Did the woman see it?"

"No."

"Did you tell her about it?"

"No."

"You're lying!"

"I am not!"

Endicott's eyes narrowed into slits. Rudy thought they looked like the windows of hell. "I saw how you exchanged looks..."

Rudy was incredulous. "What?"

"I am not blind, nor am I stupid. I heard her saying to the man in her office, 'Keep this to yourself.'"

Rudy had no idea what he was talking about. He wiped his bleeding mouth. "Why did you bring me here?"

Fathid sneered, "We thought we could talk some sense into you, but you are brainwashed by the filthy American culture."

Sahba moved in closer. "It's just like you devilish Americans to use a deck of cards to further humiliate our people. Two can play this game."

Endicott frowned at him and then turned to Rudy. "You are of no use to us except to follow our instructions."

Rudy stood. "I will do whatever you say. Please, just do not hurt my boy, my wife or Ms. Martin."

Endicott stepped back, smiled caustically, and looked around at the others. "See how he cares for her. How touching." He took Rudy by the arm and started walking toward the door. "Rudy, my friend, you will have nothing to worry about as long as you do as you are told. Be here tomorrow morning at nine o'clock. And, by the way, you'd better think of a good story about that fat lip of yours." The others laughed.

Rudy went out the door, stumbled down the stairs, out the iron gate and into his car. He pulled away from the curb and sped away. Tears burned his face as he drove toward the office garage. He looked at himself in the rearview mirror. His lip was swollen and still bleeding. He couldn't go to the garage. He had no explanation about his lip and didn't feel like making one up.

▲

The long shiny car gleamed in the night as it pulled up to the main entrance of the massive Verizon Center. Washington's 20,000-seat multi-purpose sports and entertainment venue was home to the Wizards, the Mystics, the Washington Capitals, and Georgetown NCAA basketball. And, of course, it hosted plenty of major concerts with the top music performers *du jour.*

The usual stares accompanied the entrance of the stretch limousine. Camera flashes nearly blinded Sabyl, as she stood with her PTT in hand, keeping her eyes fixed on Roberto Enrique emerging from the car. His perfect white teeth gleamed as he smiled and waved to the crowd. She felt a strange responsibility toward him. The crowd jostled her as she radioed the drivers to take the cars to the back entrance into the security lockup area along with Roberto's five hot pink, black, and gold Prevost XL II buses and his ten matching Kenworth tractor-trailers.

Roberto loved to arrive at the front entrance, much to the chagrin of his bodyguards, who held the squealing fans at bay. Sabyl was given a stage pass, which she promptly hung around her neck, and was escorted to one of his special-guest seats on the front row. The excitement of the sold-out performance was growing by the second as the attendees streamed in and found their seats. Sabyl assured him, barring an emergency, she would be there until his concert was over. The fans were young, mostly Hispanic, many yelling in Spanish their undying love for him.

As was expected, the music was so loud she could hardly bear it. From past experience, she remembered to put earplugs in her ears. It helped some, but the beat thundered through her body like a freight train. As usual, Roberto came on with an explosion of pyrotechnics, using the latest computer and digital technology, with wildly flashing lights in full effect. His crew had spent the last eighteen hours setting up their powerful state-of-the-art sound system, massive video projection equipment, pyros and hydraulic staging systems.

The Latin beat had the fans up on their feet, clapping and dancing in the aisles with the first earsplitting notes of his latest hit, *Tengo Bailar* (*I've Got to Dance*)—and dance he did. His six backup singers, three female and three male, were dressed in tight, hot-pink sequined hip huggers with pink satin tank tops. Their shoulders shimmied as they sang to the throbbing beat. The musicians wore black pants and white silk shirts with blousy sleeves. The bongo player tossed his head from side to side, smiling broadly with obvious delight to be playing for the biggest Latin star in the world. Roberto wore a spangled white tux with tails that flew as he gyrated and twirled with the other nine dancers to the perfectly choreographed steps. After the first number, he took off his tux jacket, revealing an open chest, bronzed and well-oiled, and sequined ruffles running down the length of his sleeves. The ladies shrieked and squealed with delight. Sabyl thought some of them might faint. His white patent-leather shoes gleamed in the bright lights as he swayed and whirled, thrilling his fans with amazing steps that made him seem to float. The throbbing beat of the bongos even got Sabyl on her feet.

Before coming inside the arena, she had switched her cell phone to vibrate. She felt the strange buzzing sensation, pulled it out of her jacket pocket and opened it. "Sabyl Martin," she yelled. "You'll have to wait 'til I can get to where I can hear you. Hold on!" She ducked and walked quickly across the front row to the side entrance. Security checked her pass and let her by. She got as far away from the noise as she could. "Okay, now I can hear you."

"Sabyl, it's John. I just got a call from Rudy's wife, Layla. She was crying. Rudy hasn't come home yet—hasn't called or anything. She's really upset. Maybe you'd better call her."

"Okay, John, thanks, I'll call her now. Everything else okay?"

"All quiet, for a change."

"Thanks for the heads up."

She quickly punched in the number. "Layla, it's Sabyl."

"Oh, Miss Sabyl, thank you for calling me."

"John said you called. What's wrong?"

Layla spoke hoarsely with her soft Egyptian Arabic accent. Sabyl could tell she had been crying. "I am not one to interfere in my husband's work, but is something going on that I do not know about? Is his job in jeopardy? He is not himself."

"No, Layla, his job is not in jeopardy. I've noticed he's been acting strangely too. In fact, I was going to call you and ask if his health is okay."

"As far as I know, unless he is keeping something from me, because I asked him if he was feeling all right and he said he was fine. But I know something is wrong."

"I'm sure there's a logical answer, Layla, but I'll have a talk with him tomorrow and I'll call you. Now, don't you worry, okay?"

"He has not come home. That is not like him."

Sabyl looked at her watch. "His client keeps him very busy. I'll see what I can do. Try not to worry, okay?"

She sniffed, "I will try."

"All right, dear. And if he comes in anytime soon, have him call my cell."

"Thank you, Miss Sabyl."

"You're welcome."

She put her cell back in her pocket. She wasn't imagining things after all. If she didn't hear from him tonight, she would call him in the morning.

⅄

Scott pushed himself away from the table. "That was awesome, Crystal. Neil told me you were a good cook, but that was incredible."

The petite blond smiled and thanked him. Her pregnancy had been the topic of the evening. They were beginning to think they were not going to be able to have children, and just as they got serious about adopting, she got pregnant. Scott ducked questions about Sabyl as much as possible without out-and-out lying. He wished she was there.

Crystal said, "You two go on in the den and I'll clean up these dishes."

"You sure you don't want me to help, hon?"

"No, but thanks. I know you guys have things to discuss. I'll bring dessert in later."

After Scott settled himself on the sofa, Neil brought in the large box he had gotten from Donna Bradford. "I've looked through a lot of these. There must be hundreds of photos. Haven't found anything so far, but figured we could go through them together."

Scott leaned forward and peered into the box at his feet. "I don't know what I'm looking for."

"Everything is dated, but nothing's in order. It's almost like it's been rummaged through. Just look for a photo of a Middle-Eastern man that is dated anytime in 2005."

They dug through the box for a half an hour. Crystal brought apple cobbler and ice cream, with a healthy portion for herself. They were getting close to the bottom of the box when Scott pulled out a photo and handed it to Neil. "Is this him?"

Neil let out a sigh of relief. "That's him."

Scott frowned, "Not sure how I'm going to run this through the data base when I'm no longer..."

"I'll take it to them. I'd like to talk to your boss about this guy anyway." He started putting the other photos back into the box. "By the way, the *Washington Post* had an editorial about the 'Five-Card Draw' poker notes."

Scott polished off the cobbler and handed the plate to Crystal. "Thanks. That was great. Yeah, I saw it. Everybody's got an opinion." His face was glum.

"Something on your mind, Scott?"

"So far nobody's been able to come up with the meaning of this last poker riddle."

"Yeah?"

"There are a hundred scenarios—none of them good. I have a thought about this, but I hope I'm wrong."

Neil turned to him with serious eyes. "What?"

"FOR OLD TIME'S SAKE. What does that mean to you?"

"I don't know—like reminiscing or something."

"Right. If you're reminiscing about something, then obviously something has happened to reminisce about, right?"

"Rrright." Neil looked puzzled.

"What has happened before that would be important to these guys?"

"That they've killed three of our top leaders?"

"Not that recent. What would be important to a terrorist?"

"Nine-Eleven?"

"Exactly."

"What about the upside down card?"

"If I'm right—you don't wanna know."

"What?"

"What's 911 upside down?"

Neil thought for a moment. "116?"

"Yeah. What's tomorrow?"

"January the 16th! One–sixteen! No *way*!"

"Better pray I'm wrong."

⋏

Layla looked at her husband suspiciously. "Rudy! Where have you been? What is wrong with your mouth?"

"I bit it when I was eating my lunch."

"You bit it? How can you bite your lip on the outside?"

"Don't worry about it."

She helped him with his coat. "Miss Sabyl wants you to call her."

"She called here?"

"No, I called her." She folded the coat over her arm. "Rudy, you must talk to me. I'm so worried about you."

"I'll call her after supper. When will it be ready? I'm hungry," he lied.

"Go wash up, I'll take it out of the oven. It's probably ruined by now."

Rudy washed up and sat down at the small kitchen table. He picked at his supper and finally pushed his chair back.

Layla looked at him with worried eyes. "When are you going to call Miss Sabyl?"

"Not now."

"Rudy, you promised!" She reached for his hand. "When are you going to tell me what is wrong?"

He saw the pain in her eyes and wanted to comfort her, but there was nothing he could do or say. He stood up and looked her in the eyes for the first time in days. "I want you to go visit your sister in Newark for a few days."

"Why?"

"It would be a nice change for you. You haven't seen her in a long time. Go call her and tell her you're coming for a visit."

"I am not going anywhere until you tell me what is wrong!"

He picked up his plate and put it in the sink. "I'm going to bed." He walked slowly up the stairs and went into the bedroom. His body ached with grief. Slumping down on the bed, he picked up the pillow and buried his face in it, wept and prayed. "God, please keep David safe. Please don't let them harm him." His chest heaved with sobs. He heard Layla downstairs slamming cupboards. "Lord, give Layla your grace and peace. Only you can comfort her now." He lay back on the bed and stared at the ceiling. He had to do something. He couldn't just let them continue their evil plots. "God, please give me wisdom and courage."

⅄

Ron Keefer leaned forward and shifted his phone from one ear to the other, listening closely as Scott gave his take on the last poker note. He was silent for a moment.

Scott frowned. "Are you there?"

"Yeah, I'm here. Sounds like they're planning something big."

"I'd say so."

"We got another riddle today. DHS sent it over a couple of hours ago."

"What does it say?"

"It says, 'THIS TIME WE'LL PLAY A WILD CARD. IT STINKS, BUT IT'S A HOME RUN HITTER.'"

"That's weird."

"Yeah. But you've been pretty good at coming up with the answers, so what does this one mean?"

"I'll think about it."

"Don't think too long. If you're right about the other, the Nine-Eleven thing, they're probably tied."

"Thought I was suspended."

"Can't suspend your brain."

"So you said before." He sighed, "Give me the exact wording again."

Keefer repeated it.

Scott scribbled it on a note pad. "I'll think about it and call you if I come up with something."

⅄

The bodyguards swept Roberto Enrique past the screaming devotees out the back entrance and into the waiting limousine. Sabyl sat next to him smiling. "Great show as always, Roberto."

"Sabyl, *mi querido*. As always, you make everything nice for me."

"Seriously, Roberto, your show gets better every time I see it. You're a real star."

"Not so big. I am still doing coliseums. I want to do movies."

"You will. You wait and see."

"What about you, Sabyl. How have you been?"

"Couldn't be better," she lied. "Staying busy—unfortunately, not the kind of business we would like. All these funerals."

"Ah, *si*. It is terrible what has been happening. We considered canceling D.C., but my manager said no. He thinks it makes me look very, how you say, *valeroso,* ehhh, courageous to come here at this time."

"I know that's not the only reason you came here, Roberto."

"No, you are right. I love to perform. It is my life." He squeezed her hand. "And I wanted to see you, my friend."

Just then Sabyl's cell vibrated. "Excuse me, Roberto." She answered, "Sabyl Martin."

"Sabyl, it's Scott. Where are you?"

She was shocked to hear his voice. "I'm at the Verizon Center. What...?"

"Something big may be going down tomorrow. I can't explain now, but just want you to be extra careful."

"What do you mean?"

"Just be careful. Especially tomorrow. Talk to you later."

"Scott..."

She looked at her cell and held it motionless for a moment. "Your plane leaves soon, Roberto. You'd better get going."

"*Si*. I am flying out of Dulles."

"Good." She kissed him on the cheek. "Now, get out of here."

Friday, January 16

Neil Harper sat across from Keefer's desk. "I hope you know by now Scott's as honest as they come."

"'Knew it all along."

"Then why did you suspend him?"

Keefer ignored his question. "It's too bad about your photographer friend. When did you say he died?"

"End of November. His wife was kind enough to let me look through his files and photos."

Keefer once again looked at the black and white photograph Neil had brought him. "Thanks for sending this over We ran this photo through our most wanted database. It doesn't match anything we've got."

"What does that tell you?"

"It tells me that Shatir is most likely Talib Sahba, one of the most dangerous operatives on our list. And we've never been able to get a clear photo of him. Plus he's a master of disguise."

"And a chemical engineer with the know-how to make the basketball bomb and the ricin pod."

"Exactly."

"So, what happens now?"

"We'll put this in London's latest FDC database."

"FDC?"

"Yeah. Facial Detection Cameras."

Neil nodded, "Ah, yes. Biometrics. I read that the privacy advocates are having a hissy fit over those."

"Yeah. False matches are possible. But that's changing. They're much more reliable now. Even though it's useful technology, there's still about a five to ten percent failure rate. It's definitely a work in progress. The Brits have the best technology so far. Maybe they'll come up with something."

"So what is it—pattern recognition?"

"Sort of. There are hundreds of uniquely identifiable points—peaks and valleys on the face—but there are always ways to get around it. Some apply prosthetics that can be ordered from theatrical makeup suppliers—like puffier cheeks, a larger nose, enhanced chin. Some even have plastic surgery done just to get past the surveillance cameras."

"Seems easier to stay honest."

"You said you saw him over on Van Ness. Guess he was checking out where to do his dirty work. How did he look?"

"Bald, that unmistakable offset jaw and the one long eyebrow."

"So he looked pretty much the same as this picture?"

"Yeah, only with no hair."

"The hair won't matter to the FDCs. Did he see you?"

"No. And even if he did, I doubt if he would recognize me. Back then, I was skinny, had long hair and a beard."

"Okay." Keefer stood up and offered his hand. "We appreciate this information. Thanks again for coming in."

Neil got up and shook hands with the Special Agent in Charge. "Hope you nail these guys soon."

"Yeah. We'll be in touch."

⋏

Scott's brain felt like it had a cramp in it from umpteen cups of coffee and trying to figure out the latest poker riddle. He went from his kitchen to the living room just to have a different place to think. It didn't help. He wanted to be out there looking for—something. There was so much legwork to be done. Right now they needed his brain—and it was fried.

Keefer and Martz walked up to his door and rang the bell. Scott went to the door in his pajamas, toting his coffee mug. He looked through the peephole and opened the door. "What are you guys doing here?"

Keefer said, "We miss your smiling face. You going to let us in?"

He shrugged, "Yeah, sure." They sat on the sofa and Scott sat down across from them. "Want some coffee?"

"No thanks. What'd you come up with?"

"Nothing."

Keefer frowned. "Martz seems to think we can do better if we brainstorm together."

"Not sure I have any brains left to storm."

"Give it a try."

Scott took a sip of his lukewarm coffee. "You got any ideas at all?"

"Nothing," said Martz, dejected.

Scott looked at the ceiling. "Great. This could be the day for complete disaster and we have nothing."

Keefer frowned, "We're not the only ones working on this. The FBI, the CIA, DIA, DHS are all over it."

"Good thing. Okay," he sighed, "Let's go over it again. It says, 'WE'LL PLAY A WILD CARD. IT STINKS, BUT IT'S A HOME RUN HITTER.' What would a wild card be?"

Keefer shook his head. "A Joker?"

"I racked my brain on that half the night. The only thing I can think of is a Joker is not like the other cards. It's different. Maybe they're going to do something different."

"Like what?"

"Don't know. Maybe the rest of it will tell us. IT STINKS... The Wild Card stinks."

"What the heck does that mean?"

"Cards that stink. A low number?" Martz said, scratching the top of his head.

"Maybe, but I'm not sure that's the trail to go down."

"Then what?"

"Think of things that stink."

Martz folded his arms and sat back. "Lots of things, bad breath, garbage, dirty socks, poop—"

Scott sat up straight. "Poop! How about fertilizer?"

"Yeah, fertilizer. Oh, man! Fertilizer!"

"Yeah. Remember the Oklahoma City bombing?"

Keefer said, "What about the rest of it? 'It's a Home Run Hitter.'"

"I don't know—Home—the White House?"

"No, that can't be. It's blocked off. They couldn't get near enough to it with a truck full of explosives. It's got to be something else."

Scott rubbed his head as though trying to sort out the strange words, then quickly got up and went to his computer. "Seems like I saw something like that in that list of Poker terminology..." He clattered on the keyboard and brought up the site. "Here it is. Home Run Hitter." Martz and Keefer walked over and peered over his shoulder. "It means, 'A player who will make a big play that requires maximum risk.'"

Keefer said, "A big play. Sounds like it's connected to the last riddle."

"Yeah, they're going to do something big, maybe with fertilizer." Scott jumped up. "The Israeli Embassy!"

"Why there?"

"That's where Neil saw Shatir. It's on Van Ness. The street is narrow right there. A truck could get up close and personal to that embassy."

"There are a lot of embassies on that street."

"Yes, but you know how terrorists despise Israel."

"We're on it."

"I'm going with you."

"No, you're not. Stay here and keep that brain of yours on this. There may be more clues."

⋏

Sabyl had called Rudy and asked him to come into the office. The call startled him. He knew by the sound of her voice she meant business. And if he didn't, she would attempt to talk to Endicott.

Rudy collapsed his ample form into the deep leather chair across from his boss of fourteen years. She was more like a daughter to him than an employer. His heart was heavy, but he tried to manage a smile.

Sabyl leaned forward and looked at him with worried eyes. "Rudy, what's wrong? You're not yourself."

Rudy looked at her, his eyes red and his face drawn. "Boss, I am fine. Just worried about some personal things."

"What things?"

"Nothing I cannot handle."

"Rudy, we've been friends a long time. Can I help in some way?"

"No, boss, you cannot help. It will work out."

"Do you need money?"

"No."

"Is your health okay?"

"Yes, nothing like that—just some personal things."

"What do you mean personal things?"

"Nothing. I want to know how you are."

"I'm fine. Just waiting to hear the biopsy results."

"My father is praying for you, as am I."

"Thanks, buddy, I cherish your prayers and your dad's. And don't go changing the subject—"

Rudy's cell phone rang. He looked startled, jumped up quickly and answered it. "I will be right there." He moved toward the door. "I have to go now. I will see you later, okay?"

Sabyl noticed his accent thickened when he was nervous. She stood. "Rudy, you don't have to continue driving this guy."

"No! I must—I mean only a few more days," he said with pleading eyes. "I must go now."

"Are you logging your hours?"

"Yes, boss. I must hurry. I will talk to you later."

Sabyl watched him pull out of the driveway. She didn't know why, but she had a terrible feeling in her gut.

✦

Keefer and Martz headed north on Connecticut Avenue toward Van Ness Street in Northwest D.C. On the way, they called for a bomb squad to be sent immediately to the Israeli Embassy, but to move with stealth. DHS was alerted and they quickly warned the Israeli and other embassies nearby to evacuate as well and to try to avoid being seen on the Van Ness side of their complexes. Immediately, ambassadors and their staffs in embassies to the south of the Israeli embassy, Ghana, Bangladesh, Ethiopia, Bahrain, started working their way toward Tilden Street. They moved through the trees and shrubs, helped each other over fences, and down the steep hill. Embassies on the north side of Van Ness, Malaysia, Nigeria and Pakistan, moved out onto Reno Road, and UDC was being evacuated as stealthily as possible, getting everybody out on the northeast side.

Keefer turned left onto Van Ness. Martz saw it first. "That's gotta be it!"

They drove slowly past the twenty-five-foot motor home with its hood up, feigning mechanical problems. They could see that someone was still inside pulling the curtains to cover the windshield. "You smell that?"

"Yeah. Fertilizer. Can't mistake that smell—like ammonia."

Keefer turned left into a parking area in front of the embassy. Two Israeli agents approached them. They got out and showed their ID and brought them up to speed. "Have you evacuated?"

"Yes. Thank you for the warning." He and Martz stood talking with them, trying to look as casual as possible.

Keefer's cell beeped. "Keefer here."

"You on it?"

"Yeah, Scott, we're on it. We got some of the last part of the riddle—the "Home" part. It's a motor home."

"Oh, man!"

"There's someone still inside."

"Do you think they'll blow themselves up with it or do it with a remote detonator like McVeigh did?"

"Wish I knew."

Maybe that Home Run Hitter means they'll hit it and run—use a detonator."

"Could be. Gotta go."

Keefer radioed the bomb squad and told them to approach from Reno Road and not to make their presence known yet. "We've got a delicate situation here. There's somebody still inside the motor home. If we spook them, they might set it off. But if these guys are mercenaries, they most likely will use a remote device. We're betting on the latter."

The agent on the other end said, "You'd better be right."

"Pray they don't see the people evacuating—wait a minute!"

"What!"

"They're getting out."

Two men stepped out of the motor home, looked around and started walking east toward Connecticut Avenue. Keefer looked at Martz and said quietly, "Let's go."

They crossed Van Ness and walked past the motor home following the two men. "When I give the signal, you take out the guy on the left, I'll get the one on the right. We can't let them hit that detonator. Drop 'em the first shot."

One of the Israeli agents ran inside their embassy to make sure the ambassador and all his staff got out safely. The other agent watched the four figures walking toward Connecticut Avenue and said a silent prayer.

⅄

Rudy pulled up in front of the Lafayette House Hotel. Endicott watched as the car approached, looked at his watch and then looked north as though eagerly waiting for something. He looked at his watch again, frowned and then got into the car and ordered Rudy to take him to the brownstone.

Protestors were gathered at Dupont Circle. Endicott looked at them curiously. Their placards said something about profiling, but he couldn't make out the rest of it. Traffic was heavy as it always was on Fridays. They continued past Union Station, onto Maryland Avenue, and turned right toward E Street.

Rudy wanted to ask for his cell phone back, but he didn't dare. He hated feeling so helpless, but he couldn't jeopardize David's life. It sickened him that he was driving the very assassins that were systematically murdering his beloved nation's leaders, prowling about in the dark limousine like jungle cats after their prey, no doubt making sinister plans to complete their list. If there were only some way he could warn the authorities without tipping off the ones who held his son hostage. *Maybe I should call Scott Terhune. He would know what to do. Maybe he could find David and bring him to safety. Do I dare risk it?* He looked at the heartless killer in his back seat. He was afraid to try to call Scott. He would pray.

⚔

Keefer and Martz continued following the two men, knowing they had to drop them before they got near the street corner where there were always dozens of pedestrians. The two suspects ahead of them walked slowly, one with his hands in his pockets. Keefer figured he was the one with the detonator. Knowing that what he was about to do was completely without precedent. To shoot someone in the back without fully knowing the facts went against everything he had been trained to do. But at this point he had no choice. Everything pointed to their conclusions about the bomb and a detonator. He knew he was putting his career and Martz's career on the line. If they merely shot and wounded the men, they could still detonate the bomb. If they were both killed, there was a chance that the one who was in charge of setting off the bomb may not yet have his finger on the button. He saw no other way out. Keefer looked at Martz and said, "Now!" Simultaneously, they pulled their weapons, aimed carefully and fired. Both dropped like dead men. The agents hoped they were. The Israeli agents held their breath. The motor home was silent. Keefer and Martz cautiously approached the two men lying on the sidewalk, blood gushing from their heads. The man on the right still had his hands in his pockets.

"His finger might still be on the detonator." He radioed for the bomb squad. "Get here now!"

A crowd started gathering. Keefer yelled at them to get out of there as fast as they could. The bomb techs approached the scene. Special Agent Keefer spoke with a dry throat. "The detonator may still be in his pocket."

The head bomb tech frowned and said, "We've got to get that thing out of his hand without the button releasing."

"Can you just deactivate the bomb?"

"We'll work it from both ends." He turned to one of his men. "Johnson, check out the motor home. See if it's booby trapped."

The bomb tech squatted down beside the body, took his heavy gloves off and opened a little toolbox that one of the other techs handed him. He pulled out a small pair of scissors and cut the pocket away from the dead man's hand, while the other tech held his hand in place. He slowly pulled away the cloth. The small black detonator was in his hand, his thumb on a button.

Martz whispered, "You were right, boss." Keefer closed his eyes and breathed a sigh of relief. But relief was quickly replaced with apprehension as to whether or not the bomb squad could pull it off. But these guys were the best in their field. If anyone could do it, they could.

The bomb tech cautiously placed his thumb next to the man's and, with excruciating care, began to nudge it over one millimeter at a time until he could feel the rim of the button on the edge of his thumb. He could not let the slightest pressure be released from the button or the bomb would detonate. Keefer and Martz silently watched them work. Martz wondered if they had ever been schooled in this particular dilemma.

Keefer's cell beeped, causing the tech to flinch ever so slightly. Keefer quickly turned away and spoke in a gruff whisper, "Keefer here."

"What's going on over there?"

"Scott, you nearly got us all blown to bits!"

"How'd I do *that*?"

"You—never mind. What do you want?"

"I want to know what's going on!"

Keefer filled him in.

"Oh, man! I didn't know you guys were doing brain surgery over there."

"Close to it. Hold on. These guys don't need chatter..."

The tech's thumb moved another millimeter. Scott listened as hard as he could over the phone.

The other tech continued to hold the dead man's hand in place as he watched his partner work with precision. The Israeli agents stood at their post, watching and wishing they could do more, but knew the American bomb squad was well trained. If anyone could pull this off, they could.

The people gathering down the street were being held at bay by the local police whom Keefer had called on the way over. Someone in the crowd shouted, "What's going on? Why did you kill those men?" Others pulled out their cell phones and began taking pictures and yelled the same question. The agents ignored them and continued watching the bomb tech with his staggering task.

Scott held the phone to his ear, listening for the slightest sound. He could hear Keefer's shallow breathing. His stomach felt like it was on one of those sadistic amusement park rides.

The tech's thumb moved another millimeter. "Got it!" the tech said with great relief. Everybody exhaled and said a small prayer of thanks. The other tech let go of the dead man's hand and helped his partner up. They carefully deactivated the detonator. He radioed the rest of the squad. "What do you have up there?"

"It's not booby trapped."

"Awesome."

"Just stinks to high heaven."

Keefer called an ambulance to come collect the bodies.

Rudy pulled up to the brownstone. Usually, whenever Endicott was let off, Fathid would be there waiting with his camera equipment, but not today. Endicott seemed agitated. He got out of the car and finally gave Rudy his cell phone back. "Come back in one hour." He went up the steps and disappeared through the door. One hour. Not enough time to go back to the garage. He would merely have to turn around and come back. He missed seeing the guys and Sabyl. He missed his son. He thought about calling Scott but didn't have his number. *How can I get it?* Then he remembered he had it in his phone from two years ago when he was engaged to Sabyl. Still, his heart raced at the thought of jeopardizing David's life. He shook his head and drove away.

Sabyl was taken back slightly when Scott suggested Three Doves. The popular restaurant had been one of their favorite places. It occupied three adjoining row houses on Maryland Avenue. It seemed a bit too romantic with its cozy, semi-private dining nooks and plush wingback chairs, but she knew that he had suggested it because of the private alcoves. They could draw the curtains and talk privately. Obviously, the conversation would be emotional.

They met at seven o'clock to beat the crowd. The maître d' led them to a small round table nestled in one of the alcoves. In the center of the table was a small exquisite bouquet of flowers. Sabyl looked at them and felt her face flush. He helped her with her coat and pulled the chair out for her. *Always the gentleman,* she thought.

Sabyl wore a new camel colored suit, the jacket collar and lapels trimmed in black velvet, a black satin blouse, and black suede boots. They sat across from each other. Sabyl unfolded her napkin and put it in her lap. She was uncomfortable, and wanted to get it over with.

She had forgotten how handsome he was. He wore gray cords, a gray turtleneck and a tweed jacket. Her heart was feeling claustrophobic from being barricaded for two years. She could almost feel it scratching to get out, pushing at the door. She folded her arms tightly as though trying to keep it in.

"You look beautiful," Scott smiled.

"Thank you."

The wine steward came in with the list. Scott chose one and menus were brought. A young woman dressed in black introduced herself. "Hi, my name is April and I'll be your server. I'd like to tell you about our specials tonight." She recited the delicacies of the evening with passion. "I'll give you a few minutes to decide."

Scott leaned forward and smiled weakly. "Thanks for agreeing to have dinner with me. It's wonderful to see you." Her tiny diamond earrings flashed in the candlelight.

"Scott, I'm not sure why I agreed to meet with you. I suppose I should give you a chance to explain, but—"

He looked down and shook his head. "I should have told you this a long time ago. I—"

The server opened the curtain and closed it behind her. "Have we decided?" Sabyl ordered the Eggplant Rollatini and Caesar salad and Scott the

New York strip. She left and the wine steward arrived with a bottle of merlot, which he opened ceremoniously, poured, and left.

Scott picked up his glass and held it up. "Here's to old friends."

Sabyl raised an eyebrow. Was that what they were? Friends? She smiled benevolently and lifted her glass slightly. "To old friends." She took a sip and put her glass down. "I'm glad you weren't on Brassfield's detail." The words were out of her mouth before she could stop them.

The care in her voice, masked as it was, gave him a glimmer of hope. "Yeah. A shame about Dodson."

"The agent that was killed?"

He dropped his head. "Yeah."

She adjusted the silverware nervously, lining them up perfectly with her long, delicate fingers. "Have you heard anything? I mean, anything you can tell me?"

"No. Just that the investigators are looking into every imaginable lead."

A young lady brought a basket of bread and April brought their salads and left.

Sabyl took a deep breath. "So! You want to explain—"

"Would you mind if we wait 'til after dinner?"

Sabyl shrugged one shoulder. "Sure." She waved it off as though it didn't matter.

As they ate their salads, Scott stole glances at her beautiful face whenever he could. It broke his heart that he had been the one who put such pain in her eyes. How he loved that face. When he was with Sabyl it was as though color came back into his life—like when Dorothy stepped out of her house in Oz and suddenly everything went from black and white to Technicolor. Lately, seeing her and talking to her intermittently on the phone was like color that flicked on and off on a TV that was going bad.

Small talk was awkward. The evening should have been one of sheer joy for Scott. He was with the woman he adored, in a place they both enjoyed, the food was perfect, the wine exquisite. But he felt a heavy dread over him like a shroud; the weight of it was nearly unbearable. And she, under normal circumstances, would have been her easygoing, charming self; she would make direct eye contact, smile playfully, touch his hand and astound him with her wit and intelligence. But she sat with her arms folded defensively, cool and uncharacteristically ill at ease. Her eyes, once so warm and inviting, were now icy pools, daring him to trespass.

They finished their meal, and after passing on dessert, the server left the check and closed the curtain. Sabyl pushed back from the table, crossed her long legs and clasped her hands around her knee. She cocked her head to one side and smiled coolly. "So all of a sudden you've become conscience-stricken." Releasing her fingers, she folded her arms, leaned them on the table and leveled her eyes at him. "This had better be good."

Scott took a deep breath, looked directly into Sabyl's eyes and said, "My mother died of breast cancer when I was ten."

Sabyl dropped her arms in her lap. "My God, Scott, why didn't you tell me this before?"

"I couldn't. When you told me you had—it was like living it all over again. I hate what I did to you. I've thought about it over and over. About you, how I hurt you." He gulped hard. "When you told me you had breast cancer, I—I just fell into a black hole. I didn't know what to do— I just couldn't go through losing—"

"I'm sorry about your mother. I really am. But how do you think *I* felt?" Sabyl threw her head back, looked up, and waited for the dreaded tears that were welling up to subside. Finally, she looked at him and said, "You're the big macho Secret Service agent—trained to protect important people, even to take a bullet for them. But you weren't there for me when—" Her voice caught. "—when I—needed you."

Scott looked at her sadly. "Unfortunately, they don't train you in matters of the heart."

She looked at him through tears. "Where do you draw the line between courage and moral courage?"

"I've had to ask myself that over and over."

They sat in silence for a few moments.

"Okay. What am I supposed to do now? Take you back and pretend it never happened?"

He leaned forward and looked into her eyes. "Look, all I know is I still love you. I never stopped loving you."

She turned her head aside and could no longer stop the tears. "Scott, don't—"

"I can't help it. I love you and I always will." He reached across the table and took her hand. "Sabyl, I am sorry. I truly am. Can you ever forgive me?"

She pulled her hand away, dried her tears with her napkin. "Scott, I can forgive you, but I don't know if I can ever trust you—I don't know how."

The server came in again and took the check with Scott's credit card and left.

"Sabyl, I hate what I did to you. I've had to rethink everything since then; about my life, what kind of person I am, what I stand for. I've changed, Sabyl—and I still love you."

She dug around in her purse for a tissue. "I don't know what to say to that," she sniffed.

April brought Scott's credit card and receipt. He took his card and put it in his wallet. "Thanks." The conversation was at an end, he knew.

April took the signed receipt and said, "Thank you and I hope you had a nice evening."

"It was lovely," Sabyl said weakly, and blew her nose.

"The food and service were perfect, as always."

She once again backed out of the alcove and closed the curtain.

Sabyl dabbed her eyes and then stood. She couldn't look at him. "I have to leave now. Thank you for a lovely dinner." He got up and helped her with her coat. She picked up the little vase of flowers, "And for these. Thank you, they're beautiful."

"I'll carry them out for you."

She nodded stiffly and handed them to him.

"May I call you?"

"No. Not for a while. I've got to have some time to absorb all this."

"Okay," he said with resignation. "I'll walk you to your car."

"No need. The valet parked it."

"Then I'll wait with you."

They walked out into the cold night air. Sabyl gave the valet her claim ticket and pulled on her gloves. Scott handed her the bouquet of flowers. She stood there in the soft glow of the streetlamp. Her warm breath formed little wisps of vapor, and her cheeks, still damp from the tears, felt as though tiny crystals would form on her face. She shivered a little. Unspoken words hung in the air. She could feel his gaze—almost like a caress. He wanted to put his arms around her and hold her close. But he could only stand next to her with his hands deep in his overcoat pockets and hope that they might at least be able to see one another from time to time, but he had little hope that she would let him back into her life. He cleared his throat. "I, uh, I've been suspended."

She looked up at him, surprised. "What? Why?"

"They think I leaked the Five-Card Draw riddle."

She frowned and shrugged, "That's ridiculous."

A loud blast erupted, reverberating through their bodies, nearly knocking them off their feet. Sabyl dropped the flowers. The vase shattered at her feet. She screamed and instinctively reached for Scott. He held her for a moment, then told her to stay there and ran toward the explosion. He stopped in his tracks when he saw that it was Sabyl's car that was burning. "Oh, my God," he whispered.

The manager of Three Doves ran out yelling, "What was that?"

Scott told him to call the police. "I'm afraid your valet—"

"No! It can't be! This is terrible!"

A crowd began to gather. "Whose car was it?"

Someone said, "I'll bet it was another attack!"

The flames leapt into the night air, melting the paint on the cars next to the burning SUV. The acrid smell of melting rubber and the blast of fire truck horns and sirens filled the air. A fire engine from a nearby station pulled up and firemen quickly began pulling their equipment out. Scott screamed, "There's a man in that car!" The firemen aimed their hoses at the inferno and water gushed in a powerful arc onto the flames. Due to the damage of the explosion and fire, they quickly assessed that a rescue attempt would be futile.

Scott walked over to Sabyl. She fell into his arms and wept for the young man who died in her place.

Saturday, January 17

Security was always at a peak in and around the White House and other executive offices. Normally, there were around 1,200 UD (Uniformed Division of the Secret Service) and more than 2,800 plainclothes agents posted 24/7 at the executive residence, at embassies, and other diplomatic operations in the capital. But now, due to the recent terror activities, those numbers were nearly doubled. Every intelligence and security agency was stretched to the max to make sure that nothing else would penetrate their boundaries. Especially the Secret Service, whose job it is to protect the Chief Executive, the President of the United States.

For decades, the Secret Service had worked out every possible scenario to protect the White House and its occupants. Constantly facing the unexpected, the Service had to come up with new ways to do its job. Many intruders had tried to make their way to the famous mansion by going over the fence. That problem was taken care of by initiating teams of armed agents hidden in the shadows of the lawns and gardens. Plus, sensitive alarms are positioned in strategic places around the perimeter just beneath the ground and special infrared sensors placed above the ground to detect intruders. Those emergency response teams' jobs are to rush the intruders before they can reach the White House doors. But now with the new threat of UAV's (Unmanned Aerial Vehicles), or RPAS (Remotely Piloted Aerial Systems), the

Secret Service had a new source of anxiety: how to protect the air over and around the President's residence from drones.

Since radio waves are used for most drones' remote controls, it was decided by the CIA, that jamming was their best solution, which caused havoc to nearby GPS signals and cell phones in the area, much to the chagrin of the public. Although there were countless Wi-Fi dead spaces in D.C., the area around the Executive Mansion was the worst. White House officials already used phones with specially programmed signals and other devices to be able to go about the business of running the country. Now technology had to be even more advanced. Young CIA computer specialists worked feverishly to come up with new ways to deal with the problem of drones. So far, jamming was the only way the CIA could figure to keep the air space safe, other than putting up nets over the Mansion but the president declared a decisive and resounding, "No!" to that suggestion, stating clearly, "It's bad enough to live in a bubble. I'm *not* going to live under a danged net!"

A

Air Force One lifted into the gray morning sky heading for Omaha. President Anderson and the First Lady would attend the double funeral of their friends, Wayne and Gloria Brassfield. There was a collective sigh from the agencies in D.C. seeing the beautiful blue and white customized Boeing 747 safely on its way to Nebraska, but those protecting POTUS while away from the capital were on high alert. After the funeral in Omaha, he would fly to his home in Indiana for the weekend. The Advance Team was already there. The pressure on them was more than ever.

But now the agencies in Washington were laser-focused on the Vice President who would be attending the memorial service at National Prez.

The capitol grounds were being used as the staging area where multiple cars lined up for the procession. Homeland Security was nervous with so many heads of state in one place. Every car had either a Secret Service agent riding with them or some sort of special security.

Not only was every vehicle in the procession swept for hidden weapons, but every individual as well, no matter who they were. The D.C. Joint

Terrorism Task Force bomb squads were standing by. Dozens of UD agents, skilled as handlers with their specially trained canines, gingerly approached each vehicle. The dogs sniffed around them inside and out. Suddenly, one of the dogs started barking ferociously at something in the trunk of one of Sabyl's limousines. Agents with weapons drawn surrounded the car and screamed, "Get out of the vehicle!" Maurice and his passengers with stunned faces scrambled out of the car. A bomb squad carefully approached the limousine. The dog's handler with a single command ordered him away from the suspicious object. A bomb tech in protective gear slowly reached down into the trunk and picked up the dubious item. It was a bottle of *Windex*.

After the sweep was completed, Sabyl's cars lined up behind the Vice President's motorcade and the military limousines. The Secret Service had swept the area between the Capitol and the National Presbyterian Church for bombs or anything unusual and set up hidden cameras and surveillance vans all along the route. The procession was held back until Vice President Carl Bridges' motorcade reached its destination; then they would be allowed to proceed.

The VP's motorcade turned onto Mass Avenue moving toward Nebraska Avenue. Two Metropolitan Police cars with strobes blazing and sirens howling led the way. Behind them were two identical limousines with U.S. Park Police motorcycles surrounding them, red and blue lights flashing, the Counter Assault Team (CAT) cars, in two black Suburbans with several of the U.S. Secret Service's most elite units known as "the baddest of the bad boys" inside carrying an arsenal of weapons. Next came the staff cars, the Vice President's physician, two press vans, an ambulance and two more police cars bringing up the rear. Onlookers watched as the imposing motorcade sped by.

They crossed Wisconsin Avenue and entered a plush residential area. A garbage truck pulled out of the driveway of the massive Greentree apartment complex in front of the motorcade, nearly running over the two motorcycle cops blocking the entrance. The agent in the first limousine grabbed his radio and shouted, "We've got a situation! Bootleg on three! One, two—oh, *God!*" A man at the bus stop wearing a heavy overcoat shot the policeman standing in front of him, ran over and threw himself against the back door of the first limousine and blew himself up. The car flipped on its side and rolled onto its top, its wheels spinning and on fire, killing the two agents inside.

Agents jumped out of the CAT cars with weapons drawn and signaled the motorcade to bootleg and take off. All the drivers slammed it in reverse and backed up in perfect precision to the count of five. *"Now!"* Just as they began to slide around, they threw it in drive and floored it forward.

The CAT agents, brandishing Uzi submachine guns, SR-16 carbines and MP5 automatic weapons, surrounded the garbage truck and quickly arrested the driver and his cohort and put them in handcuffs. They found the bodies of the two trash collectors in the back of the truck with their throats cut.

The ambulance that was a part of the motorcade pulled up. The EMTs could see that no one could have survived such a blast. Sirens from approaching fire trucks echoed through the posh neighborhood. The Vice President in the second limousine had escaped unharmed. The Secret Service whisked him and his wife off to an predetermined place of safety.

⚔

Scott watched the scene on TV. They played the same footage over and over. He had been wrong. They were not all mercenaries. A suicide bomber. Unbelievable. Or maybe the mercenary pulled in some religious fanatics to do his dirty work. Very clever. There had been no warning for this attack—no riddle. He figured they were probably angry that they had spoiled their big upside-down-stinking-hit-and-run scheme. Two of their players were dead. He had hoped that would slow them down, but now here was another attack right on the heels of the would-be embassy bombing. He could feel the rage building within him. *Three of our leaders are dead, their wild card didn't play out, and their plot to kill the Vice President failed.* He wondered if they would go for other targets to make up for their losses, or would they go straight for the Ace. The President of the United States.

⚔

Due to the terrorist attacks, the Brassfield memorial service at National Prez was postponed to a later date. The would-be attendees returned to their homes and hotels and watched the latest coverage of the assassination attempt on the

Vice President on TV. Sabyl's drivers returned their cars to the garage, most got in their own vehicles and went home. Part of the crew decided to stay and watch the divisional playoffs on the big screen TV on ESPN, the only channel not covering the suicide bombing. The sports channel had briefly considered canceling coverage of the game, but decided the nation needed some relief from all the bad news.

Sabyl pulled into her parking space in the new SUV she had acquired early that morning. Her dealer friend, Fred Clark, from whom she had bought her last three vehicles, took her late-night call when she got home from Three Doves, and assured her he would have a car at her doorstep by seven a.m.

She walked in and was surprised to see Frank at his desk. "Why are you here, Frank? It's Saturday."

He tossed the Washington Post onto the end of his desk. "Have you seen this?"

She walked over and picked it up. The headlines read:

"CAR BOMBING NOT LINKED TO ASSASSINATIONS. A local business-woman's car was bombed last night at a popular restaurant in Northwest D.C. Sabyl Martin, CEO of Martin Transportation, was the apparent target..."

"No, I haven't had time to read the paper." She handed it back to him.

"The police have been here. Wanted to interview some of the drivers, but of course, being Saturday, most are at home; I gave them phone numbers. A few were out on various runs, but I think some are back now. Probably watching the game. Oh, and I just got off the phone with Dotty. She heard about the car bombing. She's pretty upset. Said she hasn't cried this much since John-John died. Maybe you should give her a call."

"I will."

"I can't believe what happened to you last night. Why would anybody want to kill you?"

She shook her head and looked heavenward as though looking for answers. "I don't know."

"You think it's the same guy that followed you the other night?"

"No. That was just some creep that's been attacking women in that area."

"Do you think the car bombing is connected to these assassinations somehow?"

The question startled Sabyl. It had never occurred to her. "No!" She got a sick feeling in the pit of her stomach. "Wh—why would it?"

Frank realized he had upset her. "I'm sorry, Sabe. I—uh—see you got your new car."

"Yeah. I liked my other one better." She went into her office and sat down at her desk and put her head in her hands for a few moments and thought about what Frank had just said. She called Dotty, and assured her she was fine and then tried calling Rudy.

Frank stood with his hands in his pockets staring at the TV in his office. *I'm such an idiot. He* slowly walked into Sabyl's office.

She hung up and looked up at him. "I called Dotty and assured her I'm okay. Then I tried calling Rudy. Still no answer. That's not like him to be out of touch."

"He came in earlier. Looked like he hadn't slept. His eyes were red—he left without saying anything. I'm kind of worried about him. Nothing rattles that guy. He and his wife okay?"

Sabyl stood up and walked over to the tinted window in her office that overlooked the brick circle drive. "I don't know what it is, but it's not that."

"Maybe he heard about what happened to you and it shook him up."

"No, he was acting strangely before that happened."

"Yeah, I guess you're right."

Sabyl turned and looked at Frank pensively, "You don't suppose this Endicott character has anything to do with his behavior."

"Can't imagine how. I mean if the guy is being a jerk, Rudy knows how to handle himself."

Sabyl folded her arms. "Still, I get this creepy feeling about Endicott. She unfolded her arms, walked over and sat down at her desk. I'm going to check him out. "Get Chief Max Hawks at Metro Police on the phone for me."

"It's Saturday."

"Try anyhow. I imagine everybody's working overtime with these killings going on."

"What am I supposed to tell him? That one of our clients is giving one of our drivers a hard time?"

"Let me worry about that. Just make the call, please."

"Why don't you ask Scott to look into it?"

"He's been suspended."

"What?"

"It's a long story."

Frank shrugged, and muttered, "Nobody ever tells me anything around here," and went back to his desk and made the call.

She sat back down and stared at her desk. A multitude of thoughts whirled around in her brain. Just then the phone rang and Sabyl picked it up. "Sabyl Martin."

"Sabyl, it's Scott. I need to talk to you about the car bombing."

"Oh—yes, okay," she said, still staring at her desk.

"Who would want to kill you?"

"I don't know. Maybe some client didn't like his—"

"I'm serious, Sabyl."

"I know you are, Scott. I'm sorry. I just can't seem to concentrate today. I'm worried about Rudy."

"Rudy?"

"Yes. He's been acting very—I'm sorry, you wanted to talk about the bombing."

"I'd like to talk to the drivers, if I may. Never know what they might have seen or heard."

"Seems like they would have said something to me if they had any kind of suspicions."

"They may have seen or heard things, but thought they were too insignificant to mention. That's why I need to talk to them. Are they around now?"

"Let me check." She put him on hold and buzzed the garage. "George, who all's down there?"

"Stubby, Burt, and myself."

"Okay. Scott wants to talk to you about the car bombing."

"When?"

"Now, I guess. I'm leaving town. See you when I get back."

"Okay."

She pushed the button. "Uh, Scott, there are two others besides George."

"Okay, I'll be right over."

"I probably won't see you. I'm leaving town."

"To Pennsylvania?"

"Yes."

"We really need to talk about this. Will you call me?"

"Yes, I promise."

"You have a car?" He paused. "I guess that's a stupid question. You have a whole fleet."

"I had a car delivered this morning. Uh, hold on, Scott."

Frank walked in. "Chief Hawks on line two."

"Scott, I have to go now, but I'll call you when I get to Pennsylvania, I promise."

"Are you going out after you get there? I mean—"

"No, I'm staying in. I have a lot to do. Give me your cell number again." She wrote it down, said goodbye, and punched in line two. "Hi, Max."

Chief Hawks greeted her warmly. "Did my men get all the information they need about last night's car bombing?"

"Yeah, I talked to them last night and again early this morning."

"We'll get to the bottom of this, Sabyl."

"Thanks, Max, I know you will. But that's not why I called." He listened as she told him about Endicott. He asked for information. She gave him the info she had, which was practically nothing. Not a driver's license, not a credit card number, nothing. She kicked herself mentally for not insisting on getting some sort of ID from him. Hawks said he needed more than a name. "But I'll run it through the database and see if anything comes up and get back to you on Monday."

She heaved a sigh. "Okay, thanks, Max."

After hanging up, she pulled out the contract and stared at Endicott's signature. It was a scrawl and nothing more. She sat back in her desk chair and frowned. Maybe she should simply talk to Endicott face to face and pull Rudy off the job. She knew Rudy would object—or would he? She looked at the calendar and back to the contract. Three more days. Putting the contract back in the folder, she buzzed the garage. "George, is Beau with you?"

"He's right here watching the game with me."

"I'm getting ready to leave. Put him in my car, will you? Oh, it's the black Nissan Murano."

She buzzed Frank. "I'm outta here."

⋏

George, feeling foolish, said, "We thought he might be a sleeper or something, so we followed him one night."

Scott frowned, "Why did you think that?"

Stubby hung his head. "Aww, it was something he said." They told him the whole story.

Scott rubbed his forehead. "I'm afraid that's not enough to implicate him as a sleeper. But just out of curiosity, where did he go?" They gave him the address. "I'll check it out."

⋏

Sabyl had her feet up on the coffee table thinking about the task before her. The fire sizzled and the flames sputtered. Her tea was hot, the music dreamlike. Her eyes closed and then fluttered open at the sound of the ice maker dropping its load in the freezer. Shaking her head to wake up, she got up, went into the kitchen, fixed a small salad and poured herself a second cup of tea. She picked at her salad. Beau sensed something was wrong. Nuzzling her hand, he whined quietly. She rubbed his ears and spoke softly, "What's the matter, huh, boy?"

After tidying up the kitchen, she tried calling Rudy again. Still no answer. Next, she called Layla and told her to tell Rudy to call her on her cell when he got in, no matter what the hour.

Her tea had gotten cold, so she reheated it in the microwave and walked into the sitting room next to the den and sat down in the wing-backed chair and stared at the bookshelf. Her eyes roamed across the books and the framed pictures and then rested on one of her mother's hatboxes. She closed her eyes and waited for concentration to come to deal with her mother's things. Instead a profound sadness engulfed her. The face of the young valet emerged in her mind. She thought, *This is the second person who died in my place. Lord, thank You for letting me live but my life is not worth that young man's life.* She wept quietly. *My heart breaks for that boy's family. I've got to write to them.* She wondered, *What can I possibly say?* She sighed, reached for a tissue in her pocket, and blew her nose. Puting her head back, she asked God to help them through this nightmare.

After a quiet time of prayer, she took another sip of her tea. Who would do such a thing? Who wanted to harm her? Was the car bombing somehow connected to the Georgetown incident? She thought of the Oswald brothers. Had she underestimated them?

She picked up her parents' faded wedding picture. They looked so happy; so in love. What had happened? It was a question she had asked herself many times. Why did her mother hate her so? She shook her head sadly. She couldn't deal with her mother's things tonight as she had planned. Exhausted, she sighed and thought *I'll do it later.* Returning to the den, she turned on the TV to watch the news. The anchor reported, *"The first order given by the newly sworn-in Secretary of Defense, Vernon McMillan, was the placement of the Sentinel Radar System and the Humvee-mounted Avenger air defense missile systems in strategic areas around the capital city."*

Sabyl stared at the screen. *Good heavens, has it come to this?* The chirping of her cell phone startled her. She answered, "Sabyl Martin."

"Sabyl, it's Dr. Solomon. Forgive me for calling so late."

She quickly muted the TV. "Oh, yes, Doctor. Do you have the results?"

"Yes. Sabyl, I'm afraid it's malignant. It's a slow growing tumor near the chest wall. We need to get it out as soon as possible."

She felt the breath go out of her. "You're sure?"

"Yes."

Sabyl tried to swallow. "When do you—"

"Right away."

She swallowed hard and pressed and fumbled to get to the calendar icon on her phone. "The twenty-first is the soonest I can do it."

"Alright. I'll have my office set it up. Hopefully we found it in time."

"Yeah . . . hopefully."

He apologized for being the bearer of bad news. They hung up and she sat in stunned silence and stared at the leaping flames in the fireplace. No longer able to hold back the tears that she had held in for so long, her chest heaved with sobs. Beau put his head on her knee and looked at her with his soulful eyes and whined. She rubbed his head and grabbed a tissue and blew her nose. "It's okay, boy," she said quietly. "I beat it once, I'll beat it again." After a few minutes she got up and went up the stairs to take a shower and get into her pajamas. After she undressed, she stepped into the bathroom and looked at her breasts in the mirror. *Why? Why do women have to deal with such an insidious thing?*

⏶

Scott pulled up in front of the house and looked at his watch. Eight o'clock. He got out and walked up the steps to the door and rang the bell. An elderly woman answered the door. She spoke through the locked screen door with heavy black grillwork over the screen. "Yes?"

"Hi, ma'am, sorry to bother you. I'm with the Secret Service Agency and I'd like to ask you some questions if I may." He held his breath, hoping she wouldn't ask to see his ID, which he sorely missed.

"About what?" she asked warily.

"Do you happen to know a man by the name of Jamal al Hamid?"

Her face softened, "Oh, yes! Jamal!" Her face grew somber again. "Is he in some kind of trouble?"

"No, ma'am, not at all."

"Please come in." She unlocked the door and opened it. Scott stepped inside. The house was furnished with a southwestern flair in soft earth tones with ancient looking stoneware and pottery all about. There was a fire crackling in the fireplace. A multicolored woven rug lay on the floor in front of the hearth. A fat yellow cat lying on the rug stretched and squeaked out a greeting to Scott. The woman looked to be in her early seventies, of Native American descent. Her eyes were bright and friendly. She wore a pale blue chenille robe that had seen better days. Her salt-and-pepper hair was pulled back into a long braid that fell gracefully down her back. She took his coat and offered her small, bony hand. "Sit down, won't you? My name is Grace Bell. You may call me Grace."

"Scott Terhune."

"That's a nice name. I was just about to have some tea." She carefully laid his coat across the back of a corner chair. "How is it that you know Jamal?"

Scott didn't want to cause alarm. "Uh, he works for a friend of mine. May I ask the same of you? How do you know him?"

She smiled showing perfect white teeth contrasting her smooth sepia skin. "He comes once a week for pottery lessons."

Scott's eyes widened. "Pottery lessons?"

"Yes. I teach pottery." She leaned forward as though telling him a secret. "The old-fashioned kind of pottery like my ancestors used to make." She leaned back again and smiled, "I teach it every Wednesday night. There are only a handful of students, but it's enough to keep me in supplies and Lewis and me fed."

"Lewis?"

"Yes, my cat. I found him behind my house in Santa Fe when he was a kitten. He was abandoned and starving, poor little thing. I brought him with me when I moved here to be near my daughter. She works for the Department of Interior." She leaned forward again to tell another secret. "I think Jamal is kind of sweet on her. At first I thought he only came to the lessons because of her, but it turns out that he is quite a gifted potter. Let me show you!" She got up and hobbled as though her knees hurt, and disappeared through a door that led to the back of her house.

Scott wanted desperately to call Sabyl.

Grace came back carrying a beautiful vase the color of terra cotta painted with an unusual design that looked like loose thread floating in the wind. "This is one of his pieces. I fired it only day before yesterday. Didn't it turn out well?" Before Scott could reply, she continued, "I have the clay sent here from New Mexico. Sometimes I can't get it from there, so I buy it from North Carolina, around the Seagrove area. Now there's a real potter's dream! Anyhow, you see these fine little lines? It's not painted with a brush, but with a piece of the yucca desert plant."

"Uh, Ma'am, would you excuse me for just one moment? I need to make a call."

"Oh, of course, I'll just see about our tea." She turned and walked back through the same door that apparently also led to the kitchen.

Scott pulled out his cell phone and tried to call Sabyl, but his battery was dead. "Oh, man!" He stared at the phone as though it had betrayed him.

Grace came in and sat a tray in front of him on the coffee table and poured them both a cup of tea. "Would you like sugar?"

"No thank you, ma'am. Um, may I use your phone? My cell battery is dead and I need to make an important call."

"Certainly! I'll get it for you. I have free minutes on weekends," she announced gleefully.

⋏

A mental reminder to call Scott once again nagged at Sabyl. *After my shower,* she thought. Hanging her robe on a brass hook on the back of the door, she turned the water on, waited for it to warm up and stepped inside the glass doors. A few moments later she could hear the phone ringing in her bedroom. She hesitated to interrupt her shower, but thinking it might be Rudy, she grabbed her terrycloth robe and ran to the phone by her bed, but it was too late. Whoever it was had hung up. Her caller ID displayed a phone number she didn't recognize. *I hope it wasn't Rudy. No, I would see his name on the caller ID.* She went back into the bathroom and continued her shower, turned off the water, and dried off with a creamy towel. Just then, Beau began to bark fiercely. She put her robe back on and headed down the stairs. "Beau! What's the matter? What are you barking at?"

⋏

"No answer." Scott handed the phone back to Grace. "I'm sorry, ma'am. I have to leave." He took an obligatory sip of tea. "Thank you for showing me your beautiful work, I mean Jamal's—I, uh, hope to meet you another time." He started backing out toward the door.

She stood and went to fetch his coat. "I'm sorry you have to go," she smiled. "Please come back some time for another visit." She handed him his coat. "And if you ever want to learn about pottery, you know where to come."

Scott nodded, said a quick goodbye, jumped in his Camry and sped off toward his apartment, hoping Sabyl would call there. He mentally kicked himself all the way home for not charging his cell.

A

She knew from the ferocity of his bark that something was terribly wrong. With trembling hands, she went to the hall closet and pulled out her father's old shotgun. There were no shells for it, but she hoped that if anyone looking in saw it, they'd think twice before chancing her using it.

Beau barked fiercely, running back and forth in front of the sliding glass door. "Beau! What is it, boy?" She thought she saw someone moving across the back yard. Her heart felt like it would attack her. Suddenly a loud crack sounded and glass shattered everywhere. Beau yelped and fell to the floor, blood gushing from his neck. She screamed, *"Nooo!"* A hand reached in the broken glass to unlock the sliding glass door. She hit the hand as hard as she could with the butt of the gun. She heard a loud curse and then a foot hit the glass door, shattering the rest of it. Sabyl screamed as a man in a ski mask stepped inside. He reached for her. She hit him again with the gun and turned to run, knocking over a lamp. The shade fell and the raw light blinded him momentarily. He grabbed at her and tore the arm of her robe. He leveled his gun at her.

A shot erupted in Sabyl's ears and the man fell against her, nearly knocking her down. A policeman stepped inside and moved Sabyl's shaking body away from the intruder. Sirens filled the air. Blue strobes darted through the windows and lit up her yard. Sabyl was sobbing as she moved past the man lying on her blood-reddened carpet and knelt beside Beau. Two paramedics stepped through the glassless frame of the door.

"Please!" she pleaded. "Please, save my dog!" A paramedic checked the pulse on the masked man and looked at his partner. "He's dead." They shrugged and began working on Beau and then carefully placed him on the stretcher while Sabyl called her veterinarian. They took Beau in the ambulance to Dr. Janice Ortega's animal clinic, five minutes away. One of the policemen offered to drive her to the clinic. She ran upstairs, yanked on her jeans and a sweatshirt, grabbed her purse and jacket and headed out the door.

"I'll stay here 'til the coroner comes," offered a deputy, as he radioed for the coroner.

"Thank you!" She got in the police car and they sped away. Neighbors gawked out of their windows; some stood in their yards in the cold night air wondering what was going on. Sabyl didn't see them. She was too busy praying. She never prayed harder in her life.

⅄

The coroner arrived and ducked under the yellow crime-scene tape that now surrounded Sabyl's house. Another ambulance sat in her driveway, there to remove the dead body of the intruder. The police photographer was taking pictures of the scene, carefully stepping around the body. Glass was strewn all over the floor. Cold air gushed in through the empty doorframe.

"Whose house is this?" he asked one of the policemen.

"Sabyl Martin."

The coroner removed the ski mask. "The Limo Lady? Who's the dead guy?"

"Don't know. There was no ID on him."

"We'll run his prints and see what we come up with."

"Somebody slashed her cat's throat last week," the policeman said.

"You suppose it was the same guy?"

"Hard to say. She thought it was one of her neighbors."

"Her neighbor? Why would he do that?"

"She wanted him to clean up his yard."

"That mess down the road there?"

"Yeah."

"Not a lot to ask."

⅄

The waiting room of the animal clinic was familiar to Sabyl. It was where she had brought Beau from the time he was a puppy. Still shaking, she answered the officer's questions between tears.

"You're a brave lady, Ms. Martin."

"Not really." She sat with her arms folded and pulled tight across her stomach. She searched the eyes of the officer. "How did you know he was there? I mean, you were right there. I didn't even have time to call 9-1-1."

"We got a tip from a Mr. Terhune in Washington, D.C. Said he was a Secret Service Agent and he needed our help."

"Scott?"

"Yes, ma'am. He said you might be in danger and asked us to keep an eye on your place."

"Scott?" Tears flowed like a river.

"Yes, ma'am."

The veterinarian walked in. Sabyl quickly brushed her tears away, jumped up and with pleading eyes, waited for her words.

Dr. Ortega looked at her and smiled. "Beau's going to be fine."

Sabyl grabbed her and hugged her, nearly causing her to lose her balance. "Oh, thank you, God! Thank you, Janice, thank you!"

When she got her balance, the middle-aged veterinarian continued, "The bullet just missed the carotid artery. If it had hit it, he'd have been a goner. I stitched him up and dressed the area. He's going to be all right, but I need to keep him overnight."

"Oh, thank you! May I see him?"

"Sure, but just for a few minutes. He needs to rest."

Sabyl walked slowly—almost tiptoed—into the operating room. Beau lay on his side with an IV in his front leg. He tried to raise his head, but had to put it back down. His tail gently thumped against the examining table. "Heeey, there's my boy," she said quietly. "How are you, buddy? Huh? You okay?" She gently rubbed his ears and kissed the top of his head. Beau's tail slowly stopped wagging and he fell asleep.

Dr. Ortega checked the IV. "He'll sleep all night. Call me in the morning. We'll see how he does through the night."

"May I stay here with him? He might wake up and be scared."

"He won't wake up, trust me. I've given him a sedative. Go home and get some sleep. Sounds like you've had quite a night yourself."

She answered reluctantly. "Okay, thanks, Janice. I will."

Sabyl came out into the waiting room and walked over to the policeman. He stood and picked up his hat from the chair and put it on. "I'm real glad about your dog, ma'am."

"Thanks, officer. May we leave now or do you have more questions?"

"Uh, the coroner just radioed me. They've already removed the intruder out of your house. He needs you to ID him."

Sabyl was paralyzed. "I'm sure it's my neighbor, Oswald."

"If you don't mind, I need to take you by the morgue."

Sabyl blanched at the thought. "Uh, okay."

They drove to the back entrance of Fairview Hospital, got out and went inside. Sabyl hadn't been in the building since her mother died. She folded her arms and followed the policeman through the double doors into Pathology. A strange odor assaulted them as they entered. The coroner introduced himself and led her over to the body lying on a steel table in the middle of the room with a sheet over it. Buzzing fluorescent lights lit up the area. The coroner looked at her sympathetically. "You ready?"

The policeman watched her closely to mentally record her reaction.

Sabyl took a deep breath and nodded. The coroner pulled the sheet back. She gasped as she looked at the face of a man she had never seen before. She turned away and shook her head. "I don't know who he is."

The policeman once again asked, "Any idea who would want you dead?"

"No. I'm completely shocked."

"We'll need as much information as you can give us. Any disgruntled employees, boyfriends, whatever."

"I have fired a few employees for different reasons over the years. He's not one of them."

"We need their names."

"Of course. I'll have my secretary send the information to you."

"That would be good." He handed her his card. "My fax number is on here."

"Okay. If there's nothing else, I'd like to go home and get some rest."

The policeman looked at the coroner. "Anything further?"

"No, that's it for now."

"You know you've got a crime scene in your den there. I've got to ask you not to touch anything."

"No, no, I won't," she said, meaning it.

Sabyl rode in the front seat of the blue and white cruiser thinking about the face of the man lying in the morgue. Who was he? Why would he want to hurt her? And Beau? Her mind couldn't seem to take it in. Suddenly, she remembered that her house was exposed. "My house—the back door is shattered—it's wide open—"

The officer said, "I called my son, Jimmy. He's over at your house now putting sheets of plastic over your door and window and sealing them off with duct tape." He smiled sheepishly. "He said he had bought a bunch of it when, uh, you know, there was that alert a few years back. Said he was glad to finally find a use for it."

Sabyl smiled, "That's very kind of him—and you."

The policeman turned onto Sabyl's street. "I'll have an officer guard your house tonight. Plastic and duct tape won't keep much out."

"No, not really." She tried to smile.

It was almost one a.m. when Sabyl got to bed. Her first instinct was to wait until morning to call Scott, but she thought better of it. Sitting on the side of her bed, she picked up the bedside phone and dialed his number. "Scott, it's Sabyl—" I'm sorry it's so late, but I had to call and thank you—"

"Thank God, Sabyl! I've been calling all night! I was nearly out of my mind when you didn't answer. You probably didn't recognize the number on your caller ID. My cell went down and I had to borrow a phone."

"What time was that?"

"Around 8:15. I just had a gut feeling that something was wrong. And then when you didn't answer your home phone or your cell—"

"That was you?"

"Yeah, you told me you would call me when you got to Pennsylvania and that you would be at home all night—I thought—"

"I was in the shower. Scott, if I had answered that call, I'd be dead now! You would have thought everything was okay and you probably wouldn't have called the police!"

"Are you alright?"

The impact of it all began to sink in. "If you hadn't warned them, I'd be dead right now." Scott could hear the exhaustion in her voice.

"I had to go to the morgue and identify him. I thought it was my neighbor, but it wasn't. It was some man I've never seen before. It was...horrible!" She reached for a tissue. "How can I thank you?"

"Just so you're alright. I wish I had been there for you," he almost whispered.

His words echoed a longing she'd had for two years. "You were there for me, Scott. You saved my life."

"I wish I were there now——." He longed to hold her in his arms and comfort her.

"I can't believe such a horrible thing could happen. He shot Beau! I thought he was dead! I nearly lost it when he——." She choked up at the thought of it.

"Beau? He's been shot? Is he going to be okay?"

"Yes," she sniffed. "I might even be able to bring him home tomorrow."

Scott let out a sigh of relief. "When do you think you can come back to D.C.?"

She blew her nose. "Depends on Beau. I really don't want to spend another night here, but I've got to get my house back to normal. There's blood everywhere, and glass——"

"Can you get someone to help you with that?"

"Yes, I have a couple that looks after my place when I'm not here. They'll take care of everything."

"Good. Sounds good. Uh, I'd like to see you when you get in."

"I want to see you too. There are some things I need to talk to you about."

"Okay. And we need to talk about the car bombing."

"Do you think this same man——?"

"It's possible. We'll get to the bottom of it."

Suddenly she felt drained. "Okay, I'll talk to you tomorrow."

"Try to get some sleep. Let me know how Beau is."

"I will. G'night."

DAY 14

SUNDAY, JANUARY 18

Sabyl's cold fingers were having a hard time separating the thin paper coffee filters. Finally one came loose and was placed in the basket of the coffee pot; she poured the water in and pushed the start button. The rhythm of her morning tasks somewhat gave her a sense of a return to normalcy. She even started to open a can of dog food before thinking, shook her head and put it back in the cabinet. Looking out the kitchen door, she saw an officer standing outside in the cold by the plastic-covered door, his arms folded and his cheeks red from the cold. Grateful for his presence, she opened the back door and spoke to him. "Good morning! May I offer you a cup of coffee?"

"Oh, no, thanks, miss."

"Have you been here all night? I hate to think—"

"Oh, no, miss, we take shifts. Um, if you're okay and all, I'll be going now. You'll be getting a call from the investigator soon."

"Yes, I'm fine, thanks. And thank you for being here."

"Glad to, miss."

She closed the door and locked it. The officer drove away.

The coffeepot finished its rumbling and huffing. She poured a mug full, walked into the dining room and cranked up the heat. The French doors that led into the den were closed. No way was she looking in there. It seemed surreal. Her lovely room was now a crime scene. Wrapping her long fingers around the warm mug, she took her coffee into the sitting room and curled up in the wing-backed chair and pulled a furry throw over her legs. The steaming liquid warmed her as she sipped it slowly and closed her eyes and thanked God once again for sparing her life. Beau was greatly missed. She wondered how he was doing. At least he was going to be all right. What would she have done if he had—she wouldn't think about that. He was going to be alright and she would have him back soon. It was too early to call the vet or Jerry and Kate. She would wait a few more minutes.

For the first time ever, Sabyl dreaded going back to Washington to the lurking terror there. But then she had been terrorized in her own home. She'd had enough to last her for a lifetime. Her head swam with thoughts of all that had happened and all that needed to be done. Both the intruder's and Beau's blood were in the carpet. She would have it taken up and replaced. The grandfather clock in the den struck seven. Sighing loudly, she looked thoughtfully at the bookshelf once again. What would she do with all those hatboxes? Part of her wanted to just throw them in the back of her SUV and take them to the dump and part of her wanted to keep them. The only times of happiness she remembered were when her mother wore her hats to church.

Like a daydream, Sabyl's mind went back to a Sunday morning when she was nine years old. She and her family were sitting together in church and the pastor invited the children to come forward for the short "Kid's Sermon" that he gave each week before the regular sermon. She remembered shyly walking down with the other children and sitting on the steps of the platform, their eyes glued on the kind face of the pastor who had sat down with them.

She remembered how he started out asking if they knew what the word "fellowship" meant. He said, "You know, doggies like to hang out with doggies and people like to hang out with people, but God is a Spirit; who do you suppose God wants to hang out with?" One of the little kids said, "A spirit?" The pastor replied, "That's right! But God had this problem because He had made these little dirt people. Can you imagine fellowshipping with a little clod of dirt?" Sabyl smiled, recalling they all laughed. He went on, "But God fixed that; he breathed His very own Spirit into those little dirt people and He made them living spirit people, and then He was able to fellowship with them spirit-to-spirit. And then He said, 'Okay, you may eat of every tree in the garden except that one; if you eat of that one, you will surely die. Well, we all know they ate of it and they didn't keel over and drop dead. What died?" Same kid: "Their spirit?" The pastor answered, "That's right! And that was the fall of man. And so we're all born with this little dead spirit laying there and God said, 'I sure miss fellowshipping with my kids down there. So He sent His very own Son to become the final Lamb to die for all the sins of the whole world." The little boy sitting behind Sabyl asked, "Why?" The pastor answered, "Because God's own blood is the only thing holy enough to wash away all the sins of the whole world. And so God became a man and His whole purpose in life was to get that holy blood from the manger to the cross. He did a lot of neat stuff in between; He did a lot of miracles to prove He was God; and He taught many wonderful things, but it just made people mad. So they put Him on the cross. But He wasn't surprised, and when those nails went in and that holy blood came out; that took care of all the sins of the whole world; a holy God can't fellowship with sin, so when we are sorry for our sins and we ask Jesus to come live in our hearts, He sends His holy—" Same kid: "Spirit?" The pastor said, "That's right! And He comes in and He joins with that little dead spirit and He wakes it up and we become born again! And that's what's going to heaven."

Sabyl closed her eyes as she recalled praying the prayer the pastor led them in and that a wonderful peace had filled her being. Realizing that she was alive today only because of God's mercy, she again prayed, "Lord, thank you for sparing my life last night and for sparing Beau's life. Please forgive me for not walking more closely to you. Thank you for always being with me."

A warmth began to engulf her soul. Just acknowledging His presence brought peace.

⋏

Rudy's phone rang early, waking him from a fitful sleep. It was Endicott. "Pick me up in an hour." Rudy started to protest that it was Sunday, but he didn't dare.

"I'll be there."

Layla stirred in the bed. "Who is calling so early?" she said sleepily.

He patted her arm and told her to go back to sleep. She turned over in bed, but she didn't go back to sleep. She lay there and prayed for her husband.

♦

Scott sat on the sofa and watched the Sunday morning press shows. "Meet the Media." was on. They were discussing the attempted bombing of the Israeli Embassy. Questions were raised whether the two Secret Service agents who shot the would-be bombers did so legally. Scott turned off the TV. He couldn't sit around all day listening to them debate. There was work to be done. There were assassins out there and one of them might have even tried to kill Sabyl. Somehow he felt the car bombing and the break-in at her house were connected with the terrorists, but he couldn't put it together. Why would they want to hurt her? He had to find out. He decided to call Rudy. No one knew Sabyl better. Maybe he could shed some light on all this.

♦

Sabyl returned to the same hatbox her eyes had been drawn to last night. She put her coffee mug down, reached over and picked it up, sat it in her lap and carefully removed the lid. It contained a small beige pillbox hat wrapped in yellowing tissue paper. Sabyl remembered it and the beige suit her mother wore it with. Upon picking it up, she noticed another object wrapped in several layers of tissue beneath it. Slowly, she folded back the thin, aged paper. A small diary lay in her hands, the kind that came with a little lock and key that was sold in dime stores back in the fifties. She dug around in the tissue, but there was no key. She stared at it for several moments and then tried to force it open. When she couldn't, she cast the furry throw off and ran for her kitchen scissors and returned to the chair. A mixture of guilt and excitement filled her as she cut the plastic strap that held the clasp in the lock. She laid the scissors down. Her heart rate quickened as she opened the little book to the first page and began reading her mother's diary.

The handwriting was so familiar, yet stronger and more youthful than it had become over the years. The first entry was dated June 3, 1959. That meant she was ten years old. She noticed that even then she flared her P's and

J's with a loop at the bottom and then a sweep up to join the next letter. For an hour, Sabyl read each entry. Page after page she read words that wrenched her very insides. Her mother's father and all five of her older brothers had sexually abused her for years. The words took her breath away. For the first time, Sabyl saw into her mother's heart and mind. When she finished, she held the small book to her breast and sobbed like a child. When the tears finally subsided, she whispered, "Oh, Mama, I'm so sorry this happened to you." A sob caught in her throat. "Mama, I forgive you. I finally understand."

⋏

Rudy pulled into the hotel entrance. Endicott was waiting with his hands in his overcoat pockets. Rudy got out and opened the door for him.

Endicott glared at Rudy and said, "Drive me to Union Station."

Rudy hoped he was leaving town, but was certain that he probably was not. He had no luggage and he knew his dirty work was not finished. He hoped he was not meeting another cohort. Endicott rode in the dark cabin of the luxurious car in silence. Rudy avoided looking in the rearview mirror at his evil cargo. He would only see his passenger's steely eyes staring at him.

His contract with Rudy would end the next day, but Rudy dared not say anything as long as they held his son. At the beginning, Endicott had told him two weeks or perhaps longer. He hoped it would not be longer. Would he be leaving soon? Would he leave without releasing David? Would he let him live? Fear gripped his heart again. How he yearned to see his son—to talk to him—to hold him. He prayed silently for his safety and begged God to help him do—something.

⋏

Sabyl sat with one leg tucked under her in the wing-backed chair with her head back and her eyes half open. It had been a long time since she had felt this close to God. Fresh tears formed in her eyes—tears of peace and joyful release. The answer had come. She had found the truth among her mother's things, just as she knew she would. A little pile of tissues lay in a rumpled heap on the table beside her. Wrapping the diary back up in the tissue paper was like wrapping a gift. She carefully placed it in the hatbox.

The phone rang, startling her. It was Dr. Ortega. "I knew you would want to know as soon as possible about Beau's night."

"Oh! Yes, Janice!"

"Beau slept well. The wound looks good and I think the best medicine for him right now would be for you to come take him home."

"You mean that? I can come get him?"

"Yes. Whenever you're ready."

"Uh, what about taking him to D.C.?"

"That should be okay. Just keep him comfortable. He's pretty sore. You'll have to lift him in and out of the car when he needs to make a pit stop."

"Wonderful! Thank you! I'll be there as soon as I get dressed!"

She hung up the phone and it rang again immediately. It was the investigator. "Just wanted to let you know that we'll be finishing up the investigation probably by tomorrow. You can have the carpet cleaned or whatever after that."

"Okay, thanks. I'm heading back to D.C., if that's okay. I have someone who will be taking care of everything here. I gave their names to the officer last night."

"I see no problem with that. Your dog able to travel?"

"Yes, he is."

"That's great, ma'am. We have your number down there in Washington if we need you. Have a safe trip."

Sabyl called Jerry and Kate and told them the whole story and what needed to be done. They were aghast as they listened and assured her they would take care of everything. "Don't you worry about anything, Sabyl. We'll deal with the carpet, glass, all of it. You just take care of yourself and Beau." She thanked them, ran up the stairs, dressed quickly and headed for the animal clinic.

ᛚ

Layla had just finished breakfast alone at her kitchen table when the phone rang. "Layla, this is Scott Terhune."

"Mr. Scott!"

"Layla, is Rudy there? I'd like to talk with him if I may."

"No, Mr. Scott. He left early this morning after he received a phone call. This is the second Sunday we have missed church," she said sadly.

"I guess in the limo business he has to be available on Sundays too, eh?"

"Yes, sometimes; especially since he has been driving *this* client." She nearly spat out the last two words.

"Would it be okay if I called him on his cell?"

"I'm sure he would not mind." She gave him the number and they hung up.

Scott punched in Rudy's number. He answered immediately. "This is Rudy."

"Rudy, this is Scott Terhune."

Rudy was silent. He looked in the rearview mirror. Endicott's eyes were fixed on him, his brow deeply furrowed.

"Rudy?"

"I cannot speak with you now. I am with a client."

"Is there some way we could get together, Rudy? I have some questions I'd like to ask you."

"No!" He quickly shut off his phone. Endicott glared at him suspiciously.

Scott frowned. *That's strange. That's not like Rudy at all. And Layla sounded strained.* He walked into his bedroom and sat down on the bed. He wasn't used to praying but he bowed his head and said, "God, it's me, Scott Terhune. But I guess you already knew that. I just want to thank you for sparing Sabyl last night. That was pretty scary for her and for Beau. Please comfort her and please help us find the people who are doing these killings. Oh, and…" His voice lowered. "Please show me how I can have faith like Sabyl has. I'll, uh, sign off for now. Thank you again. Amen."

As he showered, he thought to himself, *I've got to talk with Rudy. One way or another, I've got to find out what's going on with him. Something is very wrong.* He got out of the shower, dried off, shaved, dressed and, out of habit, reached for his holster and weapon. He felt as though a part of him had been amputated. Adjusting his tie he thought, *I've got to get out of here and do something—anything.*

⋏

Sabyl drove as delicately as possible, trying to avoid as many bumps and pot-holes as possible, a real feat on the Pennsylvania Turnpike. After a short stop for gas, she took the Breezewood Exit and headed south toward Washington on I-70. Beau was resting comfortably in the back in his doggie bed. She pulled over at the end of the ramp and dialed Scott's cell.

He was sitting on a park bench on the mall trying to sort out his thoughts when his phone chirped. He saw Sabyl's name on the caller ID. "Sabyl! Are you okay? How's Beau?"

"We're both fine. He's asleep in the back of the car. I'm on my way to D.C."

"Great! When can I see you?"

"I don't know. I'm staying in tonight. Going to let Beau rest."

"Good idea. I tried calling Rudy a little while ago and he sounded very strange—Layla too."

"You called Rudy? Why?"

"I need to ask him some questions about the car bombing."

"But why Rudy? He knows nothing—"

"Just trying to find a link, that's all. I want to know if he can tell me anything at all to get to the bottom of this, and Rudy knows you better than anybody."

"He hasn't been around lately."

"What do you mean?"

"He's been driving a man named John Endicott from London for two weeks. We hardly see him anymore."

"Is that unusual?"

"Not really. Clients often want to keep the same driver while they're in town for a period of time. This client is new, though. We don't know anything about him. He's staying at the Lafayette House Hotel so we know he has money, but that's about it." Sabyl wanted to tell him that she had a bad feeling about Endicott, but decided to wait until she could talk to Rudy.

"Rudy sure didn't sound like himself."

"We've noticed he's been acting kind of strange lately."

"Like what?"

"I don't know. Like he's carrying the weight of the world on his shoulders. I talked with him last Friday. I asked him if his health is okay and if he and Layla were all right and he said it was nothing like that; that he had some personal problems, and that he would work them out. I asked him if he needed money. He said he didn't."

Scott cleared his throat. "I talked with George and some of the other drivers. I'd like to talk to the rest of your drivers as soon as possible. I just want to know why anybody would want to hurt you, and if the attack last night was connected to the car bombing."

"Yes, I'd like to know that too. It makes no sense, but I appreciate your concern, Scott."

"Let me know if you hear from Rudy."

"I will."

"I'll call you later."

"I'll be home."

$$\blacktriangle$$

The black extended sedan pulled up to the curb at Union Station. Endicott got out of the car and told Rudy to pick him up in precisely forty minutes. Just before he left, he ordered Rudy to hand him his cell phone. He reluctantly complied. Endicott glared at him as he put it in his pocket and went inside Union Station. Rudy's heart thudded in his chest. He hoped Endicott would not check the last number that had called him. He circled around and parked in his usual place and hoped security wouldn't make him move. He shut the engine off and prayed.

$$\blacktriangle$$

Beau grunted and whined a little when the doorman gently picked him up and carefully placed him in his doggie bed he had put on the luggage cart along with her bag. Sabyl tipped the young man and gave him her parking space number. He got in her SUV and drove towards the garage entrance.

Beau's questioning eyes looked straight into Sabyl's. "It's okay, boy." She maneuvered the cart into the elevator and pushed the seventh floor button.

The elevator stopped on the fifth floor and an older gentleman and his wife got on. The lady complained to her husband, "I told you the elevator was going up!"

"So we'll take the scenic route! Relax!"

"What happened to your dog?" the lady asked, eyeing Beau's bandage.

Sabyl smiled feebly, "You wouldn't believe me if I told you."

They looked at one another and shrugged. The elevator door opened on the seventh floor and she pushed the cart out. "Have a nice day," they said, still wondering about the beagle.

⭐

Finally, Rudy saw Endicott coming out of Union Station. His countenance was sullen; his eyes fixed on Rudy. He got out and opened the door for him. Endicott did not get in. He stood with his face just inches from Rudy's and said coldly, "Who is Scott Terhune?"

Rudy's heart went to his knees. "I do not know—"

"Don't lie to me. He called you. I saw his name on your incoming calls. Now tell me who he is."

"I started to say, I do not know why Scott would call me, except that he is my boss's ex fiancé, and wants very much to get back with her. He probably wants to talk to me about her."

Endicott glared at him. "What does this Terhune do?"

"Um, he works for the government."

"Who in this town does not work for the government? What does he *do*?"

"Sir, I do not keep up with my boss's boyfriends."

Just then, the Park Police approached them. "Going to have to move along, Rudy."

Endicott got in the back seat.

The officer said, "You okay, Rudy? You look kind of pale."

"I'm fine, Hank." How he wanted to tell him the man in the back seat of his car was the one who had been orchestrating the assassinations. "Thank you for asking." He got in the car and was relieved to find that Endicott was engrossed in a phone conversation on his own cell phone. He wondered if he would give him his phone back. He spoke a silent prayer. "Thank you, Lord. I did not have to lie."

⋏

Scott slowed down each time he saw a black limousine. They all looked alike. How would he be able to tell which one was Rudy's? What, if anything, did Rudy know? If only he had something to go on. He remembered Sabyl saying this Endicott guy was staying at the Lafayette House Hotel. He decided to park near there and watch to see if Rudy might show up. For now, he couldn't think of anything else he could do. He parked across the street from the historic hotel and waited and watched.

⋏

Sabyl listened to Beau's soft snoring in his doggie bed on the floor beside her. She sat up with pillows behind her back, rubbed her legs with lotion and after her hands no longer felt slippery, picked up the remote and flipped through the news channels. Nothing about last night's attack. But then why should there be? They don't report what goes on in a country house in Pennsylvania. A young blond woman on CNN reported, *"More traffic patterns have been changed in the nation's capital, much to the annoyance of those who travel in and around the monuments and government buildings deemed to be possible targets. Parking has become more of a nightmare than usual—"*

She flipped it to FOX News. *"Special surveillance cameras have been set up at every angle around the nation's capital."* They showed demonstrators carrying signs of protest, saying, *'BIG BROTHER IS WATCHING MORE THAN TERRORISTS'* and *'INVASION? OR INVASION OF PRIVACY?' And the controversy is still heating up about whether or not the Secret Service agents were acting within their authority to shoot the two would-be bombers.*

Sabyl turned off the TV and picked up the newspaper. Editorials and political cartoons told the same story. Citizens were unhappy at the extra time it took them to get to and from work because of the blocked-off areas. Sabyl put the paper down and sighed. "Don't they have anything better to complain about?" she thought aloud. She opened her nightstand drawer and took out a bottle of nail polish and touched up her toenails. Beau snored contentedly. Sabyl wondered what time Scott would call.

⋏

Scott had waited in his car near the Lafayette House for hours. Finally, after seeing no sign of Rudy, he left, stopping for a bite to eat on his way home. When he got there, he quickly changed into his jogging sweats and headed back to his car.

The drive to Bethesda was a nice change from sitting in one spot. He turned onto Rudy's street, which ended in a cul-de-sac, and looked carefully as he slowly passed his house. Not seeing his car, and knowing there was only one way in and out of his street, he parked and waited. The skies changed from blue to deep lavender with orange streaks edging the lingering clouds, and finally royal blue with stars trembling in the distance. After waiting a half hour, he got out and strolled along the well-lit sidewalks, as though he belonged in the neighborhood, to see if anybody else was watching Rudy's house. He made mental notes of every car on the block; people walking their dogs and those jogging by. He saw no out-of-state tags or anyone sitting in their car. Then at nine o'clock, he went back to his car.

Within moments, Rudy pulled into his driveway in his own small car. He was alone. Scott got out of his car, quietly approached him and spoke his name. Rudy swung around, his eyes filled with fear. Scott knew then that something was terribly wrong.

"Rudy, how are you?"

Looking around as though fearing someone might see them, he said, "What are you doing? Why are you here?"

"Just act like I'm a neighbor that stopped for a chat. Now what's going on with you, big fella?"

"Did my wife call you?"

"No. Sabyl did. You either tell me what's going on, or I'll haul you in and we'll talk at Headquarters," he lied.

"Nothing is wrong. I am struggling with some personal things, that is all. I am fine."

"You don't sound fine."

"Please, don't call me again while I am with a client. They do not like that."

"Rudy, you're in some kind of trouble, and I want to help. Now let me, will you?"

The words were nearly formed on Rudy's tongue. He so longed to tell him the whole story—about David—about the men he was driving—but he could not. "You cannot help me. No one can. It is something that I must work out myself."

"I'd like to help if I can."

"I must go in now."

"Someone tried to kill Sabyl last night."

Rudy's eyes widened in horror. "What? What do you mean tried to kill her?"

"A man broke into her house in Pennsylvania, shot Beau and then tried to kill her, but the police stopped him."

Rudy felt sick to his stomach. "Is she all right? Is Beau—"

"They're both fine."

"Thank God." Layla was looking out the window. "I must go inside now. My wife will be worried."

"You won't invite an old friend inside?"

Rudy's sad eyes looked away. "I—I am sorry. I cannot."

⋏

Sabyl's phone rang at nine-fifteen. "Sabyl, it's Rebecca. I hope I'm not calling too late."

"Rebecca! No, not at all. How are you?"

"I'm fine, dear. I haven't heard from you and just wondered what was going on."

Sabyl told her what had happened in Fairview.

"Oh, Sabyl, that's horrible! Are you all right? And Beau?"

"We're both fine. He's lying here next to my bed snoring away."

"I'm speechless! How terrible that you had to go through that alone!" She paused and whispered breathlessly, "So, what happens now?"

"Of course, there will be a full investigation."

"Oh, Sabyl, that's so frightening!"

"I know. I—I still can't believe it happened."

"You don't suppose that's what Beau was barking at last week when—"

"I don't know. I can't imagine—"

"What about your house?"

"The couple I told you about, Jerry and Kate, are going to replace the carpet and have the door and window repaired. I'm so fortunate to have them."

"Indeed you are." Her voice softened. "Poor Beau! You must have been terrified! And what about Scott?"

"He saved my life, Bec. He's the one who told the police they needed to watch my house. I owe him my life."

"And how do you feel about him now?"

"I—wait a minute; somebody's calling me on the other line. Hang on..." She punched the call waiting button. "Hello."

"Sabyl, it's Scott."

"Oh, Scott, hold on, I'm on the other line—let me tell her—hello, Rebecca, I have to take this call."

"Okay, but before you go—what about the biopsy?"

"It's malignant. I'm having surgery the twenty-first. Wednesday."

"Oh, God, I'm so sorry. I'll take you to the hospital, okay? I'll call you tomorrow and we'll work out the details."

"That'll be great. Thanks, Bec—bye...I'm sorry, Scott."

"That's okay. How's Beau?"

"He's great. Sleeping like a baby."

"I saw Rudy."

"You did?"

"Yeah. I went to his house. Something is bad wrong, alright. I asked him to let me help—he just looked terrified and said he had to go inside."

"What could it be?"

"I don't know, but he's not talking."

Sabyl sighed in frustration. "That's for sure. Scott, uh, what about your job?"

"Still don't have one, but I think it'll work out. The truth usually comes out in the end."

"That's true." she smiled and nodded, "That's so very true."

Monday, January 19

Dotty kicked the front office door with her foot. Frank came running and opened it wide. He whistled, "Those flowers are gorgeous! She's going to flip! Here, let me take them." She handed him the huge bouquet. He took it into Sabyl's office and carefully set it on her desk. Dotty took off her coat and hung it on the rack. "Hey, Frank. You make coffee?"

"Yeah, it's fresh."

"Here, be sure to sign this card and then I'll get the guys in the garage to write something in it."

Frank read the card and looked up to the ceiling as though looking for inspiration. Finally he wrote something and handed it back to Dotty. She took it to the garage and told them to get it back to her before Sabyl arrived. She went back inside, poured herself a mug of coffee and turned on her computer. Frank leaned against the door. Did you get that information faxed up to the police in Fairview?"

"Pulling it up now. Have you heard from Sabyl?"

"Yeah. She's taking Beau to be checked out by her vet out on River Road."

"So tell me the rest of what happened in Pennsylvania."

Frank poured himself a cup of coffee. "Well, after she got Beau to the vet, she had to go to the morgue to ID the guy."

"Gross! I'd rather baptize a cat!"

"Tell me about it."

"Imagine. He might have been stalking her for days—maybe planning this a long time. Gives me the willies."

Frank added creamer and stirred it in. "Yeah, last weekend, when Rebecca Carriere was up there with her, he might have planned to get Sabyl then, but when he saw she had someone else there—"

"He killed her cat instead. What a psycho."

Frank shook his head. "The thought of what might have happened—"

"So, Scott basically saved her life."

"Yep. That's what she said."

"Who knows? Maybe she'll take him back," Dotty said with a little smile.

"Never know."

Karen walked in with an armload of files. "Never know what?"

"Never know if Sabyl and Scott will get back together."

"Girl, if she doesn't want him, I'll take him. He is—like—hot!"

Dotty looked at Karen and smiled sideways. "Like—in your dreams. Hey, do me a favor. Run down to the garage and see if the guys are finished signing that card and then get everybody in the back office to sign it. Is Floyd back there?"

"Yeah. And Jenny. Ohhh! Look at the pretty flowers! Sabyl's going to—like—croak!"

⅄

A light rain fell as though the heavens were weeping. The funerals for the agents killed in the Vice President's motorcade were held two hours apart. Scott attended one at nine that morning and was now at the other at eleven. He stood holding a large black umbrella, listening to the minister softly speaking words of eternal hope. He watched the brave young widow comfort her children. Scott's jaw tightened. *Nobody has a right to do this to another human being.*

The brief service ended. Scott made his way over to the family and quietly spoke his condolences. One last look at the coffin and then he turned to leave. The rain began to let up as he walked along the wet paved paths of the cemetery. Ron Keefer caught up to him. "Hello, Scott."

Scott stopped and looked at him for a moment and then continued walking. The two men walked together in silence toward the gate. The sun broke through the clouds and bathed their shoulders with warmth. The men shook their umbrellas and folded them. Scott stopped and faced his boss. "We've lost three good men in the last few days and I'm on hold while—"

"We found out they leaked the story themselves. Guess they like the press attention."

"When did you find this out?"

"This morning."

"When were you going to tell me about it?"

"I just did. Come pick up your stuff. We've got work to do."

"But hasn't my clearance been suspended?"

"I never turned it in."

⚓

Sabyl held Beau in her arms and managed to get the heavy front door open to the animal clinic. Beau looked at Sabyl with trusting eyes as she followed the attendant to a small room. Carefully, she laid him on the examining table and patted him and rubbed his nose. The veterinarian came in, sat on a short stool and listened as Sabyl explained his injuries.

He shook his head. "Sounds like both of you are lucky to be alive."

"Yes, we are."

"Let's have a look here." He spoke softly to Beau, who responded with a wag of his tail. The doctor changed the dressing and repacked the wound. When he was finished, he sat back down on the stool and wrote something on the chart. "Looks like he's doing fine. Just continue making sure he gets plenty of rest. And, of course you know to keep him from jumping on or off the furniture or in or out of the car."

"Yes, of course."

"Bring him back in a week."

"Um, I'm having surgery Wednesday. I'll have my pet sitter bring him in."

He looked at her concerned. "Sorry to hear it." He didn't press the issue. "Will Beau be with someone he knows really well while you're in the hospital? I don't want him to become fretful or upset while you're away."

"Yes, I'll definitely arrange that. Thanks, Doctor." She rubbed Beau's head. "Did you hear that, buddy? You're doing great!" He responded with a large squeaky yawn.

The attendant helped her take him out to the car and carefully placed him in his doggie bed in the back of the SUV and said goodbye to Sabyl. "See ya, Beau."

As she drove to the office, she once again thanked God aloud for His mercy. Beau wagged his tail seemingly in agreement. At a stoplight, Sabyl speed-dialed Conrad and asked him if he could stay with Beau at her condo while she was in the hospital.

"No prob," he said easily. "I'll be glad to stay with him. My roommate is driving me crazy with his rap music. I can use the peace and quiet."

"Perfect, thanks, Conrad."

Sabyl parked in her private parking space. George saw her pull in and came out to help with Beau. "Hey, boss, you okay?"

"Yeah, I'm fine. Thanks for asking, George."

The garage manager opened the back door of the Murano. "Hey, old man, how you doing, eh?" Beau's tail thumped and wagged with delight. George lifted him carefully and headed for the office door. Sabyl grabbed his doggie bed and followed close behind.

Dotty opened the door wide and greeted Beau with puckered lips. "There's my good boy. He's our hero, yes he is." Beau licked her chin, thoroughly enjoying the attention. Dotty looked at Sabyl with motherly eyes and hugged her as she came in the door. Sabyl hugged her back with her free arm and went in her office and placed Beau's bed beside her desk.

George gently laid him on it and patted his head and looked at Sabyl. "Must have been pretty hairy, huh?"

"That's an understatement."

"Glad you're okay." He grunted slightly as he stood up, pecked her on the cheek and stepped back waiting for her to say something about the huge bouquet of flowers on her desk.

She looked at Dotty's grinning face and smiled playfully, "Whose are these?"

Dotty grinned, "Whadaya mean whose are these! They're yours, of course! Open the card!" Frank, Floyd, Jenny and Karen crowded in.

She pulled the tiny card from the plastic holder and opened the envelope and read it. "To our boss with love from all of us."

"We tried to think of something funny to say, but none of us thought it was funny. Here's a real card. Everybody signed it." She handed her a beautiful card that had scrolled lettering on it that said, "Thinking of you." She looked at the signatures, each one having found their own little space on the card—some saying something special, others merely signing their names with love.

She hugged them one at a time. "Thank you so much. The flowers are beautiful. This means a lot to me. George, tell the guys I said thanks. And I'll tell them myself when I see them."

"Okay, boss," he grinned. "See ya later." He headed for the garage.

Floyd pulled his glasses off and wiped his eyes. He bent down and patted Beau. I'm so sorry about what happened, Sabyl. I can't imagine…"

"Thanks, dear." She took a deep breath and smiled, "Okay, you're going to make me cry. Back to work, everybody." She shooed them out like she was shooing chickens and sat down at her desk. Jenny and Karen waved and headed back to their cubicles.

Dotty stood in front of her desk. "This is all just too weird. I can't stand the thoughts of what you went through." She blew her nose.

"I know. I'm just grateful to be alive and that Beau's going to be okay."

"God's looking out for you, for sure. I faxed the info you asked for up to Fairview."

"Thanks, Dotty."

"Well, I gotta get back to work." She turned and went back to her desk.

Frank leaned on the doorjamb with his hands in his pockets looking at Sabyl and shook his head slowly. "So, you get followed in Georgetown, somebody kills your cat, blows up your car and now this? What the heck is going on?"

She leaned back in her chair. "I have no idea, Frank."

"George and Stubby and Burt seem to think we've got a sleeper among us."

Sabyl's eyes widened, "What? A sleeper? Who?"

"Jamal. You'd better talk to them."

"Okay," she frowned. "I will!"

"So what did the vet say?"

"Beau's doing fine. Just can't let him get too excited or jump around."

"Glad to hear it." Frank turned slowly to go back to his desk.

Sabyl picked up the card and headed to the garage to thank the drivers.

Frank settled down at his desk. The phone rang and he answered, "Martin Transportation."

"Hi, this is Rebecca Carriere. Is Sabyl in please?"

Frank couldn't speak.

"Hello?"

"Uh, hi, Ms. Carriere. This is Frank, the day dispatcher. Sabyl's down at the garage. Can you hold while I buzz her?"

"Oh! Frank! At last we meet. I've heard so much about you!"

Frank chuckled, "Well, maybe we can be friends anyway."

Rebecca laughed, "No, it was all good."

"I love your books, especially the second one."

"Why, thank you, Frank. That's very kind of you."

"Uh, Sabyl just walked in. It was nice talking to you." He punched Sabyl's extension. "Rebecca Carriere on line one."

She smiled knowingly at Frank through the glass windows and picked up the phone. "Hi, Bec."

"Hi, dear. How's Beau?"

"He's healing just fine."

"That's great."

"So, about Wednesday. That's the twenty-first, right?"

"Yes, day-after-tomorrow."

"What time do you want me to pick you up?"

"Surgery's at 8:30. I need to be there by 6:30. Sorry it's so early."

"No problem at all. I'll pick you up at 6:00. That should be enough time with traffic, don't you think?"

"That'll be fine. You're a dear."

"Who's taking care of Beau?"

"Conrad. He's going to stay at my condo so Beau will be comfortable—you know—in his own environment."

"That'll work. Okay, dear, if I don't see you before, I'll see you Wednesday morning."

"Oh, and Rebecca, you made Frank's day."

Sabyl hung up and saw Dotty standing in the doorway waiting with some papers for her to sign, looking pained.

"I would have been glad to take you to the hospital."

"I know, dear, but Rebecca already offered, so I told her yes."

"Then let me stay with Beau."

"I need you here, Dotty. I'm counting on you to keep the place running smoothly. Knowing you're here will put me at ease."

Dotty smiled, satisfied. "Okay. You saw the guys in the garage?"

"Yeah. They were sweet, and so glad I'm okay. They all want to see Beau. I told them he needs to rest right now. He's already had a big morning."

"Oh, by the way, Chief Hawks called and said to tell you he came up empty. Said you'd know what he meant."

"Okay, thanks," she sighed. "I guess now is as good a time as any for you to give me a rundown of everything I need to deal with before I go in the hospital. Not sure how long I'll be in—well, you know what I mean."

"You're going to be okay, honey. I know it. I feel it right here," she said, tapping her ample bosom.

"Thanks, Dotty," she smiled. "I believe it too."

⋏

Scott walked into his office for the first time in five days and was greeted as though he had never been gone. When he picked up his SigSauer and his shield, he felt almost whole again. Almost. He would feel whole when he and Sabyl were—*No time to think about that now.* He briefed Keefer and Martz on what had been happening to Sabyl and said he wanted to talk to her other drivers.

Keefer cocked his head to one side. "Why? What's this got to do with these assassinations?"

"Not sure that it does. I just have a gut feeling. I mean, why would all these things be happening now—while these other things are going on?"

"She's not a government leader."

"No, but she might know something or—"

"That's a stretch, Scott," Keefer said. "No pun intended."

"Just let me talk to the rest of her drivers, okay?"

"Sorry. These assassinations are priority."

"Right." He exhaled and clenched his jaw.

Keefer handed him a file. "You and Martz take a few of these leads and check them out."

Scott took the file. "We're on it."

⅄

The Director of the Secret Service agency was still taking heat for the shootings of the would-be motor home bombers. He stood solidly behind his agents. The President called them heroes. The Israeli ambassador personally thanked Keefer and Martz for their bravery. Letters of commendation came from the surrounding embassies, as well as the corporate offices of Intelsat, housed in an enormous glass building on the corner of Connecticut and Van Ness, who sent a letter of thanks. And with a note of humor, added, "We're grateful that your agents are such good shots; otherwise all of northwest D.C. would have been picking glass out of their behinds for the next year."

⅄

"Close the door." George and Stubby sat down in the two leather chairs across from Sabyl's desk and Burt took the side chair against the wall. "Okay, what's all this about your thinking Jamal is a sleeper?"

None spoke for a few moments, waiting for the other to reply. Finally, Stubby said with his head down, "Aw, we didn't like something he said." He proceeded to tell the whole story about Jamal's "freedom-fighter" remark. "We told Scott and he was pretty nice about it, but basically told us we were out of line."

She sat back in her chair. "I agree, although I can understand why his remark made you feel uncomfortable. Have you talked to him about it?"

They looked at one another sheepishly, "Naw, we just let it fester and decided to follow him."

"Yes, I heard you gave Scott the address." She tried to suppress a smile. "Seems he's been taking pottery lessons."

"Pottery lessons?"

"Yes, and according to his teacher, Mrs. Bell, he's quite gifted at it. I think you owe him an apology, but I'm going to leave that up to you to do whatever you think is right."

They looked at one another. "I guess the least we could do is talk to him. I mean, that remark—he was just asking for it."

"Okay. Talk to him about it. Let me know how it turns out."

↟

Rudy wanted desperately to ask Endicott when his last day would be and then wondered if he would live to see it. For some reason, the brooding man seemed to be more uptight than he had been for the past several days. Rudy hoped he would be leaving soon, but was sure he and his cohorts had one more target.

That thought was not only in Rudy's mind, but everyone else's within the beltway and, for that matter, the rest of the world. Would the assassins attempt an attack on the President? It seemed likely that he would be next. For now, the President was out of town, hopefully safe at his home in Indiana. But they would wait, Rudy was sure, for an opportune moment. It seemed, thus far, they had done their homework well.

Rudy knew that Sabyl had been trying to reach him. He had gotten his cell phone back, but was ordered by Endicott to keep it turned off except certain hours when he needed to get in touch with him. Rudy looked in the rearview mirror at the cold-blooded killer who held his son, who had threatened to kill him if he didn't cooperate, and even threatened his wife and Sabyl. It took everything he had to keep from hating him. But he had been taught that hatred is a disease of the soul and that it never brought about good.

Having learned about the bombing of Sabyl's car and the attack in Pennsylvania, Rudy was grateful that she was not harmed, but he was terrified for her. Of course, it was possible they would attempt to harm her again. He felt so helpless—unable to tell anyone—to warn Sabyl—to warn the authorities.

Knowing that she had never known fatherly, protective love, he had always felt somehow it was his place to give her that. And then Scott came along. But the professional protector caused the most pain of all. And now this. Never had he felt so completely powerless. *And now my son,* he thought. It all came crashing in on him. If he couldn't protect his family or Sabyl, what good was he? He felt like a pen that had run out of ink. Its usefulness gone—empty. He clenched his jaw. I *must do something. God, are you there? Show me what to do! Please!*

🛦

It had been a long day. Sabyl tried several times to reach Rudy, but to no avail. She had Frank check the GPS to see where he was, but Rudy had turned it off. Frank thought that was very strange.

Conrad came to the office to pick up Beau and took him to Sabyl's condo while she went grocery shopping. She piled her buggy high, getting several extra things for Conrad to enjoy while he stayed at her place during her hospital stay. The grocery clerk chatted amiably with the customer ahead of her. He paid for his purchases and left. After she loaded her groceries on the conveyor belt, Sabyl stood looking at the headlines of the gossip publications, and was aghast to see herself on the cover with headlines screaming, SABYL MARTIN TERRORIST TARGET. And then the sub headline: DC LIMO LADY CAR BOMBING TIED TO TERRORISTS? She felt the bottom drop out of her stomach. The cashier stared at Sabyl in a way that unsettled her. Looking around, she pulled her hat down over her face, hoping no one would recognize her. After paying the cashier, she pushed her cart out the double doors to the underground parking garage, pulled out her keys and hit the unlock button. The lights blinked and a short honk echoed in the cavernous parking garage of the *Giant Food* store. She put her bags in the back and got in and put the key in the ignition. She held her breath and said a little prayer each time she started her car. The face of the young valet appeared in her mind as she turned the key. When it started, she exhaled with relief. She sat quietly for a few moments and realized she must write to his parents. The thought of it overwhelmed her. *What can I possibly say to them?* She shook her head. *I'll have to wait until I can think more clearly.*

She pulled out her cell phone and called the office. "Hi, Karen, it's me. You about ready to go home?"

"Yeah, it's—like—pretty quiet around here. Have you talked to Layla?"

"No, why?"

"She called and was very upset."

"Okay, I'll call her as soon as I get these groceries home."

"Better call her now. She was—like—crying."

"Oh, okay. Where's Dotty?"

"She already left. Frank's in the john."

"Okay, I'll call Layla now."

Sabyl punched in Rudy's home number. "Hi, Layla, it's Sabyl. What's wrong, dear?"

"Oh, Miss Sabyl! David is missing. Our son David is missing!"

"What do you mean missing? How do you know?"

"His roommate at the university called and asked where he was. He hasn't seen him since Tuesday."

"A whole week? Why didn't he call before now?"

"I don't know. I felt something was wrong when David had not called. He always calls us—he is such a good boy." She sobbed, "I tried to tell Rudy something was wrong, but he just got angry and told me to stop talking like that. That is not like Rudy, Miss Sabyl. I don't know what to do."

"Call the Bethesda Police. That'll at least get things moving. I'll call Scott right now and tell him about it."

"Oh, thank you, Miss Sabyl."

"Just pray, Layla. I'll be back to you." She dialed Scott's cell phone and got his voice mail. "Blast!" She left a voice mail, "Scott, it's Sabyl. I need to talk to you. It's urgent."

She put the phone down, drove to her condo, and pulled into the parking garage and down around the ramps to her parking space. Pulling her fold-up aluminum cart out, she loaded it up with her groceries and headed for the elevator.

ᐱ

Scott was following up a lead in College Park, Maryland. He and his partner, Martz, were interviewing a man who claimed he knew who was doing the assassinations. Certain it was his ex-wife, he vehemently argued his case that she should be picked up and immediately locked up. They assured him they would look into it, and headed for their car.

"Man! What a nut job."

"You're telling me." Scott looked at his watch. "We're going to hit some serious traffic."

The beltway was a parking lot. Every lane was stopped cold. After sitting still for five minutes, Martz radioed in to see if it was just beltway traffic or something else. Keefer informed them that a tanker-truck had overturned near the Georgia Avenue exit carrying several thousand pounds of calcium carbide, closing both east and westbound lanes of the beltway. "Emergency response teams are all over this thing. If this stuff gets wet, it becomes a potential Haz Mat."

"Isn't it forecast to rain?"

"Yeah."

"Great," he said wryly. "Anything we can do?"

"Yeah. You can catch up on your paperwork. You're going to be there a while."

They turned off the ignition and began filling out reports.

ᐱ

Conrad opened the door for Sabyl and took the grocery cart into the kitchen. She dropped her keys and called Layla back. "Layla, I'm not able to reach Scott. Did you call the police?"

"Yes. They're sending someone out right away."

"Okay. Call me as soon as they leave. I want to know what they're going to do."

"Thank you, Miss Sabyl. Oh! I think they are here now."

⸎

After dinner, Sabyl gave Conrad instructions for Beau's care. "I'm not certain how long I'll be in the hospital, Conrad. Totally depends on what they find. It could be just overnight. I don't know."

"I'll be here for as long as you need me."

She patted his arm. "You're a jewel. Sorry you have to come here so early in the morning."

"No prob." He stood up and picked up his dishes.

"I'll get those."

"My mom would turn over in her grave if I didn't take my own dishes to the sink."

"Well, we wouldn't want that," Sabyl smiled, confident that he would at least keep the dishes picked up.

"I've gotta run. Have another client to sit with tonight—a poodle named Zenobia—a real hot number. Beau'd like her."

"Okay, but while I'm gone, no sleepovers. I don't care how hot she is, Beau's just not up to that sort of thing yet." They both laughed. Conrad thanked Sabyl for dinner and left.

Sabyl punched the remote and took the rest of the dishes into the kitchen. The familiar voice of the local anchor spoke in the background. *"Emergency crews are going door-to-door warning residents of the potential danger. The Virginia Highway Patrol is rerouting all northbound vehicles, and the Maryland Highway Patrol has completely closed down the beltway until the spill can be cleaned up. The chemical was being transported in dry form in 4,000-pound containers. Thankfully, not all eight containers spilled. Calcium carbide, when wet, can generate acetylene, an extremely flammable gas. And it looks like rain is coming our way. We'll now turn it over to chief meteorologist, Kelly Wilson. Kelly."*

"Thanks, Dana. We'll keep our fingers crossed that the emergency response teams can get the spill cleaned up soon. As we can see here, a band of showers is headed our way..."

Sabyl ran the garbage disposal, put the dishes in the dishwasher and turned it on. She finished tidying up the kitchen and went into the living room and nestled in her favorite spot on the sofa. It wasn't until that moment that she realized how tired she was. On the screen there was an aerial photo of the beltway at a standstill with all its arteries clogged. She looked at her watch and wondered why she hadn't heard from Scott.

Rudy saw police cars in front of his house and nearly panicked. He got out of his car and quickly walked inside. "What is wrong?"

Layla ran to him and threw herself into his arms. "David is missing. His roommate called and said he has been gone for a week."

Rudy sat down hard on the sofa and put his face in his hands. The police asked him questions. He told them he knew nothing. He felt he would die if he couldn't tell the truth, but he was terrified. The police took his statement and said they would file a missing persons report and that they would send someone out to talk to David's roommate and his friends.

"What about the FBI?" Layla asked.

"That's for kidnapping cases, ma'am."

"But maybe he has been kidnapped!"

Rudy sat frozen, his voice silent.

"We'll talk to his friends and then we'll decide what to do from there." They assured them they would do all they could do and left.

Rudy felt sick to his stomach and went upstairs to the bathroom and locked the door.

At eight-fifteen, Sabyl's cell phone chirped. It was Scott. "Sorry, I just now got your message. I've been sitting on the beltway for two and a half hours. What's up?"

"David is missing."

"David?"

"Rudy's son. He's a med student at Johns Hopkins. Layla said his room-mate hasn't seen him in a week."

"Maybe he's with friends."

"No. He's missed classes, didn't pack anything."

Scott thought a minute. "Did Layla call the police?"

"Yes. They're going to talk to David's roommate and his friends."

"I've got a buddy in the FBI. I'll give him a call. They handle kidnappings, but, of course we don't know that he was kidnapped."

"I told Layla I'd have you call her."

"Where's Rudy? Have you heard from him?"

"I talked to him this morning. Yesterday was supposed to be his last day driving this Endicott character, and when I asked him to come into the office, he begged me to let him drive him a couple more days. I knew then something was wrong. He can't stand Endicott." Rain pecked at Sabyl's window like a flock of chickens trying to get in. "Did they get that spill cleaned up?"

"Yeah. Just in time too. That could have been a real disaster. Tell me about this Endicott guy."

"I told you all I know. He's from London, here on business, staying at the Lafayette House Hotel. Strange man—sullen, cold but polite. Or at least he was to me. I don't know how he treats Rudy."

"Okay, I'll call my friend Jason at the Bureau and see what he thinks. I'll call you back. You going to be up?"

"Honestly, Scott, I'm exhausted. I'm going to take a shower and go to bed. Please call Layla and then call me in the morning and tell me what your friend said."

"Will do. Try to get some rest. You've had quite a week."

"Thanks, I will."

Sabyl hung up, undressed, got in the shower and prayed for David.

✦

George, Stubby and Burt sat in the lounge and eyed Jamal warily. They had talked among themselves and decided now was as good a time as any. "Hey, Jamal. We need to talk to you."

He slowly laid down his crossword puzzle. "Yes, so talk."

George began, "Well, we thought that freedom fighter remark you made last week was pretty rotten with all that's been going on."

"Especially after Nine-Eleven," Stubby added.

Burt put out his cigarette and said, "Makes us kinda uncomfortable to think you feel that way."

Jamal leveled his eyes at them. "I have been thinking about what you said. Stubby, you asked how crashing into buildings brings freedom to anybody's cause—it doesn't." He stood and put his hands in his pockets and started slowly pacing. "If one is to be called a freedom fighter, then that one must fight for freedom. There is no freedom in the killing of innocent human beings. Only bondage to one's own hatred."

Stubby frowned skeptically. "Go on."

"Yesterday, I drove a client to the Vietnam Veterans Memorial. I have been there many times and usually stay with my car, but my client asked me to walk with him. I looked at the names on that wall." He frowned deeply and swallowed hard as though taking a bitter pill. "It took me a while to comprehend the enormity of the human loss and for the first time realized—those names—those men were real freedom fighters."

George looked at the other two and whistled softly.

Stubby whispered, "Wow."

Jamal continued, "Even though they did not live to see the end of it, they fought for freedom. This country has fought on foreign soil for nothing but other nations' freedom. That is quite remarkable." He sat back down and added, "While I may not agree with a lot of things that go on here in the U.S., I do not think it is reason for these attacks. Excuse my remark, please."

They shook his hand and pounded him on the back. George smiled, "You see, Jamal. Our government is kind of like Noah's ark. It's a stinking mess, but it's the best thing afloat." They all laughed and Stubby and the guys invited Jamal to watch the game. Ricko made something hot and spicy and, as always, they passed around the antacids.

Tuesday, January 20

Rudy left his house before daylight to beat the traffic and headed for the garage. No one was there yet. He used his key to get in and sat down in the rich leather seat of the limousine, pulled the cassette player out of the glove box and inserted his father's latest tape. Listening to the loving voice of his father, he wept, wishing he were there and that he could talk with him. His father's gentle voice said, "God tells us to pray for those who despitefully use us so that we will not sustain a bitter spirit within our souls, a cancer that can wreak more havoc than almost anything we can imagine. When we pray for those who mean us harm, it opens the door for God to work things out for our good."

He ejected the tape. *How can I pray for these men?* Deep inside Rudy knew the answer; he knew that hatred was what motivated these men. He didn't want the same in his own heart. "Lord, help me. I cannot forgive these men. You alone can give me the grace to—" He took out his handkerchief and wiped his eyes. "Please work somehow to bring an end to all of this and to set my son free. And help these men—if it is possible—open their eyes—" He began to feel a relief in his spirit. He heard someone come in and quickly started the car, put it in drive, and waved as casually as he could to George as he pulled out onto the street.

⋏

Scott wasn't able to get in contact with his friend, Jason, until late that morning. Within a half-hour, two FBI agents visited Layla. She gave them the information about David, his address, phone number, and his roommate's name. They asked about his professors, his classes, friends and habits. Scott had told Jason about Rudy's strange behavior and about Endicott. They, like the police, didn't see the connection, but agreed that if David's disappearance was somehow connected to Endicott, they had to move cautiously.

⋏

Dotty buzzed Sabyl. "Mr. Eisendoffer on line one." The phone rang again. "Martin Transportation."

"Hi Dotty, it's Scott."

"Oh, Scott! Hey! You're the man-of-the-year around here, dude."

Scott chuckled, "I am, eh?"

"Sabyl's on the other line, but I'm sure she'll want to talk to you. Hold on, okay?"

Sabyl drummed her fingernails on the desk. "I must spend one third of my life on hold," she sighed as she leaned back in her desk chair. Dotty walked into her office and motioned to her she needed to speak with her.

"It's okay, I'm on hold. What's up?"

"Scott is on line two."

"Okay. Hello, yes, Mr. Eisendoffer, may I call you back? I have an emergency. Yes, I'll call you right back. No, of course you're important too. I'll call you—he hung up." Sabyl punched line two. "Scott?"

"Hey."

"Did you talk to your friend at the Bureau?"

"Yes, they're out talking to Layla now."

"Scott, I couldn't sleep last night thinking about all this. I know this is going to sound strange, but I think—" She hesitated. It sounded so incredible she could barely form the words. "I think I know who's been doing these killings."

Scott stood up at his desk, almost knocking his chair over. "Who?"

"I think it might be Endicott."

He sat back down. "Endicott?"

"Yes. The day he first arrived here, he lost something in Rudy's car and was quite upset when he thought Rudy may have read it."

"What was it?"

"A small book with lots of writing in it—in Arabic."

"Did Rudy read any of it?"

"No, he only looked for the owner's name. Frank said he thought it was some sort of list of names, addresses and dates. Rudy didn't discuss it with me. All but one of the killings have taken place since he arrived here."

"All but one?"

"Fredericks."

"He wouldn't have to have been here for that. It had been set up for months. So why do you think it's him?"

"If he thinks Rudy read his little book, I'm sure he wants to keep him in his control. Rudy hasn't turned in any log sheets—he's been under tremendous stress ever since he started driving Endicott. And think about it. A limousine is perfect. They have a driver who knows his way around D.C., there's a divider between them so he can't hear what they discuss, it has tinted windows so nobody can see in, they have plenty of room to make all sorts of evil plans back there."

Scott took notes as she talked. "Go on."

Hearing herself saying it sounded ridiculous. "I—I know it sounds crazy—"

"Can't say the thought didn't cross my mind."

"Really?"

"Yeah, but I just couldn't put it together."

Sabyl frowned, "It's hard to believe he would lose such a valuable item, though. The little book, I mean."

"The only good thing about terrorists is that they're human and they make mistakes."

"Another thing about them using a limousine is that Rudy knows the Park Police. They sit in their cars and shoot the breeze all the time. They're used to seeing Rudy at different locations around town so they're most likely not going to bother him."

"Where is he now?"

"I don't know. George said he left early this morning without saying anything."

"What time?"

"Around 6:30. And Scott—"

"Yeah?"

"He's turned off his GPS."

"Why would he do that?"

"No clue. Maybe they made him do it."

"The only way they could make him do something is if they've threatened him somehow."

Sabyl stood up. "David! Oh, Scott, poor Rudy!"

"Sabyl, did you see the little black book too?"

"No, Rudy just put it in his lost box. When I was told about it, I knew Endicott had already gotten it back, so I didn't think about it anymore."

"Endicott might think Rudy discussed it with you."

Sabyl gasped, "The car bomb?"

"And maybe the break-in at your house."

She sat back down with a thud. "Oh, my God."

"I'm going after Endicott. Call me if you hear from Rudy."

"Please, be careful, Scott."

"I will." He was warmed by the concern in her voice. "You too. Talk to you later." He hung up, jumped in his Camry and headed for the Lafayette House Hotel.

⋏

Rudy drove around for hours. The rain had finally stopped. He was to pick up Fathid at 9:00 a.m. He needed time to think—time to pray. Finally, with trembling hands, he dialed Scott's cell phone. His heart thudded in his chest. Scott's voice mail message said that he was not available. He tried again. Same message. No way would he leave a voice mail, knowing that he might try to return his call after he picked up Fathid. Another try. No answer. Fathid came out of the brownstone. Rudy quickly put his cell phone away, but kept it on, knowing Endicott might try to contact him. He wasn't sure why he hadn't heard from him yet, but he was glad he hadn't.

Fathid got in and instructed him to go to a drive-through on Wisconsin Avenue. He ordered an egg sandwich and then told him to drive around while he ate it. He seemed to be killing time. Finally, after riding around for twenty minutes, Fathid told him to go to the Washington Monument parking area. Rudy pulled into the usual place. The flags encircling the monument, heavy with rain, were still at half-mast.

"Turn your cell phone off and give it to me."

"Why? Mr. Endicott may try to call me."

"Just do as I tell you." He turned off his cell and handed it to him.

"Now open the sunroof."

Rudy pushed the button and it slid open.

⚓

Scott parked at the Lafayette House Hotel and went inside the historic hotel and showed his I.D. to the desk clerk and asked for Endicott's room number.

"He's already checked out, sir."

"When?"

"About an hour ago."

"Did he have a limousine pick him up?"

"No, sir, he left in a cab."

"Did you call the cab for him?"

"Yes, sir."

"Which company?"

"Capital."

"Were there others with him?"

"I'm not sure."

"Has his room been cleaned?"

"Uh, let me see—" He clacked his keyboard and peered at the monitor. "No, sir, it has not."

"Don't touch it. I'm sending a forensics unit over right away."

The desk clerk's face flushed with excitement. "Yes, sir!"

Scott knew he would have to go through the Operations Center to send Forensics. He called the cab company. After much wrangling with the dispatcher, who was reluctant to give out information, he was told that one of their cabs had picked up three other men prior to Endicott and drove them to Union Station. Scott called Keefer.

His boss listened with interest and made notes as Scott filled him in. "This is pretty far-fetched, but we don't have anything else. Hang on." He put Scott on hold, punched in some numbers and ordered several agents to Union Station and put the word out for all trains to stand down. He then ordered Forensics to go to the Lafayette House Hotel. Back on the line with Scott, he asked him if he had gotten the address where the other three men had been picked up. "Yes, an address on E Street." Keefer's phone buzzed. "Hang on, Scott—Yeah."

"Secretary Killian on line one." Another poker riddle had come in. Keefer told Killian that Scott had been successful in figuring out the others.

"Get him on it," Killian ordered.

"Got him on hold now."

He gave Scott the riddle. THREE OF A KIND. WE'LL LAY ONE DOWN AND THEN WE'LL FOLD—FOR NOW.

A forensics unit was quickly dispatched to the brownstone. They found a black Labrador retriever and the body of a young man.

⅄

At Andrews Air Force Base, the President and First Lady, looking rested from their weekend at their home in Indiana, stepped out of Air Force One, walked down the long steps to the tarmac, and were greeted by more Secret Service agents than they had ever seen on a protective detail. His chief of staff came down the long stairs behind him along with several other staff members and waited until the President finished his greetings. Giving him a chance to stretch his legs, the President usually walked from the massive blue and white plane to the waiting helicopter that would take him to the White House. But today, he was whisked into his hardened limousine and driven the three hundred feet over to Marine One. He stepped out of the long, shiny car and into the dark green helicopter, a *Sikorsky VH-3D Sea King,* smartly saluting the Marine standing by the steps.

Once safely aboard the helicopter, his chief of staff got into one of the limousines and said, "Okay, let's go." The driver took him to the gate where an Air Force guard promptly stopped him. "You can't leave until the President has lifted off, sir."

"Look, I'm his chief of staff, for crying out loud. Let me pass."

The guard pulled his weapon. "We're on a tarmac freeze an hour before he arrives and an hour after he leaves. You're not going anywhere, sir."

"Aw, Geeeez."

⋏

Fathid unrolled the blanket. Rudy got out, as he had done on so many occasions, to hand the camera to Fathid after he spread the blanket and got his tripod set up. He opened the back door and noticed the blanket was on the floor and the camera was not there. Fathid screamed, "Get back in the car!"

Rudy frowned deeply and reluctantly obeyed. Fathid watched to make sure the Park Police were out of sight, and carefully placed on the roof a Stinger surface-to-air missile (SAM) with a specially-made plastic outer molding attached to it that was shaped like a camera with a telescopic lens. He quickly stood up in the sunroof and positioned himself to get the Stinger ready. His cell phone beeped. The caller told him, "The birds have flown away." Fathid knew he would have only seconds to hit his target—and a bullet for Rudy when he was done.

⋏

Frank walked into Sabyl's office. Leaning over her desk, he said, "Sabyl, look at these." He handed her Rudy's log sheets. "George just found them in one of the empty lockers. Looks like he was trying to hide them."

Sabyl studied them closely. "Oh, my God! I've got to call Scott!"

Frank's phone rang. He ran to his desk to answer it.

Meanwhile, Sabyl got Scott on the phone and told him about the log sheets.

"Have you heard from him at all?"

"No, and we have no way of knowing where he is since he's turned off his GPS and his cell."

Scott rubbed his forehead. "He tried to call me several times. I tried calling him back but his phone was off. Endicott has checked out of his hotel."

"Maybe Rudy's driving him to the airport."

"No, they left in a cab."

"Then where's Rudy?"

"I don't know, but we've got to find him. Sabyl, you know the President's coming in today."

She gasped. "Oh, no."

"Rudy's got to be with one of Endicott's goons or he would have his cell on. He'd want people to be able to reach him in case there's any news about David."

"Oh, Scott, you don't think he's—"

"Call me the second you hear anything. Gotta go."

Frank began yelling into the phone. "Why didn't you tell me?"

Sabyl jumped up from her desk. "What's wrong?"

"Stubby just called in and said he just dropped Endicott and his buddies at Dulles!"

"We can't let them get away! Call the police! Call airport security!" Sabyl ran back to her desk and picked up her phone.

Frank stood up. "And tell them what? That one of our clients is being dropped off there and to arrest them?"

"Tell them the terrorists are getting away!"

Sabyl tried to get Scott back on the phone, but got his voice mail. "Scott, they've pulled a switch. One of our drivers just dropped them at Dulles!" She slammed the phone down and held her head in her hands.

Just then Frank ran into Sabyl's office. "His GPS just came on! He's near the Ellipse Visitor's Pavilion across from the White House!"

"Oh, God bless him, he's trying to send a signal."

Karen and Dotty walked in with lunch they had picked up from *Café Deluxe* and the latest edition of the *National Enquirer*. Dotty yelled, "Hi everybody, lunch is served! Hey, Sabyl! Your picture's on the front page of the *Enquirer!*" Sabyl ran past them, out the door and jumped in her SUV.

Karen hollered at Frank, "Where's she going? Her lunch will get—like—cold!"

Dotty set the bags of food on her desk. "Well, this is just the pigs."

Frank filled them in while on hold for airport security.

⅄

Scott saw his voice mail message. He called Sabyl's office. Frank was still trying to get through to airport security when Dotty answered line two. She quickly handed the phone to Frank. "It's Scott!"

"Tell him what's happening!"

She told Scott about Stubby dropping Endicott at Dulles. "Rudy's GPS came on. He's on Ellipse Rd. just off Constitution Avenue! Sabyl's on her way over there."

"Oh, man! How long ago?"

"She just left."

Scott yelled at Keefer to warn Marine One. "The two identical helicopters that accompany Marine One! That's THREE OF A KIND!"

"Oh, my God," Keefer whispered. He got Killian on the phone. "Get those fighters in the air!"

The DHS Sec said, "Already did!"

Scott headed out the door.

⅄

Airport security took the information. "How do I know you're not some nut?"

Frank stood up and screamed, "These are the guys who've been doing the assassinations! Get them!"

"What flight are they on?"

"How do I know? Probably an international flight! Just get them!"

The security officer got on his radio and ordered all flights grounded and to be on the lookout for anything suspicious. He had no idea who he was looking for.

⅄

The Park Police saw Rudy's limousine parked in its usual place. They drove up, got out and approached the car. Shanklin bent down and said, "You can't sit here today, Rudy. No photographs in this area. The President's flying in."

Fathid turned his body a half turn in the sunroof, pulled out a gun with a silencer on it and shot both of the police in the head.

⋏

By the time the word got out that all flights were grounded, a sleek white Gulfstream V had already departed carrying Endicott, Sahba, and two other operatives. They cheered as they lifted off and congratulated one another on a job well done. "Too bad we could not have gotten the Vice President as well."

Endicott shifted his large frame in the posh seat. "Yes and the Israeli Embassy. But another time, eh?"

Sahba grinned, "Yes. Perhaps another game soon."

⋏

Frank, Dotty, and Karen heard the three helicopters pass over them as they had heard on so many occasions. One of them was Marine One with the President of the United States aboard. The other two had special-ops forces with machine guns aimed at anything that looked suspicious. Dotty said a fast prayer. "Lord, keep Sabyl safe."

Frank added. "And our President."

⋏

The sleek jet followed the flight pattern east and then turned. The pilot looked at the mahogany paneling, the leather seats and thought, *Pity to crash such a fine aircraft,* but then he felt proud to enter paradise in such style. He laughed loudly. "My brothers! You realize we will never have an opportunity like this again. We will finish what our brothers started on September Eleventh. We will hit the Capitol!"

The two operatives clapped their hands and cheered, "Praise be to Allah!" Endicott screamed, "Nooo!"

Sahba pulled out a gun. "Turn this plane back on its course or I'll kill you!"

"And who will fly the plane, eh?" He laughed loudly again.

▲

DHS Security, John Killian, was on the phone with air traffic control. "Where are they?"

"We have them on radar, sir."

"Which way are they heading?"

"They're heading east, sir. Probably heading for Europe—uh, wait a minute, they're turning southeast."

"Southeast?"

"Heading straight for the Capitol, sir."

"Get those fighters after them. Now!" Immediately, two F-16s thundered toward the small white jet.

"They're closing in now, sir."

Killian screamed into another phone, "Evacuate the Capitol!"

▲

Keefer finally got through to Air Defense on the phone. "Switch 'copters! Marine One is in danger!"

"Too late, sir. They're making their final approach to the White House." Keefer slammed down the phone and called for his car.

▲

Rudy stared in horror at the two dead officers on the ground. He pulled David's picture out of his wallet and stared at it. Tears blurred his vision. He wiped his eyes with his knuckles and said, "Forgive me, David." He reached over and pressed the button to the sunroof. It began to close, pinning Fathid in.

Fathid screamed, "Open it back up or I'll kill you!"

Just as he reached for his gun, he saw the three helicopters approaching. He dropped his gun and aimed the Stinger, knowing he would have only one chance to hit his target.

⁕

Sabyl burned rubber and laid on the horn as she jumped curbs, went up on sidewalks on Virginia Avenue, and ran red lights. She turned onto Constitution Avenue, bounced over the curb onto the Ellipse grounds, and cut across the lawn toward Rudy's limousine. She could see the three helicopters coming toward her. "Please let me get there in time!"

⁕

"Say your prayers, my brothers. We will be in paradise tonight!"

"No, you fool!" Endicott pleaded. "I'll pay you anything! I have millions!"

"There is more waiting for us in paradise!"

Sahba screamed, "We don't give a damn about your beliefs! Turn this plane around!"

"Then you are infidels and deserve to die!"

⁕

The Metro Police sitting in their squad cars saw Sabyl's SUV cutting across the Ellipse. Two units started their engines, floored it and went after her, their lights flashing and sirens twittering loudly behind her.

⁕

The soldiers manning the Avenger missiles set their instruments to target the Gulfstream as soon as they could get a bead on it. They were concerned about hitting one of the F-16's, but that was the price they might have to pay.

⁕

Alarms were going off all over the Capitol. "We're under attack! Get out of the building!" the Capitol police shouted. "This is not a drill!" They herded people toward every exit. When they approached the Capitol steps on the west side, they could see the jet in the distance heading right for them. "Run the other way!"

The Humvee-mounted Avenger would soon have the Gulfstream in its sights.

Three identical dark green helicopters flew together approaching the White House from the Potomac. Nearing the White House grounds, one of them with the President aboard began moving away from the other two. Fathid had his target. He aimed the Stinger carefully. He would not let this opportunity go by.

Rudy knew he had to do something. He opened the sunroof, scrambled out of the driver's seat, yanked the back door open and grabbed Fathid and tried to pull him down into the car. Fathid kicked him in the face knocking him back. Rudy fell against the doorpost, and onto the ground, blood gushing from his nose. He got up, got behind the wheel, started the car and just as he put it in gear, out of the corner of his eye, he saw the grill of Nissan Murano heading straight for his back door. Fathid pulled the trigger just as Sabyl broadsided the car knocking it a quarter the way around. The Stinger took off in another direction, heading straight for one of the F-16s.

The pilot of the other fighter screamed, "Jink for a SAM!" The F-16 peeled off in a sharp roll right. The heat-guided missile flew past it looking for another target. It found one. It honed in on the Gulfstream. The Stinger slammed into it. The plane exploded into flames and almost like an offering, fell in a fiery shower at the foot of the Capitol steps.

The Avenger missile was aborted. It wouldn't be needed.

Scores of fire trucks with their sirens blasting roared toward the Capitol. Once it was confirmed that the terrorists' plane was down and the President was safe, the news choppers were released. All the channels scrambled to get the story, and reporters converged on the scene by the dozens.

Eight police cars surrounded the smashed limousine. The spent Stinger fell to the ground. The police held their guns on Fathid as they pulled him out of the car. Two ambulances were there putting the bodies of the two murdered officers on stretchers. Scott pulled up and jumped out of his car and ran over to Sabyl and threw his arms around her. "Are you all right?"

"Yes," she smiled, still trembling.

Scott held her tight. "And so is the President." He reached over and put his hand on Rudy's shoulder. "And so is David."

His words didn't register with Rudy. He was still shaking violently. "My son! They have my son!"

"We've got him, Rudy! He's safe!"

His eyes widened. "Where? How?"

"The driver of the garbage truck that blocked the VP's motorcade sang like a bird. Told us everything."

"Where is he?"

Just then, David got out of one of the black Suburban CAT cars and ran over to his dad. They embraced with joy.

Fathid glared at Rudy as the Park Police led him away in handcuffs. Rudy held his son tightly and watched the man whom he had driven for over two weeks being taken away. An officer opened the back door of a police car, put his hand on Fathid's head and pushed him inside.

"What happened to Endicott?" Rudy asked. "Was he on that plane?"

"Yes. He and his cohorts. We've arrested the rest of them, including the kidnappers."

"My boy is safe! How can I thank you?" He pumped Scott's hand with gusto.

"Thank the good Lord, Rudy."

Sabyl looked up at Scott. "I'm so glad it's over. It is over, isn't it?"

"Not yet," Scott said. "We have one more terrorist we have to deal with."

Rudy frowned deeply? "What? Who?"

Scott looked at Sabyl tenderly. "Breast cancer."

She was stunned. Tears welled up in her questioning eyes.

"Dotty told me."

Rudy nodded and smiled. He and David walked toward the CAT car. "Let's go home, son."

Sabyl smiled at Scott through tears. "Are you sure you're up to this?"

"I've never been more sure of anything in my life."

She smiled, "I'm sure too."

"We've got a lot of catching up to do." He held her and kissed her tenderly.

WEDNESDAY, JANUARY 21

Scott stood beside Sabyl's bed and kissed her on the forehead. "The doc says you're going to be fine. They got it all. It was contained within the tumor."

She smiled, licked her dry lips and said weakly, "That's good."

Flowers filled the room. Sitting on the table across the room was an enormous bouquet of red and white roses with a huge blue bow from the White House. Rebecca sat on the other side of the bed wiping away tears as she watched Rudy and David tell their story on Fox and Friends.

⅄

Frank hung up the phone and shouted, "Yesssss!!!"

Dotty ran in to see what the ruckus was about.

"That was the lawyer. We won the Claude Bagot case!"

"Glory be! We gotta celebrate, Frank! Order some champagne!"

He gave her a look.

"Oh, never mind. Can't have you jumping off the wagon."

Frank jumped up from his desk. "Let's call Sabyl!"

"Not today. With that anesthesia, she wouldn't remember it if we told her. We'll call her tomorrow."

Frank hugged her so hard he lifted her off the floor.

"Ouuuffff…put me down, or I'll be suing you for broken ribs!"

The garage buzzed and Dotty answered. It was George. "Turn on the TV, Rudy and David are on!"

⅄

Fourteen of Sabyl's drivers sat in the garage lounge watching the morning talk shows. George shushed everybody as David and Rudy were introduced. Rudy wore a neck brace from the jolt he took when Sabyl's Nissan spun him around. He wore it as a badge of honor. Their story made the front-page headlines above the fold in every major newspaper around the world. Rudy, David, and Layla were booked solid on TV shows for the next two months.

⅄

Conrad and Beau sat on the sofa watching David tell how the SWAT team busted down the door and raided the place, arresting the two men and one woman who had held him for seven days. Beau cocked his head from side to side and barked when he saw Rudy.

⅄

The major news networks announced that the operatives who had been arrested were talking, especially the kidnappers.

Because the Lafayette House Hotel refused to allow Endicott to pay in cash, Scott was able to obtain a credit card number. The United State Treasury Department began investigating a money trail that they hoped would lead to the ones who hired him to attack America's top leaders. An arrest was anticipated in the near future.

⅄

Fathid's picture covered the television screens, his piercing stare glaring into the eyes of America. His photographs of the Washington Monument, the Lincoln Memorial and other sites in the capital city were confiscated. Among the pictures were photos of every conceivable angle around the White House, the Capitol, and especially the Washington Monument. One man wrote the FBI and asked if he could buy them. He wanted to sell them on eBay.

⊼

Rudy identified Ahmad al Shatir as Talib Sahba, the chemist who was responsible for making the pod filled with ricin, the basketball bomb, and the bomb made of fertilizer.

The body that was found in the brownstone on E Street was the landlord. He had gotten a little too curious about their comings and goings. The black Lab was given a clean bill of health and was immediately adopted by the agency and was scheduled for training to be a part of the canine specialty unit.

⊼

It was confirmed that the man whose assignment it was to kill Sabyl Martin, CEO of Martin Transportation, was none other than Yasar al-Afdal, known as the "Basketball Bomber."

⊼

Another of her neighbors found new courage after Sabyl got up the petition against the Oswald's and went to the police. He reported that they had more than junk in their yard—they had a crop of marijuana that was hidden behind the refrigerators and wrecked cars. When the police raided their place, they found file cabinets full of child pornography and evidence that they had been involved in the kidnapping of a missing child in the Fairview area. They were arrested and were now in custody without bail.

⊼

Jerry and Kate completed the cleanup of Sabyl's favorite room. New carpet lay on the floor; gleaming new glass was in the sliding door and window. Flowers and cards from grateful neighbors were everywhere. The whole town watched in wonder as the story unfolded on network television about what their hometown girl had been through.

⊼

A congressional hearing for the two Secret Service agents who shot the would-be Israeli embassy bombers was suspended in light of the framework of the situation and pending further investigation.

⋏

The President and the Vice President of the United States were shown coming out of the White House smiling and thanking everyone involved. They gave a special thanks to the quick thinking of Sabyl Martin and Secret Service agent Scott Terhune. An invitation to sit in a place of honor at the upcoming State of the Union address was hand-delivered to them, along with a personal note of thanks from the President to Ms. Martin and to the agent who had so adroitly deciphered the poker riddles.

The First Lady came to visit Sabyl in the hospital the next day.

THE END

You Are America's Best Defense

The United States is offering substantial rewards for information that would help locate terrorists or that could help prevent terrorism from occurring here or abroad. But we need your help. Your information could save lives and you may be eligible for a reward and relocation. Please visit www. RewardsforJustice.net to submit a confidential tip or contact the FBI or your local law enforcement agency.

REWARDS FOR JUSTICE
Washington, D.C. 20522-0303 U.S.A.
www.RewardsforJustice.net
1-800-877-3927
Email: info@rewardsforjustice.net

STOP A TERRORIST. SAVE LIVES

About the Author

Tempe Brown is a native of Oklahoma. She is a former magazine editor and is the author of an enhanced historical novel entitled, *The Seed* and a children's book, *The Little Dirt People*. For over thirty-five years, she has gained international recognition as a speaker for the *Gideons International* and serves as the Regional Speaker Trainer (RST) for *Stonecroft Ministries*. She currently resides in Greenville, South Carolina.

Made in the USA
Columbia, SC
25 August 2018